Broken Lies

A Sequel to Unspoken Truths

Jo Buer

Dedication

For anyone who has ever felt "different".

Contents

Prologue

Whoomph!

Natalie jumped, her hand knocking the mug of cold coffee on her desk. It teetered for a second and splashed a brown stain onto her planner.

Shit.

She smeared it with her palm, knowing as she did so, it wouldn't help.

Turning away from the lesson planning on her desk to the sliding doors on the other side of the room, she focused on where she had heard the impact. She homed in on the blemish where the thing had hit, and let out a sigh. Her lesson planning could wait. The storm behind her right eye had grown worse as the afternoon rolled on. Now would be as good of a time as any to call it quits for the day. The second van had already come and ferried the last students back home. Only adults were left on site. Natalie was free to leave whenever. She'd just make sure she was in early the next morning to finish preparing her lessons, before the kids arrived.

Natalie shuffled her planner and the surrounding papers into a pile on her desk, closed down her laptop and placed it on the stack. She took one glance at her coffee. A thick film had gathered on the surface of what remained. She should tip it down the drain. Actually, what she *should* do was take it back to the staffroom and put it in the dishwasher, but right now it felt like too much work.

Rubbing her eyes, she tried to cajole her headache to behave or at least wait until she got home before turning into a full-on migraine like she expected it would.

Natalie sighed and grabbed her bag from the cupboard behind her, slinging it over her shoulder. Jean jacket in hand, she gave it a jiggle to verify her keys were inside the pocket. They were.

At the sliding doors, she turned the inside lock so it would fasten itself behind her. About to step onto the deck, she paused at the sight of the small, plump body of a bird lying there. She could have stood on it.

Something pinched inside her. Poor thing. Bending down, she saw its chest still rising and falling gently. With her jacket over one arm, she cradled it in her hands. Its body was still warm although its head hung limp and its chest barely moved at all now.

It was a fantail.

She brushed away a shudder. As a little girl, she'd heard from her grandmother how some people believed fantails, or pīwakawaka as they were indigenously known, were harbingers of death, particularly if they flew inside.

Which this one hadn't, she reminded herself, although not for a lack of trying.

Others believed they were the messengers of those who had passed. Natalie stifled the sudden jolt of electricity prickling up her spine.

A memory floated to mind of her standing on a stool at the kitchen bench beside her grandmother. Natalie must have been about eight at the time. They were making caramel scrolls, one of her grandmother's favourite afternoon tea treats. It was summer. The silk tree outside the window was blossoming. Delicate pink, fluffy petals floated to the ground as the tree quivered in the breeze, and she watched them drift lazily to and fro on invisible air currents. Then the pīwakawaka appeared, making Natalie cry out in surprise. It flapped its wings against the window as if in a panic to enter. Finding no way in, it danced and flitted back and forth. Natalie had been mesmerised, and for an eight-year-old, it seemed fully believable that behind its unblinking eyes it was trying to communicate something to her. Although she wasn't sure what.

It took Natalie a moment to notice her grandmother's posture beside her. The rolling pin hovered above the pastry, no longer rocking in lullaby motion. Natalie watched, unease growing, as her grandmother slowly lowered the rolling pin to rest with a shaky hand. Her eyes were locked on the bird at the window.

"Grams?" Natalie asked.

Shaking herself from her reverie, her grandmother turned to her.

"It's okay, my moko," she replied. "It's just a little pīwakawaka, come to tell us something ..." Her voice trailed off, and her eyes followed the bird flitting in front of them. She tilted her head slightly as if listening to words unsaid.

"What's it saying, Grams?" Natalie asked, though thinking back she couldn't recall the bird making any sound beyond its wings flapping against the glass. Strange, since fantails were chatty wee things.

The older woman's eyes shone, the pale blue of her irises growing misty.

Grams turned to Natalie, pulling her close to her side with an arm wrapped around her shoulders. There was nothing as nice as the warmth of being hugged by her grandmother.

"Oh, sweetheart," she said. "A spirit has come visiting."

Grams brushed the top of Natalie's head with a kiss.

"It's the way of the pīwakawaka, to travel between worlds, to tell us of the passing of another. It's just a spirit. Come, let's finish with our scrolls." The spell was broken, and Grams sniffed and wiped an eye with the back of her hand. She picked up the rolling pin again, and the fantail gave a last flap at the window before flitting away beyond the silk tree.

Only a little later, Jerry, one of the farmhands, knocked on their door. Natalie watched curiously, peeking down the hall from the kitchen doorway, as Grams opened the front door. She remembered whispered voices. Her grandmother's petite stature did little to block Jerry's form filling most of the doorway. From behind them both, a loud sob strangled the air, and Natalie's mother pushed her way between Jerry and the door frame, brushing away Grams's outstretched hand, as she ran down the hall towards her. As time slowed, Natalie took in every detail of her mother's face. Her hair was wild and unkempt. Mascara streaked her cheeks like war paint. Grief twisted her face into something unrecognisable. Natalie shrank back further behind the doorframe, still watching. Even at eight, she had seen her mother in a wide array of emotional states. She'd become somewhat attuned to her mother's ever-shifting moods, but this ... this was new.

At her bedroom, her mother threw the door open and disappeared inside. She then slammed it shut with such ferocity the hallway pictures rattled on the walls. A deep mournful wail from behind the closed door made Natalie cover her ears, her mother's pain like fingernails dragging down her spine. Something was wrong. Worse even than when she'd broken up with the shearer from the next town over. The heaviness in the air, the leaden weight of grief that had now found its footing, Natalie realised, had been brewing even before her grandmother had opened the front door.

It was only later, much later, after Jerry had left and her mother's sobs had died down to muffled whimpers from behind her bedroom door, that Grams told her what had happened.

It was the neighbour. A friend of Natalie's mum. Maybe he had been something more. Natalie had noticed the comings and goings of many men in her short life.

Grams had told her plainly. There had been an accident on the farm. Jerry had seen it happen but hadn't been able to do anything. The tractor had driven too close to the ditch and had rolled. And just like that ... the fantail had come fluttering.

Shuddering again at the memory, Natalie peered down at the small body in her hands.

A gentle bluish tinge coloured the poor thing's eyelids. How peaceful it looked, she thought, just as its chest gave one final undulation and stopped.

Natalie swore under her breath and swallowed back a lump. Her brain raced to sort the practicalities of the moment, and as she glanced around, her eyes landed on the green rubbish bin at the end of the deck.

No. It didn't seem right. She needed to bury it. Only moments before, it had been a living, breathing thing. She couldn't just discard it now.

The school was quiet. A couple of cars were still visible in the car park across the other side of the court: Victoria's rusty-red hatchback, which meant she was likely in her office, and the new girl's white Swift. Newbie was often one of the last to leave. Trying to score points with Victoria, Natalie thought spitefully and grimaced at the sudden rush of hate.

Appraising the rest of her surroundings, Natalie decided the gingko would be as good of a place as any to bury the critter. Around the side of her classroom block, a giant gingko tree stood resolute, its green leaves fanning out over part of the playground. She could dig a hole by its roots; the kids never dug there. Although an occasional climbing spot and a shady place to rest while lining up for the pool, something about it was held in reverence. A perfect place for a bird burial, regardless of how ridiculous people might think it.

The small body was still warm in her hands as she walked with it along the deck, past her class and the other junior room, turning right around the corner of the building until she was under the shade of the gingko. Finding the perfect spot, between two raised roots and close to the trunk, Natalie placed the bird on the ground. This would be its resting place. First, she'd need to dig.

She let out a groan and placed her bag and jacket on the ground beside the bird. It seemed like a hell of a lot of effort for something so small. She'd need a shovel or something. It had been a dry few weeks, and the ground was hard. She wouldn't get anywhere using her hands alone.

She'd go rummage around the caretaker's shed to see what she could find, as long as it wasn't locked. Otherwise, she'd have to rethink her plan.

With one final glance at the bird and her belongings, she cut across the back field to where the small wooden caretaker's shed stood alone in the corner.

In all of her five years of teaching at Te Tapu she must've visited the shed maybe just as many times. She rarely had to attend to anything herself, requiring tools or gardening equipment. The few occasions when she did, there was usually someone else she could fob the job off to. More recently, Liam, for one. Gritting her teeth, she pushed the thought of him aside.

What was she thinking? She needed to get home. Her headache was now sending needles through her right eye. It was a bloody bird. If she didn't want to chuck it in the bin, she could throw it into the native garden, let nature do its thing. Only, it didn't feel right.

She strode across the field to where the caretaker's shed stood stoically in the corner. There wasn't much to it. Peeling paint. No windows. The main classroom block held a cleaner's cupboard with other caretaking supplies. This was simply a storage space for the outside stuff. An old iron wheelbarrow leaned against one side of it. She doubted anyone besides Liam ever went in there now, particularly since he was back in town and had taken over the caretaker duties for the school.

She felt a familiar ache in her chest thinking of him. Only, it wasn't really him that did it to her. It was who he reminded her of. Anna.

Sniffing, Natalie tried to push the memory away. Not now, she scolded herself.

The door was held shut by a Brenton bolt though the padlock looped through it hung open. Natalie sent a silent thank you to whatever god was listening. It wasn't like Liam to be careless, but it was a small school, a safe school. She'd never known there to be any theft. Not in the time she'd been around anyway. That was the thing with small rural communities. Everyone knew everyone. For better or for worse. And you didn't go shitting in your own backyard.

Natalie threaded off the padlock and slid back the bolt. It took a little tug on the door to make it open. Enough light for her to see by came in through the open door, and she was able to quickly trace the shadowy form of the shovel hanging on the wall beside an array of tools. She grabbed it and turned to leave.

Strange, she thought. She'd spent a mere second in the shed, and yet as she left, it was like hours had passed. Concrete-coloured clouds had obscured the blue sky and crowded out the sun. The air smelt different too. Rain. Not that there had been any sign of it before. The farmers would be happy, though.

With the sun hidden by heavy clouds, the temperature had dipped. She stifled a shiver and paused as the hairs on the back of her neck rose in warning. She'd felt this before. It wasn't the change in weather that accounted for the icy chill on her exposed skin. It was that she wasn't alone.

Standing in the doorway, shovel in hand, she peered out across the field where the back of the main school block stood with white cladding and tall windows up high.

All was quiet. As far as she could see, she was alone.

From her vantage point, she saw the lights were off in both the office and the new teacher's room. To her right, she made out a hint of her own car. She couldn't tell if the others had left, hidden as their vehicles were by the angle of the main building.

To her left, the gingko tree stood dark and shadowy. Its branches gently swayed in a breeze that hadn't been there moments before. The playground lay quiet, abandoned. The wide stainless-steel slide stood ominous, hard and unyielding. The worst type of playground equipment in her mind. Particularly in summer when the steel heated to searing temperatures. Two swings gently swayed back and forth, pushed by invisible hands. Leaning the shovel against the doorway for a moment, Natalie wrapped her arms tighter around her body, rubbing the sides of her arms to coax some warmth. Then she turned, grabbed the shovel again and stepped outside the shed. She paused. All her senses on high alert as the insidious prickling at the base of her skull again sent warning jolts through her veins. She *was* being watched.

With one hand Natalie closed the door, pushed the Brenton bolt into place and re-hooked the padlock. She'd lock it properly when she returned the shovel. Liam could thank her later, she thought. Ha!

The breeze picked up.

God, she felt it again. Like someone was behind her, over by the classrooms. Studying her. While she knew the feeling, it didn't normally come with such heaviness. It was different to what she had experienced before. She stifled another shiver.

Pull yourself together, Nat.

"You want to know whether I believe in ghosts? Of course, I do not believe in them. If you had known as many of them as I have, you would not believe in them either."

The words of a Don Marquis quote replayed themselves in her mind.

She turned around again slowly, giving a final scan of her surroundings before heading to the gingko tree.

How did it get so late? she wondered again.

She took a few paces away from the shed when her legs turned to stone and refused to take another step. What the hell was going on?

She pivoted, facing the shed again, searching for anything out of the norm, anything out of place to explain her strange reaction. This time, she could see slightly around the corner of the shed, and although it was draped in shadows, she caught a glimpse of something on the wall. She hadn't noticed it before and couldn't make out what it was. She tried to shrug off her curiosity and draw her attention back to the task at hand. She had a grave to dig.

She grimaced.

Ugh, a grave.

A heavy cloud of emotion settled over her though she couldn't discern exactly what it was. Fear? Anger? It pressed behind her ribs, squeezing at her lungs.

The pinch behind her eye got tighter. She gritted her teeth against a bolt of pain that shot through her temple before dissipating into a dull ache. Torn between getting back to the ginkgo so she could get home and checking out what it was nailed to the side of the shed, half-hidden in shadows, she let out a sigh. Damn it!

She dropped the shovel and marched back towards the shed, this time moving around its side between where the long branches of an overgrown feijoa tree brushed against its walls.

Pushing a branch away she saw it in its entirety. It was beautiful. A marbled type of wood formed a round plaque. Two hands clasping a heart with a crown on top was etched into its surface. Like a Claddagh ring. She knew the symbol well. Grams wore one on her ring finger. A symbol of love and loyalty and the like, if she remembered correctly.

But why was there one here?

Words, obscured by the shadows were inscribed in its surface. Reaching up, Natalie traced the letters with her fingertips. *Billy MacKenzie. Gwen Davies.* For a second a wave of warmth spread through her chest, then, just as quickly, it was torn away by icy fingers. Anger seemed to erupt all around her. She swivelled on her feet searching for the culprit, knowing immediately where it came from. Across the way from her, the darkness grew, menacing, furious. A human silhouette emerged from the shadows against the wall of the school block, its attention homed directly on her.

Natalie felt it, the hatred like needles tattooing her skin. Her head pounded to the point she felt it might split open. Pushing the palms of her hands against her temples, she squeezed her eyes closed, willing away the pain, willing away the figure by the classrooms.

The light. Think of a white light. Surround yourself with light. Grams had taught her how to do it. With all her will power, Natalie imagined herself encased in a ball of white light where she was safe. Superstition, New Age woo-woo – it didn't matter. The pain in her head eased enough to open her eyes again.

She could still see it. Like a mini tornado, the figure had morphed into a swirl of reds and blacks crashing in anger, pain and so much hostility. Whoever he was – and she knew it was a he – his anger and hatred were directed at her. Yet she stared it down, all the time imagining herself enclosed in white light. The man moved no closer, and Natalie held strong to her circle of light. Fuck you, she thought. Whoever you are, fuck you!

She flicked a glance once more at the plaque on the wall.

It was because of the plaque; she was sure of it. It had woken something.

Whoever had hung it there, they'd stirred something up. Did they have any idea what they had done?

CHAPTER 1

Natalie

Poe slunk out from the overgrown weeds around the side of the house and met her on the front porch. He opened his mouth wide and emitted a strangled choking sound as was customary for him. Silly cat had never got the hang of a proper meow.

Natalie bent down and gave him a quick pat, eliciting a head butt from the old fellow before he turned towards the door and scratched at it. Dinner time, Natalie thought. That cat was good at keeping her on schedule.

She steadied herself before making a move to unlock the door. Her mother's beaten up Civic sat in the driveway, its rear passenger side door showcasing a dent from one of her mother's misadventures.

Giving a sigh, Natalie closed her eyes for a moment. All was quiet in the house itself, but she knew the moment she opened that door, she'd be hit with a hurricane of drama.

Old orange paint flaked off the door and down between her feet. Poe pawed at the door again, letting another strangled mew escape as he encouraged her on.

When Natalie opened the door, the cat shot through her legs and down the hallway, making a right into the kitchen, where Natalie could hear the host of a TV game show egging on his audience.

"Nat?! You home?" a muffled voice called out to her.

Her mother, Helena. Natalie ignored her and headed to her room. Bed unmade, curtains still drawn, she scrunched her nose at the stale smell. God, she needed to get her act together. She dropped her bag and jacket on the end of the bed, then went about stripping off her clothes. She picked a crumpled Nirvana T-shirt and a pair of trackies from the bedroom floor. She had just pulled the T-shirt over her head and had one leg in her track pants when her bedroom door burst open.

"I've been calling you!" an angry voice said.

"Jeez! You could learn to knock," Natalie retorted slipping her other leg into her pants. She hoisted them up and tied a bow in the cord at the waist.

"Fuck, Nat! Open this place up, would ya?" Her mother scowled and stormed over to the other side of the room. She proceeded to pull back a curtain and unlatch one of the windows before pushing it open. Natalie stifled a growl. *Now* she wanted to act all motherly?

They had only seventeen years between them, and her mother carried her age well. Those who didn't know better thought they were sisters. Her mother was more petite with darker skin, having inherited more of her father's, Natalie's grandfather's, complexion.

"I've been calling you. I needed you home an hour ago." Helena spun to face her. Hands on hips, she jutted her chin out, looking like a petulant teenager.

Natalie rummaged in her bag on the bed and pulled out her phone. After turning it on, she saw a long list of notifications of missed calls. All of them Helena.

Helena huffed, waiting for a reply.

"I was working," Natalie said through clenched teeth. She wanted to say more. Hell, if it hadn't been for her, they would have lost the house years ago.

Helena huffed again, louder this time, and flicked her hair over her shoulder. She'd piled on the makeup. Her mascara had clumped, and her eyeliner had already smudged around her eyes. Unless, Natalie thought, that was how she'd planned it. The short skirt, cleavage re-vealing tank and knee-high boots told Natalie everything she needed to know as to why Helena so desperately wanted her daughter home. Lately Helena had been spending more and more of her evenings at the local tavern. Only three a week accounted for her bar shift. Which meant there was a man involved. There always was. For a second, Natalie wondered who the loser was this time and how long before his wife came banging on their door? Again. Her mother had a type.

"Well, I can't do this all alone, Nat! I need you here. Ma needs you here. I'm going out and someone needs to mind her." Helena waved her arm in the direction of the kitchen, where it sounded like the TV game show had taken a break for an insurance ad.

"God, Mum!" she whispered under her breath, shaking her head in disgust and pushing past Helena for the kitchen. Helena's heeled footsteps followed her.

"You can't just walk away from me like that," Helena called after her, her voice an octave higher. Not yet a screech but getting there.

Natalie stifled the impulse to plug her ears with her fingers.

"I've been working all day, you know. Plus, I got a call from Melanie Harrison. She said she'd seen Ma wandering again. Towards the woods! And I had to leave work and go collect her."

Natalie stifled a snort. Occasionally, Helena picked up a day shift. Today must've been one of those days. She clenched her teeth against asking how it was that Grams had left the house. They had a system in place, albeit not a great one. When they went out, they locked the doors. Natalie had attached a bolt to the outside of the front door to be used in emergencies only. It made Natalie feel sick when she did have to use it. But Grams was safer in the house than out on her own.

"I deserve some fun, Nat. You can't say I don't. I need this!" Helena's voice rose in pitch.

"*Deserve* this?" Natalie said incredulous, pivoting on the ball of her foot to face her mother, who pulled up abruptly.

Helena stood almost six inches shorter than her. A flicker of surprise crossed her face before giving way to a steady glare. Natalie held it with her own.

"I'm the one who works," Natalie retorted, tapping her chest with her thumb. "Me. Monday to Friday, *I* work. *I* pay the bills," she growled, hot anger rising up her chest. "You work part time at the tavern, but rent, food, utilities ... That's on me. And when you or one of your dumbass boyfriends find themselves at the station or the drunk tank, who goes along and bails you out? Me!"

She shouldn't have thrown that at her, of course she shouldn't, but she was so sick of having the same argument over and over and over again. What was it said about the definition of insanity? Doing the same thing over and over again while expecting a different result?

"That's not fair!" her mother argued, stamping her foot on the hardwood floor again.

Natalie wondered for the umpteenth time how this child, this teenager in front of her, because damn it, that was how she acted, could be her mother. How were they even related?

Natalie took a deep breath to calm her pulse. Quieter this time, she said, "You pick up a few shifts here and there at the tavern and then do what? She's your mother – you owe it to her to be here, not galivanting around town. And you know what, Mum? You owe it to me too." By some miracle she'd kept her voice calm. She didn't know how. Inside, every ounce of her was quivering with rage. Her mother's bottom lip trembled, and Natalie quickly turned away and made for the kitchen, relieved for a moment to hear silence behind her.

Grams was sitting where she always sat: on the corner chair under the window. Her eyes were glued to the small television perched on the end of the island; Poe already curled up on her lap.

"Hey, Grammy," Natalie said, kneeling down beside her and taking her hand in her own.

It was so cold, so frail. Like all of her. Grams's lips curved upward, but her eyes never left the TV. Natalie didn't for a second believe she was really watching it. She was lost. Elsewhere. Reliving another time, another place. As she most often was nowadays. Natalie could still see a hint of the young woman she had been, still was in many ways. She was sixty-nine years old now, the same as Victoria, Natalie's principal, who had as much energy if not more than all the other teachers put together.

Grams was still lithe, much like Helena. Her eyes were now a pale foggy blue, but other than laughter lines around her eyes and mouth her skin was remarkably smooth.

Natalie looked down at the hand resting in her own. The skin on the back of her hand was creped and darkened with age spots, the Claddagh ring her only jewellery. Natalie gave her hand a gentle squeeze, checking again if anyone was home. The corner of Grams's mouth twitched, and Natalie let Grams's hand fall gently to her lap.

Natalie straightened, feeling her mother's eyes on her from the doorway. Without sparing a glance in her direction, she turned to the pantry and pulled the door open to scour its contents.

"Do you want me to leave you some dinner?" Natalie cringed at the edge that had crept into her voice again.

She waited, holding her breath to see if her mother would respond.

"I'll fend for myself," was the terse reply.

Natalie closed the pantry door, finding nothing inspiring and moved towards the fridge.

"I'll be home late so don't bother waiting up," Helena finished.

"I never do." The words slipped out before Natalie was even aware what she was saying. She silently cursed herself as a humph came from the direction of the doorway. She heard her mother turn on her heel and storm down the hall.

"Bitch," Natalie swore under her breath, not sure if the curse was meant for her or her mother.

CHAPTER 2

Natalie

There was a ripple of excitement in the air. Even Natalie felt it prickle under her skin. Term Four: the final stretch of the school year. Despite being only eight thirty in the morning, the sun already packed a punch, and without a single cloud in the sky, it was guaranteed to be a hot one.

Natalie stood on the deck outside of her room ready to greet the eager faces pouring out the door of the bus, which had pulled up by the entrance. Bags on backs bustled against each other as a rampage of small bodies and shrill voices hastened through the front gate, down the path towards her.

Hers was the first classroom, and children called out greetings on seeing her. Many continued along the deck to the connecting classroom or else tore across the courts to the old school block and the prefab class across from it.

Turning her attention to the small bodies in front of her, Natalie said her greetings and listened as the excited Year Twos spoke over each other to fill her in on their two weeks of vacation. After dumping their bags on the hooks along the classroom's wall, they raced off with friends in tow towards the playground and sandpit.

They were like mini-hurricanes, and a genuine smile broke across Natalie's face. It was a strange thing to notice, but how many times had she smiled, *really* smiled, over the term break? She could probably count as much on one hand. It never ceased to surprise her how such small beings could elicit such a feeling. Her shoulders dropped; her tension eased away. They were so innocent, so free. The thought came with a small pang of jealously.

The kids showed none of the first-day nerves that accompanied the beginning of the year. By now, they all knew each other and their teachers as well as the routines and what was expected of them. Many of the older kids were aware of the encroaching end of the year, not only the joys of summer but their final term ruling the school before embarking on their new adventures at Intermediate the following year.

Natalie glanced across to the main school building. The original school building. A long concrete deck ran along the front side. At the end closest to her was the toilet block, followed by the resource room and a small teachers' office. Next to that was the Year Five and Six classroom, beside which were the staffroom and reception area.

Natalie's gaze fell back on the classroom in the middle. Its double French doors were swung open so everyone could see clearly into the classroom. It made sense considering how hot it was.

Her eyes fell upon the two figures standing inside, clear for everyone to see. One was Riley, or Newbie, as Natalie still thought of her although she had started at the beginning of the year. The broad-shouldered figure beside her was unmistakable, even from behind.

Natalie bristled as her eyes followed Riley's fingers gently brushing Liam's arm as she leaned in closer to him. Natalie imagined she heard coy tittering as they shared an intimate joke.

So that was it, then? They *were* a thing now? Natalie scowled, a tsunami of emotions turning her stomach. It shouldn't have been a surprise. She'd had a hunch they were an item for months. She'd seen the tension between them earlier in the year and had known it would only be a matter of time. It was one of the reasons she disliked the new teacher so much. She was no replacement for Anna. How could she be?

A prickle of anger crawled up her spine, and beads of sweat gathered at the base of her neck. "Bitch!" she thought venomously, her teeth grinding together. Just as suddenly, the intensity of the emotion disappeared, and Natalie gave herself a little shake.

Where the hell had that came from? She hated Liam – nothing new there – and didn't like the newbie much either. But just for a moment, an intrusive thought had taken root. She'd wanted them dead.

Natalie wet her lips with her tongue; her mouth suddenly dry.

It made no sense. What the hell did she care whom Liam dated? For all she knew, they deserved each other and deserved whatever their twisted entanglement brought them.

She felt it again. A fire, a venom that left a bad taste on her tongue.

She'd known Riley was trouble from the first moment she'd seen her. The woman brought darkness with her. It was a tangible cloud that seemed to follow her, particularly in those first few weeks of her arriving at Te Tapu. All of Natalie's senses had been heightened towards it, and as much as they could be a pain in the arse at times, she trusted them.

Still, the anger, the depth of it, it hadn't come from Natalie. She was sure of it. But neither was it the first time she'd felt such malice when seeing either Riley or Liam. She gave another involuntary shake, just as a deep voice broke through her reverie making her jump.

"Kia ora. Are you Miss Sullivan?"

Natalie blushed, startled, as she turned to face the man before her. Her heart stuttered as she took in how attractive he was. Damn. That was unexpected.

Her eyes fell to the small form beside him, hand clasped in his. A round cheeked boy of maybe seven with a large red school bag on his back.

"I'm Riki," the man said, redirecting her attention and holding his free hand out to her.

Swallowing hard and forcing a more professional composure, Natalie took it, noticing immediately how firm his grip was. A second wave of heat rose up inside her, putting to bed all the anger she'd been feeling only moments before.

Riki tilted his head as if noticing, the corner of his mouth quirking upward.

Times like this, she would give anything for more of Helena's colouring and her grandfather's genes to hide the warmth in her cheeks.

"Natalie Sullivan," she said in response, forcing professionalism she really didn't feel. It wasn't often she was caught so off guard. What was with her today?

"And who is this?" Natalie bent down, eye level with the small form before her, hoping to hide how disarmed his father made her.

The child bowed his head to his chest and refused to make eye contact, pulling himself closer to his father's side.

"This is my son Cole. The principal sent us over here." Riki waved his free hand in the direction of the court were a small group of children surrounded Victoria's willowy form.

Natalie caught her eye, and Victoria raised her eyebrows in response. A new student then.

"Nice to meet you, Cole," Natalie said gently.

The small boy said nothing, his eyes remaining focused on the ground

"Well, I'm Miss Sullivan. I'm going to be your teacher. And this" – she swung an arm towards the classroom behind her – "is going to be your classroom."

Cole continued to ignore her. His fringe shielded his downcast eyes.

First-day nerves, she thought. "Would you like me to show you where to put your bag?" Natalie extended a hand towards him, pausing to see if he would take it. Cole nuzzled his face into his father's side.

Wiping her slightly damp hands on her legs, Natalie stood up and gave Riki a knowing smile.

"Come on, bud, let's go hang your bag up, eh?" Riki shook his leg gently. Cole seemed to tighten his grip.

Riki's eyes met Natalie's again, his lips turning in a rueful manner. "He's just a bit shy. He'll come around." He placed a hand on his son's shoulder before leaning in slightly to Natalie. He whispered, "It's been a bit of a tough year." He glanced at the small form beside him.

Natalie waited for an elaboration; when none came, she said, "That's fine. It's his first day. Let's get Cole set up, shall we?"

Gesturing towards the hooks lining the wall along the outside of the classroom, she led the pair over to find a free one. Riki unwound his offspring from his leg and tried to pry the backpack from his back. Once freed of it, Cole's arms quickly wound themselves back around his father's leg.

"Would you like to come inside?" Natalie said, gesturing towards the classroom door. "I can show you and Cole around."

"Sounds good," he said. "If I can get this koala to unravel himself from my leg." He gave his leg another shake, and Natalie warmed, hearing the hint of a giggle from Cole.

Slowly, Cole released himself and took his father's hand in his own.

Natalie inwardly sighed with relief. She stole a glance through the entrance of her class at the clock on the back wall. Damn, almost bell time.

"Come on, then," Natalie said, adopting the chirpy tone she used on those children she wasn't sure would actually do as she asked. From the corner of her eye, she saw Cole steal a glance in her direction. She started; Cole had the most stunning blue eyes, accentuated by long dark eyelashes. Combined with the dark warmth of his skin, he was one cute kid.

She guided the pair through the open doors, where she set about giving a brief tour of the classroom. This was where the tote trays were for his books and pencil case. Had he brought any exercise books with him from his previous school? And oh, where was that again? Natalie continued asking questions, gently pressing for a little bit more information about her new charge, while consciously trying to push aside the flutter in her chest whenever her eyes caught those of Riki.

Two weeks of being cooped up at home with Grams had done something to her. Her emotions were all over the bloody show. Pull it together, Nat, she scolded herself. The weak-kneed, horny teenager act was her mother's thing, not hers.

Cole seemed to be losing some of his shyness to curiosity. With gentle fingers, he reached out to touch some of the seashells on the nature table, and he ran his fingers through the basket of linking cubes on the maths shelf.

When they finished, Riki gave her a grin of thanks. Cole was now pulling further away from his dad to peer outside, where some of his classmates were playing by the sandpit.

His relaxing was a good sign. Maybe Dad could even head home without leaving any tears or tantrums behind him.

"Do you want to go play?" Natalie gently probed. Cole was almost at the door now, his arm stretched back so that he was still clasping his father's hand.

Natalie crossed her fingers. It would be good just to have a couple of minutes to talk with Riki alone. She suspected there was a bit of a story to poor little Cole.

Cole looked back tentatively at his father, and Natalie caught a glimpse once more of the stunning blue of his eyes. Oh, the girls in her class were going to love him. Even at six and seven, the kids noticed things like that.

"Go on, bud. I'll be right here with Miss Sullivan."

Cole paused.

The sandpit was a covered area only ten metres or so from her classroom, in easy view from where they were standing near the entrance to the room. Little heads bobbed behind the flax and grassy tussocks of the small garden surrounding the woven wire fence bordering the sandpit. A couple of young boys and girls from her class were playing a chase game, running in one entrance and out the other in circles around and through the sandpit.

In one big breath, Cole let go of his father's hand and took off in their direction, and a surge of relief filled Natalie's chest. He would be just fine.

Turning back to the man in front of her, she willed herself into teacher mode. Keep that professionalism, Nat, she reminded herself.

Riki's eyes followed his son's form for a second, before turning his attention back to Natalie.

"Look, I'm sorry about that," he said. "Cole's a good kid; he's just ..." He paused and Natalie waited patiently as he searched for words.

It came with the job. Every kid had a story. In his face, she recognised what usually preceded an admittance of learning or social difficulties or neurodivergence. She'd lost count of how many times she'd seen parents wearing the same expression. The same wave of emotions covered their faces too, embarrassment, defensiveness, hope and fear. These things still carried a ridiculous stigma for many. And if it were a new diagnosis, parents were quite often still coming to terms with it themselves. It made them vulnerable. Oh, if only they knew how many times she had heard it all before, they would realise it was no big deal. Their child would be fine. She'd make sure of it.

So, she wasn't prepared when the next words fell from his lips.

"His mum ... she died."

Natalie fought against the initial shock. This wasn't what she had been expecting. Not at all.

She mentally chided herself. Not only had she made completely wrong assumptions only seconds earlier, but she'd also been lusting after this man who'd just lost his wife.

"I'm so sorry," she said, quietly, allowing him the space to say more if he wanted.

"Yeah, well ..." Riki said. He shrugged a shoulder, feigning nonchalance though his eyes no longer met hers. "It was eight months ago, but Cole ... well, it's been hard ..." His voice trailed off.

"I understand," Natalie said, feeling a prickle behind her own eyes.

"He hasn't completely accepted it yet. He's kind of withdrawn from others. He doesn't say much." His voice cracked. "Shit," he said. "It's been tough." He wiped a hand across his forehead, and Natalie looked away for a moment to give him time to compose himself.

"Cole. He's good. It just might take him a while to warm up to people."

Natalie followed his glance through the doors towards the sandpit. The kids from her class still chased each other, laughing and teasing as they did. Cheerful voices carried from inside the sandpit too. And there sat Cole.

Her blood left her extremities, and she bit her lip hard; her skin turning to ice. Fuck.

Cole perched alone on a large rock at the edge of the garden by the sandpit. He appeared deep in conversation, his head high, turned to the side.

Riki's hand drifted to his mouth, where he massaged his jaw with his fingers for a moment before letting his hand drop to his side.

"He make-believes she's still here and he can see her. I catch him chatting away to thin air as if he's talking to her and ... Look, I'm sorry. It's all a bit much."

Natalie noticed the bubble of emotion in his voice.

"I just thought you should know, in case he starts acting a little ... like that, I guess." He gestured at his son. "He'll be okay, though. His doctor said it'll just take time. It's a bit of a coping mechanism, I guess."

Realising she hadn't said anything, Natalie tried to regain her composure. "Of course." She forced what she hoped was a believable smile. "I'm sure he'll be fine." A wave of pity for the poor child hit her hard.

The thing was, he wasn't making believe. But neither was he talking to his mother.

Riki might not be able to see who his son was talking to, but she did. And it meant that Cole was a very special little boy indeed.

And also ...

Maybe in a lot of danger.

CHAPTER 3

Maggie

PRESENT DAY

The dream was back again. It started as it always did with her standing barefoot in the forest behind the house, eighteen again. It was night. She could see a sliver of the crescent moon peaking between the gnarled branches of the rata tree that twisted its way to the sky. The sky was the darkest of blues, the light fading so fast the trees around her were only moments away from dissolving into blackened shadows. Tree ferns and creepers, podocarps and shrubs encircled her in a natural prison.

Maggie tried not to panic. She knew it was a dream; lucid dreaming she had heard it once called. Yet at the same time, the cool breeze teasing goosebumps on her bare legs did nothing to alleviate the feeling that this was real, this was happening. She was here in the woods. Again. Alone. But not alone.

A flapping of wings above her made her heart shudder in her chest, and she peered around, knowing she only had seconds before the footsteps came for her.

Turning in a circle, she did her best to find any sign of her tormentor. If she could only see them, she thought, maybe this time she could escape. Or fight. And she had age on her side. She'd swapped her sixty-nine-year-old body for a younger model. Such was the power of dreams. Even so, what a slight eighteen-year-old, standing barefooted in her nightie in the middle of the night, could do to hurt or maim an unseen attacker, she just wasn't sure. She'd never won before.

Yes, except this time she'd fight harder, a voice in the back of her mind pressed.

She heard it now. Footsteps. They sounded as if they were coming from behind her. Standing between her and safety, the house at the edge of the woods. But every time she'd thought she'd pinned them down; they surprised her, and her attacker would appear from a different direction.

It was just a dream, just a dream, she reminded herself. And she rubbed her arms where the cold had pierced through the thin linen. She circled slowly. Still nothing beyond the footsteps. The gentle crunching of leaves and vegetation beneath booted feet grew closer. She needed to make a decision.

Choose a direction, she pleaded with herself. You don't have much time. Choose a direction and ... RUN!

A voice screamed in her head. Her own voice, but it spurred her on anyway, and she lunged forward, in a panicked sprint. Dodging the silhouetted trunks of the trees, their buttressed roots and the spindly fingers of their branches. Something scraped across her cheek regardless, like a dirty fingernail. It made her flesh burn, but it didn't matter. Her whole intent was to escape the man behind her.

Though she never saw him in her dreams, she knew him from another time, when the world had been ablaze and seared her skin, and smoke had strangled her lungs and stolen her voice.

The heaviness of his energy preceded his form. It thickened the air, making it hard to breathe, and drained the blood from her limbs so that she thought she might collapse, there on the forest floor. So she willed herself on.

Every time, he caught her. And when he did, he'd wrap his calloused fingers around her throat and fill her nostrils with the sour stench of whiskey on his breath as he leant in and whispered the word "whore" in her ear.

She yelped as a sharp pain sliced through the fleshy part of her foot. Again, she thought she'd fall, her legs turning to rubber. She stumbled and flailed her arms to restore balance.

Sounds of movement came from behind, crashing through the underbrush. He was coming for her. Her heart pounded against her ribcage, propelling her feet to keep moving. She fought her way through the darkness, pushing aside the talons that tugged at her sleeves and ripped the hem of her nightie.

A voice called her name. A glimmer of recognition sent Maggie clamouring to remember who it was. A seed of hope was sown – maybe this time she'd be saved.

Without warning, she slammed against a wall. Strong hands grabbed her shoulders, and she screamed, screamed blue murder, because that was what lay ahead. She could feel it within her bones, with all her knowing. Murder lay ahead.

CHAPTER 4

Natalie

"Grammy!" Natalie reached her seconds after Troy grabbed her. "Grammy!" she shouted again, trying to get through to her grandmother over the sound of her screaming.

"Grams, it's okay; I'm here," she said arriving at her side.

Troy was still holding the older woman by the upper arms, pinning them to her sides. Natalie manoeuvred herself in between the two of them, taking Troy's place.

"It's okay. It's okay," she soothed in a low voice. "I'm here now. You're safe."

Grams quietened until her screaming was replaced with soft whimpers and sobs. Natalie pulled her close, wrapping her arms around her so Grams's head rested on her chest. Natalie could feel her bones beneath her thin night dress. She shot a glance at Troy, who had a frown etched on his face.

"This is the third time in two weeks, Sullivan!"

"Shh, shh," she whispered to her grandmother again before turning back to him. "I've got it."

"Well, obviously you don't. I can't keep coming out here. It's a waste of police resources—"

"Oh, please. It's not like the police force out here are exactly rushed off their feet. Anyway, I said I've got it!" Natalie glared at him. Troy could be an arse, but he didn't deserve her shitting on him like this. He'd been lenient up until now. She was beginning to lose track of the number of times he'd brought Grams home when she'd gone wandering. She owed him. But she wasn't ready to admit it right now.

"Come on, Grammy," Natalie said pushing the old woman slightly away from her.

Troy shook off his jacket and draped it around Grams's shoulders.

Natalie stifled a growl. She had no reason to be moody with him, but his show of chivalry irritated her like it was secretly a judgement of her. How many other elderly ladies did he get called out to trapse after in the woods in the dark of night? Probably none. And he'd said it before: Grams should be in assisted living, getting proper care. But by God, if he mentioned it again, particularly tonight, *she* was going to scream bloody murder.

She wrapped an arm around Grams, who was now eerily silent but for her raspy breathing, and Natalie gently led her towards Troy's cruiser.

Troy shone the torch ahead of them and lightly touched Natalie's shoulder. Though she suspected it was his way of trying to make amends, she shook it off. Honestly, her fear for her grandmother was now being replaced with embarrassment, and Troy was the last person she wanted to know that.

They'd known each other since they were kids, attending Te Tapu Primary together although Troy was a year older. They'd even gone to the same college but ran in different circles. While she went into teacher education, he nestled into police training. As they all seemed to do in Te Tapu, both found their way back home again. Te Tapu, had a way of reeling people back in. Did anyone ever escape? she wondered. Troy had come closest. He resided in Maramanui, a town a mere twenty minutes away. But with Te Tapu too small to have its own police force, he was often drawn back to help the community he knew so well.

It didn't help matters that they'd slept together. Many times over the years. It never meant anything. Not to her anyway. And she'd always been upfront about that. How else was a person to entertain themselves in a village like this? Unfortunately, just like with Te Tapu, every time one of them said no more, they kept finding their way back to each other. It was like a disease.

Troy muttered something under his breath and pulled ahead, walking a few paces before her. He was annoyed with her too. So be it.

Natalie held his jacket tight across Grams's shoulders, guiding her back through the forest, trusting Troy knew the way back to his cruiser.

What was she going to do with her? Grams had been doing this all too often lately, and it was dangerous. What if she'd snuck out in the middle of the night and no one had noticed, and she'd fallen or broken something? It wasn't safe for her. Troy was right. She needed better care than what she was getting. Natalie worked and Helena mostly partied. And Natalie loved her grandmother. Only, she didn't want her left in the hands of some unfriendly caregiver, shut away in some small room, feeling alone and forgotten about. No. Somehow Natalie would make it work. Plus, with Helena barely contributing anything to household expenses, she wasn't sure she could afford it.

When her grandfather had passed, he'd left Grams with loans against the house for the farm and an excess of bills to pay. Grams had done her best to keep the farm afloat, taking small jobs here and there in the village, yet the bills kept coming. And then Helena got herself knocked up at the ripe age of seventeen. And with her mother never seeming to have aged beyond seventeen, things were never going to be easy. Piece by piece, the farm had been sold off, which had kept them afloat for a little while.

When Grams had gotten sick they'd survived on two-minute noodles and marmite sandwiches. It helped when Natalie had gotten a scholarship to university and a part-time job. Natalie's teaching job was the core means of keeping all of their heads above water. Topped up by Grams's Super and a few bucks here and there from Helena, it was nothing short of a miracle they hadn't lost the house along the way.

And bloody Troy – she kept her eyes on his back as he led the way – he had helped them out more times than she wished to recall, surprising her with extra groceries or filling the freezer with home kill, mowing the lawns or pruning trees. She should have been thankful, yet somehow it only made her resent him more. That and the fact she knew he had a thing for her despite her insistence on keeping things casual.

Her grandmother was shaking beneath her arm, making small mumbling sounds. Relief flooded her when the brush opened to a clearing. Troy pressed his key fob, unlocking the cruiser with a flash of lights and a beep of the alarm.

After opening the back passenger door, he turned and walked towards her.

"Alright, Maggie, let's get you home, eh?" he said, being careful to avoid eye contact with Natalie, she noticed. He put his arm around Grams, and Natalie let him take charge, leading her to the passenger door and helping her get in. He stood there for a moment, back to Natalie, one hand on top of the door. He ran his other hand through his hair, as if he were taking a moment to compose himself before turning back to her.

Finally, he did.

"Front or back?" he said gesturing to the opened door where her grandmother sat.

Natalie's tongue refused to move. Her anger had stolen her voice. She wasn't really angry at him, part of her knew that, but it was easier somehow. It had always been easier. Focus the anger on whoever was nearest so she didn't have to confront her own failings.

Ignoring his question, she pushed past him and got in beside her grandmother.

Troy closed the door after her with a little too much force, and Natalie stifled another pang of guilt.

CHAPTER 5

Natalie

I t was only a couple of minutes before they pulled up her driveway. They'd taken the cruiser, unsure of what state Grams would be in when they found her, and Natalie was glad they had. Grams was spry even if her mind couldn't always keep up. She'd cut across the paddock beside their house and headed into the forest, following it around the back of their property. Had she kept going, she might have reached the school.

Despite the short drive back, Grams's eyes were closed when they pulled to a stop by the front door.

Once unbuckled, Natalie got out of the car and walked around to the other side to help Grams out. Troy beat her to it. He had already unbelted her and deftly lifted her into his arms, an arm around her waist and the other under her legs, while her head lay on his shoulder.

Natalie caught herself swallowing hard as a lump rose in her throat. How innocent, childlike even, Grams looked in his arms. And so frail.

The old-fashioned linen night dress clung to her form. Bones. Clung to her bones, Natalie corrected herself.

With one foot, Troy kicked out at the cruiser's door, slamming it shut. Ignoring Natalie, he carried Grams up the few steps to the front door and waited.

Natalie rummaged in her pocket for her key. Troy stepped aside for her to unlock the door and let the two of them in. Though the hall light was on, the house was quiet. Natalie hadn't bothered to check if Helena's car was parked under the carport, but she suspected she was still out. It was equally possible she wouldn't come home at all tonight.

Troy knew his way pretty well around the house and so took no directions, pausing at the entrance of the first room on the right, allowing Natalie time to flick on the bedroom light.

The room smelt shut up, musty, old, and Natalie grimaced. She quickened her pace to reach the side of the bed before Troy did, pulling the duvet back to allow him to place Grams on the bed.

The bed stand was a mess of crumpled tissues, an old lamp and a glass of water with a film of dust settled on top and faded lipstick on the rim. A couple of books sat in a pile. Natalie took a few steps back to give Troy space.

Grams mumbled something without opening her eyes. She turned onto her side and curled her knees up to her chest, and Natalie was reminded again of a young child. She sat down on the bed beside her grandmother and gently tucked her white hair behind her ear before turning back to the figure standing over her.

"Thank you," she said. The words sounding forced.

She got a grunt in return.

"Where's your first aid kit?" Troy asked.

Confused for a second, Natalie followed the direction of his eyes. One of the soles of Grams's feet was crusted with dried blood and dirt.

"In the kitchen under the sink," she replied, trying to downplay the alarm that rose to the surface.

Troy turned his back on her and walked out of the room, his footsteps carrying towards the kitchen.

Ugh, she thought. Why did he always make her feel so horrible? He was a good-looking, salt-of-the-earth man, and for whatever reason he felt something for her. He'd always treated her well, and yet she ... treated him like dirt.

Natalie turned back to Grams. What had she been thinking? she wondered. Why run out to the forest? Who was she running from?

She could hear Troy rummaging around in the kitchen. Maybe she hadn't been specific enough.

She stroked Grams's hair again, a finger tracing where the lines had smoothed along the side of her face. How innocent she looked. Her eyelids almost transparent blue, just like the pīwakawaka's from a few weeks back; the thought floated up from nowhere.

Natalie's eyes were drawn to the books lying on the side table, one standing out more than the others. It was a collection of Edgar Allan Poe works. She deftly pulled it from the pile and opened to a random page.

"Those who dream by day are cognisant of many things which escape those who dream only by night. Believe only half of what you see and nothing of what you hear."

Natalie recognised the quote at once. As a young ten- or eleven-year-old, she would often curl up on the couch with her grandmother, who would read to her from Edgar Allan Poe's collected works. Helena would come in and, in one of her few instances of motherly concern, tell her mother off for filling her daughters head with such morbid fascinations. Yet they had never been morbid to Natalie. A little dark, yes, but wasn't that the truth of life? The seeds of darkness could be found everywhere, and Poe certainly had a way of evoking emotion through his prose. Plus, there had always been the preciousness of time spent alone with her grandmother. Just the two of them. Grams was someone who seemed to understand Natalie in a way no one else did. And she'd always felt safe with her. She couldn't say the same of her mother.

Heavy footsteps drawing near shocked Natalie from her daydream. She snapped the book closed and returned it to the pile on the night-stand.

"You need to get a new kit," Troy said on entering the room.

Natalie shrugged, then realising her rudeness, forced a smile to soften its edge. Try harder, she told herself.

Troy narrowed his eyes, not buying her sudden change in disposition which just served to annoy her more.

He planted himself down on the end of the bed at Grams's feet.

"How bad is it?" she asked, as Troy set to work washing away the dirt with a wet towel and bowl of water he'd brought with him from the kitchen.

Grams let out a small moan making them both pause and hold their breath. When Grams's eyes remained closed, Troy went back to work.

"It's just a small cut." He dipped the edge of the towel back into the bowl of water and wrung it out again. "She'll be fine. Some ointment and a plaster. Just keep an eye on it in case of infection."

She wanted to thank him again. He hadn't needed to stay and clean her up. She could have done it, yet he'd done it anyway. And she was grateful no matter how much she loathed to admit it.

"This can't happen again, Sullivan," he said, his voice low and eyes averted.

"I know," Natalie replied, shame warming her cheeks. She did. If it happened again who knew what could happen. And it had been happening more and more, Natalie couldn't deny it. Her grandmother's moments of lucidity were becoming fewer and fewer, and if something ever happened to her ... Natalie couldn't bear to think about it. Grams was all she had.

"Right. Well, she's all fixed up." He said it so matter-of-factly, she could tell he was still angry with her. He stood up, taking the bowl, towel, and small first aid kit with him. "I'll just put these away and get going, then."

"I'll take care of them," she said, reaching out for the things in his hands.

Without protest he offloaded them to her.

"You can stay if you want," she blurted out, and mentally kicked herself. She hadn't meant it as it sounded. "I can make a cuppa," she said quickly trying to amend herself.

He paused and Natalie could almost read the internal combat playing itself out in the lines of his forehead.

"Yeah-nah," he said. "I've gotta get going."

He wiped his hands on his thighs, and Natalie stood there, frozen in place as he turned away and walked out the room.

A commotion at the door only moments later, announced her mother's arrival home, just as Troy was leaving. She heard some

cussing at what sounded like Poe nearly tripping Helena in his eager-
ness to race inside. Then another loud oath as Troy filled her in on the
night's adventures.

"Natalie!" Her mother's voice came as a shrill yell, not caring a bit
for what she was sure Troy would have told her about Grams resting.
"Natalie," she yelled again, and Natalie whispered her own choice
words as she stole a glance at her sleeping grandmother.

Natalie plopped the bowl and first aid things down on the dresser.
She'd deal with them later. First, she had to deal with her mother. The
slurring and loudness of her words were a dead giveaway she'd been
drinking.

On reaching the hallway, she saw her mother wavering on one foot,
hand resting on a wall as she struggled to take off one of her boots with
the other. Behind her, the cruiser's headlights flashed as Troy pulled
around to leave the driveway.

"You're drunk," Natalie said stonily.

"Oh, screw you," Helena replied. "You're not my keeper. Where's
Mum?"

"She's sleeping."

Finally wrenching her boot from her foot, Helena threw it to the
ground and went about tackling the next one.

A new sort of fury started to well up in Natalie.

"Just leave her, okay? She needs to sleep." Natalie said.

"She was sleeping when I left. What the hell happened?!"

"Keep your voice down," Natalie hushed her. "She went walking
again. To the woods." Natalie put her hand to her head and massaged
her forehead. A new full-body tiredness hit her.

"Where were you?" Helena snapped, almost falling over as she threw her other boot onto the floor.

"I was here in my room, lesson planning. I didn't hear her." The guilt she'd tried so hard to push down rose to the surface.

"Fuck, Natalie—"

"No!" Natalie said, raising her voice a little. "You don't get to blame me for this. I'm home almost every night. I'm the one finding her and bringing her home when she goes wandering, but where the hell are you, Mum? She's *your* mother, and you're never bloody here. *Look* at you!" Natalie felt herself losing it. Her clenched fists shook at her side.

Helena stared at her, gobsmacked.

"You're never here!" Natalie repeated, her eyes welling.

A flash of anger swept across Helena's face, quickly replaced with hurt. Her mouth opened and closed as if she were trying to say something, but then changing her mind she turned on her heel and stormed to her bedroom, slamming the door behind her.

Well, screw her, Natalie thought. She shouldn't have to be her mother's keeper too. She followed suit and stalked off to her own room, dropping onto her bed fully clothed. What the hell was she going to do? Her mother was a dead weight, her grandmother was going to get herself killed one of these days, and what of her? She was trying to hold everyone together while she herself was falling apart at the seams. Grams use to tell her she was special. Gifted, even. Cursed more like. To Natalie, it seemed her whole bloody mess of a family were cursed.

CHAPTER 6

Natalie

"How is Cole settling in?" Victoria asked.

Natalie stood at the sink, stirring her coffee. Sometimes she swore Victoria was a mind reader. She had just been thinking about the little boy. He wasn't settling in. And it bothered her. He seemed to prefer to be alone to playing with the other kids. She'd tried to make him feel at home, setting up a buddy system with some of the more confident in her class. And her students had certainly tried. They loved when new children joined the classroom. At first, they'd all scrambled to be his friend, to sit with him, to teach him the class rules like where the glue sticks lived, and where the best reading spot was. But every time they approached him, he'd look away, eyes downcast. His sadness, so palpable, that after a while the other students just stopped trying.

Natalie paused her stirring for a moment, wondering what to tell Victoria. She hated the fact it had already been two weeks and she still hadn't got through to him.

Willing the crease she felt between her brows to soften, she took a breath and turned around. She had an audience.

The staffroom was small. A two-seated sofa sat on the opposite side of the room against the wood-and-glass double doors. Identical to Newbie's classroom, in the dead heat of summer they were often folded back and opened up. Right now, Newbie just happened to be sitting on the sofa. She held a mug between two hands halfway to her lips. Their eyes briefly met, and Newbie glanced away as she took a sip.

"He's doing fine," Natalie said.

Victoria narrowed her eyes.

Even Rob, the Year Three and Four teacher, cocked an eyebrow in her direction before chomping into the over-sized peanut brownie in his hand.

Sighing, Natalie stepped towards the table, plopped her drink down and sank into the nearest chair.

"His mother's dead," Natalie said by way of explanation, and took a sip of her drink.

Sitting across from Natalie, Victoria kept her eyes well-trained on her. Waiting. Saying nothing.

Natalie twitched in her seat. Again, she wondered if Victoria had some kind of sixth sense.

Rob took another large bite of his brownie, and Newbie continued to stare at whatever was in her own mug. Through the wall, Natalie could hear Sandra – the office lady in reception – on the phone. Given the loud laughter, it was a personal call. Natalie swore the woman spent more time taking personal calls than doing any real work. She turned her attention back to Victoria's steely gaze.

"He's struggling," Natalie admitted.

"What can we do?" Victoria asked, concern evident in her voice.

"I'm not sure," Natalie said, and in an instant all she wanted to do was tell Victoria everything. "When the other kids try and include him, he just doesn't respond to them. He seems to be happier on his own."

Natalie took a big swallow of her drink to soothe the lump in her throat. *Liar*, she mentally chided herself. She'd left out a key factor. He *wasn't* alone, and that was what worried her the most.

"What does Dad think?" Rob asked, still chewing. A few crumbs had gathered at the corner of his mouth.

On mentioning Cole's dad, heat rose to Natalie's cheeks. Oh, yes, Riki. She'd had a couple of conversations with him since their first meeting.

"He's taking him to see his GP." Natalie took another sip in an attempt to disguise her discomfort. Some help that's going to be though, she thought. The boy's problem wasn't something the local doctor could fix.

She stole another glance across the room at Newbie. Natalie could tell she was listening avidly even if she was trying hard to feign interest in the education magazine beside her. Not for the first time, she wondered how much she knew about the shadows who still roamed the school grounds. Natalie suspected it was more than she let on.

"Well, maybe for the moment we make sure we check on him whenever one of us is on duty," Victoria said, bringing Natalie's attention back to the conversation. "I'll make sure Brittany knows to do the same."

Brittany, the junior teacher presently on duty. Natalie shrugged her shoulders, feigning nonchalance. The truth was, she *was* worried about Cole. And his playmate.

The toll of the hand bell interrupted her thoughts, and as was normal, a collective sigh from the teachers and office lady in the next room, signalled the end of morning tea. Natalie, however, was relieved to escape the scrutiny of her principal and colleagues.

She stood and made her way back to the sink where she tipped out the last of her drink. Too many times she had made the mistake of taking her coffee back to class to have it sit there growing cold, forgotten about and accumulating dust and dead flies.

"Natalie, can we just have a quick chat before you head back?" Victoria asked.

Natalie stiffened.

"Sure," she said turning to face Victoria.

Victoria gestured towards her office on the other side of reception.

"Ooo," Rob teased as he brushed past her. "Some-one's in trou-ble," he said in a sing-song voice.

Natalie shot him a dirty look. From the corner of her eye, she saw Victoria stifle a smirk.

CHAPTER 7

Natalie

"What's going on, Natalie?"

Victoria gestured for her to shut the door, and inhaling deeply, Natalie did so. She slowly turned back to face Victoria, who perched on the side of her desk, piles of paper and books covering the surface around her. She signalled for Natalie to take a seat.

"I really should be getting back to class," Natalie said, eager to leave, the walls already feeling like they were closing in.

"They'll be fine. This will only take a moment. What's going on?" she repeated.

There was a drawn-out pause, and with a sigh Natalie propped herself up against the doorjamb.

"I heard Maggie went walking the other night," Victoria said, her voice gentler this time.

Natalie closed her eyes for a moment. Who else knew? Damn community gossip.

"I bumped into Troy in Maramanui," Victoria said, answering Natalie's unspoken question. She held up her hand to stop Natalie before she started cursing Troy and his big mouth. "He's worried, Nat. He's worried about Maggie, and he's worried about you."

The last word hung heavy between them, and Natalie felt another pang of guilt.

"I want to help, Nat. Let me help." It was a plea. Victoria's eyes grew misty.

Natalie shook her head. It wasn't the first time Victoria had offered. Victoria and Grams had grown up together. Had been best friends, in fact. Natalie had heard the stories. But things had changed, and neither had told her what exactly had happened. Their affection for each other was still there, Natalie could sense it bubbling under the surface. She could read it in Victoria's face now though it had been many years since Victoria had crossed the threshold to visit Grams, her so-called best friend. At the time, Grams hadn't been receptive to it. And yet after the second time Grams had gone wandering, Victoria had pulled her aside, just like now, offering to help with getting Grams extra care, into a home to be precise, with professionals watching after her. The best place for her, Victoria had said. Natalie had been shaky with anger. How dare she? Natalie had thought at the time. Didn't she know Natalie had everything under control? Or at least, was doing the best she could? Working, keeping food on the table and a roof over their heads, the roof that Grams had worked so hard to keep. And she was doing it all while taking care of Grams and with her pain-in-the-arse mother needing to be bailed out of trouble on a regular basis. Call it pride or not, it wasn't Victoria's business. It was family business.

Troy had approached her about it too. Natalie guessed Victoria had pulled him in, in hopes of him being able to talk sense into her. Victoria's offer had been very generous. She would assume all financial responsibility, and God that would make life so much easier. But Maggie was her grandmother, and neither Natalie nor her family were charity cases.

"I've got it handled," Natalie said to Victoria.

Victoria sighed, as if she had expected nothing less.

"You're a good teacher, Nat, but you can't keep doing everything on your own. And you don't need to. There are people here who want to help. I know it's not been easy ..."

Natalie's hackles rose and she clenched her teeth, willing herself to keep it together. Goddamn everyone's busybodiness!

"I'm fine," Natalie growled. "I've got this." Did she though? She made to leave, and in doing so noted Victoria's mouth moving as if to say something. Natalie walked out, closing the door behind her.

Victoria could be a pit bull at times, but not today. If anything, she seemed genuinely concerned. If she cared for Grams as much as she acted, why hadn't she stayed in touch and come around and visited once in a while? Instead, she used Natalie as a go-between, asking questions, sending birthday greetings and the likes. Hell, Natalie lived five minutes away; Victoria drove past every single day on her way home.

Natalie headed across the court to her classroom. She could already hear the gentle murmur of voices: "The teacher's coming! The teacher's coming!" And the scattering of little feet as her students scrambled for books to silent read so they could appear on task. What she hadn't expected was to see the bent over form of Brittany holding the arm of a student angrily facing off with Cole, who's hands were balled into fists at his side.

Natalie's heart picked up speed. Brittany would have it sorted; she was sure. Even Natalie could admit that for all her bounciness, rainbows and unicorns, Brittany was a whizz with kids. Natalie quickened her pace regardless.

Brittany was crouching down between the two children, holding back her student, whom Natalie recognised right away as being a Year One boy named Craig. He tended to tease other students, and despite being so young carried himself with a severe chip on his shoulder. The kid looked outraged without a doubt. Cole was breathing heavily, his flushed cheeks puffing in and out as if he was trying to calm himself.

As she approached, Craig yelled, "But he started it!" He stamped his foot and tried to pull away from Brittany's grasp. "Freak!" he yelled at poor Cole, who seemed to vibrate with rage, his fists clenching and unclenching at his side.

In noticing Natalie approach, Bittany looked up at her, an apologetic smile on her face. "There's been a bit of a disagreement," she said. "I think I should take Craig inside and have a chat with him, if you want to do the same with Cole, and I'll catch up with you later."

Craig was still tugging at Brittany's arm as if he wanted to lay into Cole, who continued to stand his ground breathing in and out, in and out. Though Craig was a big boy for his age, it still surprised Natalie to see Brittany struggle to hold him back.

Natalie nodded. "Come on, Cole," she said holding out a hand. "Let's go inside, we have our dinosaur pictures to finish off from yesterday." She hoped to divert his attention and have him follow. Despite holding out her hand to him, Natalie was under no illusion that he would actually take her hand in his.

Brittany stood up and, keeping a hand on Craig's shoulder, gently tried to guide him back to her classroom. Natalie caught another apologetic smile in her direction.

"Freak!" Craig blurted out again before turning his back to Cole.

Natalie was too slow to react as Cole lunged forward. With a guttural yell, he slammed one of his bunched fists into Craig's lower back, sending the boy stumbling forward and almost falling had it not been for Brittany's grasp on him.

"Cole!" Natalie blurted, rushing forward to intercept him as he continued pounding his fists over and over on Craig's back.

Grabbing Cole around the shoulders, Natalie bent down and pulled him towards her in an almost-hug, pinning his arms to his side. The thought went through her mind: no restraining kids ... unless what? She couldn't remember. They were putting someone else or themselves at risk? Well, this was definitely one of those times, and thank God he was so much smaller than her. Brittany, on the other hand, was struggling with Craig as he turned and lashed out, wailing and trying to free himself from her grasp.

Now on the deck outside of Brittany's classroom, Natalie was aware of small chubby faces and hands pressed to the window from within the classroom, watching with open mouths at the chaos.

Craig's wails grew louder as Brittany tried to shuffle him towards her classroom. Colour rose up her neck as she tried to cajole him with gentle whispers.

They're alligator tears, Natalie thought. Despite the kid's face being scrunched up, no real tears dropped. It was all a performance.

Natalie held Cole for a little longer, hearing his quiet sobs as he trembled in her arms. Tears ran down his cheeks and landed on her bare arms.

"Cole," she whispered in his ear. "It's okay. We're going to go inside now, okay?"

The little boy shook his head and mumbled something.

"Miss Sullivan? Is everything okay?" Victoria's sharp voice cut across the school grounds.

Natalie closed her eyes for a moment and silently swore. "Yes. All good," she said without thinking as Victoria drew up beside them.

"Well, hello, Mr Lomas. What's going on here?" she asked bending down to face him.

Natalie felt him stiffen in her embrace. Victoria had that effect on people, young and old.

After a moment of scanning his face, Victoria stood up and turned to Natalie. Her eyes narrowed. "I think maybe you should take Mr Lomas to the sick bay. Let him have a rest ..." She lowered her voice just for Natalie to hear. "And maybe call his dad."

Of course Victoria had seen what had happened. For the umpteenth time, Natalie wondered just how fine-tuned the woman's sixth sense really was.

"I'll watch your class." Victoria subtly inclined her head.

Natalie understood what Victoria was saying. Hitting wasn't permitted at school, no matter the reason, and he needed to be sent home. Natalie clenched her teeth again and nodded.

Releasing her grip until she was only lightly touching Cole's shoulders, she guided him towards the office. "Let's have a bit of time out, eh?" she said, keeping her voice light.

Saying nothing, Cole seemed content to go where he was led.

As they walked into the reception, they were greeted by Sandra's raucous cackling on the phone. Her eyes travelled over Natalie before dropping to Cole. With one judgmental eyebrow raised, she swivelled away from the two of them and continued her phone call.

Definitely not a work call. What exactly was that woman paid for?

Heading to the left, Natalie led Cole through the door into the small sick bay.

"Why don't you sit down here?" Natalie gestured to the low cot with the standard army-fashioned grey wool blanket, with a pile of picture books and a Guinness World Record book stacked at the end. She pushed away the stainless-steel puke bowl with her foot, under the cot, out of sight. Without protest, Cole sat on the edge of the bed, swung his legs up and lay against the pillows. Just like in a therapist's office, she thought. He threw one arm over his eyes and some muffled sobs escaped. She crouched alongside the cot, holding onto the edge to balance herself.

"Do you want to tell me what happened?" she asked softly. She listened for any indication he wanted to talk.

Nothing.

With her free hand, she massaged her forehead. God, what was she going to tell his dad? Without a chance to chat with Brittany, she didn't even know the full story, only what she had seen: Craig's insults followed by Cole lashing out.

If she thought she had a chance at pulling Sandra away from her social life to actually keep her eye on the kid, she would head on over and have a quick chat with Brittany. But given the sounds coming from the front desk, she was on her own. All she could do was tell Riki what she'd seen, and hope Cole would be a little more forthcoming with details.

She cringed. She hated this part of the job; calling parents to tell them to pick up their child. It didn't matter the reason – tummy bugs, head lice or hitting another child – no reason was ever good news for the parent on the other end of the phone. And somehow this seemed worse. This poor boy had just lost his mum. While that wasn't an excuse for hitting another child ... Craig could be a shit. She scolded herself for the uncharitable thought. Craig was just a kid too, acting out for who knows what reason. And to be fair, to the other kids, Cole would seem a bit odd. She'd seen him a handful of times chatting to himself, playing alone. Only he wasn't chatting to himself. Or alone, she reminded herself. There was no way she was she going to bring that up in conversation with anyone. Not yet anyway.

CHAPTER 8

Maggie

1964

Vicky had first bumped into Arthur O'Regan in Maramanui at the milk bar only a few weeks back. She'd been so excited when she and Maggie caught up the day after. Love at first sight, Vicky had said, which Maggie found hard to believe. Vicky was forever falling head over heels in love with someone.

They'd been friends since they were toddlers, practically growing up together. Maggie had lost count of how many times Vicky had found "the one", only to lose interest a few weeks later. The fact she was still seeing Arthur, in itself, was nothing short of a miracle.

And in Maggie's mind, it made no sense.

They were walking back from the bakery where they worked, towards Vicky's bottle-green Volkswagen, affectionately dubbed "the Bug". A few cars passed them. The passengers in one wolf-whistled

at them, then erupted into raucous laughter as they passed. Maggie
pulled her friend closer to her, heat flushing her face and neck as
Vicky twisted to face the disappearing car and flipped them the bird.
Indignation crept into Maggie's voice even as her face flushed again.

"Vicky!" she chided her.

Vicky only laughed and continued their conversation. "But seriously, Mags, come on. It'll be fun." She slipped her arm through
Maggie's and gave her a gentle elbow. "Plus, JP will be there." She
wiggled her eyebrows. "You know you're coming, Mags. I need you
there, and like I said, JP will be there too."

Maggie pulled away from her. "I've met him once, Vicky! You know
he's not my type!"

"Well, what is your type, then? When was the last time you even
went on a date?"

Maggie hated it when she acted all holier than thou. So what if she
hadn't dated anyone in a while? She'd have plenty of time when she
got out of Te Tapu and away from Maramanui. There was something
greater for her out there, she just knew it. It was why she worked at the
bakery in the first place. Maggie had plans. She was going to move to
the city, attend university and get an English degree. Her grades had
always been good; she had done well at school, she just ... she had to
make sure Mam was okay first.

"I'll tell you who's not my type – men several years our senior who
think a good time is to get high behind the primary school. Seriously,
Vicky?!"

Vicky stopped in her tracks, making Maggie do the same.

Vicky wore her long red hair loose. She was shorter than Maggie
by a head, but she was fiery. Vicky's eyes narrowed and grew darker.

Though Maggie was used to Vicky getting riled up, her chest tightened. She hated conflict, and being on the wrong side of anyone, let alone Vicky, was never a pleasant experience.

"Six years, Mags! Arthur is six years older than us. That's nothing. And JP is even younger." Vicky's voice turned steely. "And you know how much this means to me. I like him, Mags."

Maggie sighed. Regardless of what she thought of the man herself, Vicky was her friend. She owed it to her to be supportive.

"But the school?" Maggie said.

With the air of someone who had won, a smile crept to the corners of Vicky's mouth, and she threaded her arm back through Maggie's. They fell into pace again. Ahead of them, the intersection of Raglan and Herald loomed. A woman had stopped to let her terrier relieve itself on the signpost, the leash loose in her hand. She avoided eye contact with them.

"It'll be cool," Vicky said, by way of reasoning. "No one goes to the glade anymore. It can't be seen from the main road, and it's completely secluded."

Maggie knew the spot. Anyone who had been to Te Tapu Primary School knew the spot. It was off-bounds of course. A fence had been erected behind the building well before she had attended, though over the years it had fallen into disarray with loose boards and exposed nails. A boy a few years back had snuck through the fence to the glade beyond and had to be rushed to the medical centre with a nail through his foot. But beyond the risk of a tetanus shot there had been other rumours too. The land surrounding the school, in fact even the land the school itself was on, belonged to the O'Regans. The O'Regans who founded the village and had their own history of sordid rumours. The place Vicky was talking about hardly suited the name "glade". It was a dumping ground of discarded broken desks and chairs amongst bushland, a wild, untamed forest that stretched on through ravines and over rolling hills. The forest was one of those places often spoken of with a mix of horror and awe. Gossip said a murderer had escaped justice by hiding there and resided there still, and restless spirits roamed the forest at night. Sometimes, people said, you could hear the sobbing of a woman. God forbid you heard her scream, for if you did, you wouldn't be alive long enough to tell the story.

Superstition passed down from older siblings to the younger ones. Stories parents would tell their children to stop them wandering too far into the forest's depths. She had heard it all. Te Tapu had always been rife with superstition, and although Maggie knew the worst of it was that the O'Regans would slap you with a trespassing notice, she still felt a chill when she thought of the place.

Vicky, on the other hand, had no such qualms. The rumours and superstitions were no doubt part of the big appeal to her.

"And it's not like we'd be trespassing," Vicky read her mind as they turned the corner, the Bug now in sight, parked outside the hardware store. "It's O'Regan land, so really it'll all be Arthur's one day anyway."

"Then why do we have to go through the school. Can't we just access it from the road?"

They had reached Vicky's vehicle. Vicky sifted through her purse for the keys, growling slightly in agitation and impatience.

"Got 'em," she said; holding the keys up for Maggie to see. Vicky unlocked the driver-side door and sidled in before reaching over to the passenger door and unlocking it for Maggie.

Maggie settled herself in her seat and closed the door beside her, then reopened it again and gave it a harder slam. The Bug had been a gift to Vicky from her dad, who'd received it for free for doing some work for someone in town. It still needed a bit of work. Regardless, it suited Vicky. It was as temperamental and tenacious as she was and yet she couldn't help but feel a good deal of affection for it, even being just a car.

Vicky stuck the keys in the ignition and gave it a turn. The Bug gave a loud rumble then roared to life. The whole car vibrated.

"Well?" Maggie asked again.

"Well, what?" Vicky said as she pulled out into the street.

This was just like Vicky. Even after all of the years of knowing each other, Maggie still couldn't be completely sure if Vicky left questions unanswered simply because her brain was elsewhere or if it was an intentional ruse to avoid answering questions she didn't want to answer.

"Why do we have to go through the school?" It just felt wrong. Schools were meant to be a place for innocence, not for four adults who knew better, to go skulking through to find some off-the-grid place to make out and get high, because she suspected that was exactly what was on the agenda. And if Vicky thought that she, Maggie, was going to do either, she had another think coming. Her stomach did a flip-flop at the thought.

"What if someone sees us from the road? Or if we're seen parking on the berm and climbing over the fence? No one will see us if we enter through the school. It's much less suspicious that way," Vicky finally answered.

Maggie disagreed. "You don't think people will get suspicious seeing us skulking around the school during the weekend?" Maggie cringed at the whininess that had crept into her voice.

Vicky took the corner too fast, and Maggie gripped the edge of her seat as she slid towards the door. One day her friend was going to get her killed with the way she drove. There was no slow and steady with her; everything was full tilt or not at all.

"We'll park at Arthur's. It's a bit of a walk, but we can cut through the school from around the back. No one will see us. We'll head behind the junior classes where there's a gap in the fence, some loose boards. We'll be fine."

Sure sounded like she'd followed the same course before. Recently. Maggie stifled a humph.

"It's completely private. You'll see," Vicky said, turning to Maggie. Maggie's fingers dug deeper into the seat until Vicky turned her gaze back to the road.

Maggie had been there as a child. Had Vicky forgotten? She was talking about it like it was a new discovery of hers. And as for her mention of it being completely private, that just made Maggie think there'd be no witnesses to hear their screams ...

But it wasn't worth the fight. If Vicky was just looking for a make out spot, several came to mind that didn't involve trekking through the school into the forest.

Even so, Maggie knew Vicky would inevitably wear her down. She always did. Besides, Maggie would go because Vicky wanted her to. Someone had to keep her safe, make sure she didn't get into trouble. She held back a snicker. Like she would ever be able to keep Vicky out of trouble.

CHAPTER 9

Maggie

1964

Maggie hadn't slept well the night before. Her mind kept her up half the night thinking ahead to what was in store for her today. As much as she didn't want to go, she couldn't in good conscience leave Vicky alone with two older men in a secluded "glade". And this was where her imagination got the better of her. Worst case scenarios crashed together until a sweat broke out between her breasts, her heart galloping at an unnatural speed. Her stomach turned, and she lay in bed, willing the nausea to dissipate. It had, replaced by a restless shadowy sleep, where she dreamt of the forest. Skeletal limbs reached for her as she ran, scraping at her face, clawing at her skin. She needed to escape ... who? She was never really sure. She never saw him; just knew it was a man. Arthur maybe? She didn't like him, so it would make perfect sense. Yet she knew it wasn't him – it was someone else. Someone whose energy was darker, heavier somehow.

She woke tangled within her bedsheets. Her head pounded, and her body ached as if she really had run through the forest from a predator for most of the night.

It took most of the morning for her headache to ease, and by the time Vicky picked her up in the Bug, it was only a dull aching band across her forehead.

Vicky was her usual perky self, pressing on the horn and waving frantically out the driver-side window, a smile stretched across her face, trying to hurry Maggie along as she closed the front door behind her and rushed down the front steps. Maggie grimaced as the blare of the horn threatened to bring her headache back to full force. But for Vicky, always for Vicky, she returned a smile and feigned happiness.

"Come on, come on, we're late," Vicky urged.

Maggie barely had a moment to close the car door. She slid across the vinyl seat and slammed her arm into the door handle as Vickie peeled away, spitting up gravel as she U-turned and headed towards the main road. Maggie counted herself down from telling her off. She'd been waiting a good fifteen minutes for Vicky to arrive. Them being late had nothing to do with her.

Maggie had never been to the O'Regans, although she, like all of Te Tapu, knew where they lived. Her mouth went dry as Vicky pulled the car up the long, tree-lined driveway. Pulling the car off to the left, Vicky nestled the nose of the Bug into the base of a towering toetoe bush.

"This way, we won't be in the way of anyone leaving," she said, killing the ignition.

A couple of vehicles were parked close to the house; one she recognised right away as being Arthur's. The other, she supposed, could belong to JP, and the third, parked under the carport, likely belonged to one of Arthur's parents. Gosh, what if they were home? The thought made her stomach drop. She had never pieced together the full story behind the animosity between her family and the O'Regan's, but she had heard enough to be reminded for the hundredth time that maybe this had been a bad idea.

She only had rumours to go on. And depending on who you heard it from, the story twisted and changed. Some said her own brother, Billy, had killed Jake O'Regan, Ol' Man Tom's firstborn son, and Arthur's uncle. Of course, some townsfolk said the exact opposite. Mam didn't say anything. No one at home spoke of Billy, and as Maggie had never met him, she let it be. He had been her half-brother after all, Maggie's dad being a Carrie, rather than a MacKenzie as her sisters were.

But would the O'Regans recognise the family tie?

Maggie shivered at the thought, and then forced her attention back to the moment at hand. Vicky was already hurrying up the gravel drive to the house, and Maggie had to almost run to catch up with her. At the top of the steps to the front door Vicky paused, smoothing the sides of her dress and readjusting the belt that cinched at her waist. With a quick patting of her hair, she swung around to face Maggie.

"You ready?" she asked, a sparkle in her eye.

Maggie raised a shoulder. Was she ready? She wasn't sure. Her heart had somehow found its way to her throat, and she would have sold her soul right then and there had the devil come knocking, for one ounce of the confidence that Vicky was exuding right now.

Vicky raised a fist and beat it three times on the wood-panelled door. At first there was nothing. No noise. Nothing. And Vicky tapped a foot with impatience.

This was always the way with her. She had more energy than anyone Maggie had ever met. And when she was excited or agitated, it found other forms of release. Maggie moved beside her, surreptitiously wiping the palms of her hands on her skirt. When Vicky raised a hand to knock again, Maggie grabbed Vicky's fist and stayed her. She put a finger to her lips.

There it was, in the distance, the gentle sound of footsteps on floorboards moving towards them.

Maggie took a step back and Vicky did the same.

The door opened to a tall woman, perfectly coiffed with her brunette hair falling in waves to her shoulders. A few strands of grey reflected in the light. Even so, Maggie inhaled sharply. She was beautiful.

She had seen Mr and Mrs O'Regan many times, but never up close. They attended almost all of the school and Te Tapu community functions; funding most of them, in fact. They had always seemed charming, if not somewhat intimidating, although that might have had more to do with the name they carried.

Mrs O'Regan wore a pant suit better suited for wearing in the city than a small village like Te Tapu. Hard eyes raked Vicky up and down before falling upon Maggie and softening. A small smile, both warm and sad, Maggie thought, tugged at her lips. Mrs O'Regan's eyes hovered over Maggie, and Maggie resisted shuffling under her gaze.

"Afternoon, Mrs O'Regan. Is Arthur here?" Vicky asked, seemingly nonplussed by the strange lack of attention she was being offered.

Mrs O'Regan glanced at Vicky. "Of course," she said, her mouth turning ever so slightly downward as she did.

Maggie wondered for a moment how Mrs O'Regan really felt about having her twenty-four-year-old son still living at home.

"Arthur and John Paul are around by the hay shed. They said they were expecting visitors. Just follow around the side of the house there," she pointed to their left, and Maggie shifted under the gaze that now rested on her again.

"If you head through the gate around the back of the house, you'll see the shed. You won't miss it."

"Thanks, Mrs O'Regan," Vicky said tugging at Maggie's arm, eager to run off in search of Arthur.

Maggie held her ground for a moment. Mrs O'Regan was still staring at her. Was it sympathy she saw in her eyes? Pity maybe? There was no malevolence, she was sure of it.

Mrs O'Regan shook herself and offered a wide smile before waving them off.

Vicky ran, pulling Maggie along after her. A feeling of unease replaced the fear of meeting Mrs O'Regan. Mrs O'Regan *had* seemed to recognise her, but there was something else too. Despite her parting smile, it had never reached her eyes. Running along beside Vicky, the sun beating down and warming her skin, Maggie felt a foreboding prickle. Something was wrong.

CHAPTER 10

Maggie

1964

Schools were eerie places without the sound of children. Eerier still when you were knowingly trespassing and skulking around the classrooms with two older men, one of whom had a backpack with, Maggie guessed, beer or liquor if the sound of clanging bottles was anything to go by. They cut through the paddock behind Arthur's house and climbed the fence into the school grounds. From there, they made their way behind the main classroom block towards the playground. Maggie heard the voices as Arthur and JP walked ahead.

"Do you hear that?" Maggie whispered to Vicky. Her senses had been on edge since she'd woken up that morning, but now they were worse.

Vicky gave her a quizzical look.

She heard it again. A soft murmuring on the other side of the main block, followed by a chuckle or a child giggling.

JP froze mid-step, making Arthur stagger before also coming to a standstill.

Whoever it was, they were coming closer.

Arthur let out a low growl.

"Ignore them," he said. "Whoever they are, we have as much right to be here as they do." He turned on his heel and continued marching towards the playground.

JP threw a sympathetic look at the girls, then followed suit.

"Come on," Vicky said, tugging at Maggie's arm. "We have as much right to be here as anyone else."

It irked Maggie, Vicky repeating Arthur's words, but she went along with her anyway.

As they caught up with Arthur and JP, the invisible giggling turned to raucous laughter. A young boy came running out from the side of the main building block ahead of them. His knees knocked at weird angles, and wrists hung limp at the end of his arms as he loped an awkward gait towards the swings. All the time he was laughing and making strange noises, and Maggie's chest swelled with relief.

She knew him. They all did. Gavin Jenkins had been born differently from most children. Along with uncoordinated movements, his speech was difficult to understand. His brain worked differently. Some people said slower. They called him names. She'd seen kids throw stones at him even when he'd been out walking with his mother and little sister. People could be cruel. His "otherness" scared them. Maggie saw him as a little boy who exuded so much joy on seeing such a simple thing as a swing. She quietly giggled along with him, his happiness almost palpable.

"Bloody retard! What's he doing here?"

Arthur's words felt like a slap, instantly chilling the air, and Maggie inhaled sharply. She noticed Vicky appeared taken aback as well.

Maggie stopped in her tracks, refusing to go any further. Vicky looked at her confused, and then followed her line of sight. At a much slower pace a woman rounded the corner, a little girl's hand in her own.

Had she heard? Maggie thought. Oh, God! They needed to get out of here.

No doubt, Mrs Jenkins had heard. She picked up her daughter in her arms, and with a hunched back, hustled towards where her son was swinging.

Arthur turned around to Maggie and Vicky.

"They're freaks. Nobodies. Hurry up!" Arthur continued on his path with JP, Vicky following and Maggie lagging behind, unsure what else to do.

Arthur led them around the side of the playground, past the gingko tree and towards the back boundary fence. Maggie's heart lodged in her throat. For the millionth time, she wondered what Vicky saw in the brute.

She tried to do as the others did, ignoring Mrs Jenkins completely as they passed her, but she couldn't help a side-glance in her direction. Mrs Jenkins appeared flustered, like she was locked in an argument with Gavin, trying to pull him away from the swing. Maggie suspected Mrs Jenkin's wanted to leave as much as she did.

Vicky, Maggie reminded herself. She was doing this for Vicky, and when she had her alone, she was going to have some stern words with her. In no way was Arthur's attitude okay. He was a pig, making comments like that about a child. For the moment, she felt like she had no choice beyond following them and blocking out the intermingled cries and laughter of the boy on the swing.

CHAPTER 11

Maggie

1964

The smoke was harsh. It burnt her throat and set her lungs alight, causing a spasm of dry coughing. Maggie's hand flew to her face, trying to hold back the hacking. Tears burned her eyes as she passed the reefer back to the man opposite her.

"Easy on there," he said, leaning forward and taking it from her fingers.

Maggie swallowed, willing the ache in her chest to disappear. She squeezed her eyes shut to calm her breathing, and a tear let loose. She wiped at it with the palm of her hand. A giggle floated in the air beside her, and an elbow playfully jabbed her in the side.

Reluctantly she opened her eyes to see two faces watching her. Vicky giggled again, rocking beside her, teasing her with a grin. Across from her, JP sat cross legged. His mouth stretched wide. He gave her a wink and took another swig from the beer bottle in his hand. Only Arthur sat stiff faced, the reefer pressed between his lips. His long legs stretched out before him and crossed at the ankles.

Maggie gave another involuntary cough.

"Well?" Vicky asked, wrapping an arm around Maggie's shoulders and giving her a squeeze.

Well? Maggie wondered. Did she feel any different? A little dizzy maybe. Nauseated? She wasn't sure. Her throat felt raw, and her chest ached.

"You sucked it in too far," Vicky told her.

Since when had she become an expert?

She took a moment to study Arthur. He leant back on one hand while his other hand clasped the neck of a black flask, a short joint poking out between his fingers, sending up a small spiral of smoke as he lifted the mouth of the flask to his lips. Surely his fingers must be burning, she thought, yet no emotion crossed his face.

And that's what bothered her about him. No emotion. With the exception, of course, of the odd times he cocked an eyebrow, narrowed his eyes or sneered in her direction. Maggie checked herself. He did have emotions, just not the sort that was particularly endearing to others. Yet, somehow, he'd managed to put a spell on Victoria.

Victoria was right with one thing: he wasn't hard on the eyes. Tall, lean, rakish. Toned shoulders and biceps evident in his white tank top. His dark hair hung past his ears, sideswiping his eyes. But he never smiled. His strong jawline never shifted, making him nearly impossible to read. Maybe that was what had attracted Vicky, she thought. His whole bad-boy demeanour.

It could have been other things too. His eyes for one. They were dark, piercing, of the kind she had never seen before. He was also an O'Regan, which meant something in Te Tapu. But the man himself … he made her uncomfortable. That was the crux of it.

Why Arthur had chosen the glade in the woods behind the school as a place to smoke up, she wasn't sure. In itself, it felt wrong. Yet here she was anyway. All thanks to Vicky.

Vicky moved to snuggle up to Arthur, tucking her legs half beneath her. Maggie looked away uncomfortably. Arthur casually draped an arm around Vicky's shoulders. He chewed on a piece of dried grass, which hung out the corner of his mouth.

Vicky was smitten. It wasn't the first time Maggie had seen her this way. Vicky was impulsive and passionate. But until now, the men had always been of a similar age. Not that twenty-four was really a huge leap from eighteen, Maggie reminded herself, Vicky's words echoing back to her.

Except …

Arthur bothered her. She didn't like him, and it was more than his holier-than-thou broodiness, although it certainly hadn't endeared him to her. It was something else. Like a shadow lingering close by. A darkness that hovered just on the periphery whenever he was around. Sometimes she thought she'd caught a glimpse of a figure standing behind him. Each time a rush of cold ice had trickled down her spine, and she had to physically shake herself to rid herself of the intrusive feeling.

There was no one there. How could there be? A person couldn't be *haunted* …

Yet the thought persisted.

Seeing her best friend act all doe-eyed with him turned her stomach.

Maggie shuffled backwards a little on the ground, putting distance between her and them. As she did so, her hand brushed JP's knee, as he'd taken to sitting as close to her as possible.

She flinched without glancing up. "Sorry." Her whisper was automatic, and she retracted her hand quickly.

"No problem here," JP teased in a low voice.

Heat flooded her chest and up her neck. JP clasped her hand in his own. She wanted to pull away, but her eyes met Vicky's, her attention having finally turned to her. The corner of Vicky's mouth quirked upwards, and she winked in Maggie's direction.

Now Maggie's cheeks were on fire. Vicky was incorrigible!

She let JP place her hand on his lap. He wasn't horrible. In fact, he seemed nice enough, which begged the question why he was hanging with Arthur O'Regan. And JP obviously liked her, but despite Vicky's encouragement, Maggie just wasn't interested. He was older than her, and she had dreams, dreams that would take her away from Te Tapu if everything went to plan.

Maggie shifted uncomfortably, not sure how to escape. Because she wanted to, she really did. What were they even doing here, hiding in the bush behind the back of the school? Seriously?!

Vicky owed her big for doing this.

Oh God! Maggie struggled to keep her stomach in its rightful place.

Arthur had discarded the dry straw from the corner of his mouth, and he'd pulled Vicky even closer. They were making out, devouring each other. Maggie turned away, wishing she were anywhere else.

Something in her movement must have made JP see it as an invitation, and he leaned closer to her, his warm breath moistening her neck. For a second, she closed her eyes, panic rising, unsure what to do.

She needed to leave, needed to get out of there. What was Vicky thinking? Getting high. Making out with older men.

JP edged even closer, startling her into action. She pulled away and launched herself to her feet.

"Maggie? What are you doing?" Vicky's words were full of surprise.

JP's eyes were wide, equally as surprised. She guessed he had thought kissing her was a certainty.

"I ... I ..." her mind stumbled helplessly through a myriad of excuses. What exactly was her plan right now? Was she really just going to leave Vicky here?

She bit her tongue to stop from saying the first thing that came to mind – that she needed fresh air. Being out in the glade, there wasn't really a shortage of fresh air, if she would only allow her breaths to return to normal.

Her whole body burned, exacerbated by the confusion etched between Vicky's eyebrows. Did she really have no idea?

"I need the little girls' room," she said, wishing desperately that the ground would open up and swallow her.

Her eyes darted from one face to the other. Confusion and maybe a little embarrassment on JP's, puzzlement on Vicky's, and nothing, no emotion on Arthur's whatsoever. Darkness hung around him like an aura, and she shuddered.

"I won't be a moment," she said, faking a smile.

Vicky mouthed, "Are you okay?"

Aware, that other eyes were still focused on her, she nodded and hoped the forced smile was believable.

God, she wished she could just tell Vicky the truth. They needed to leave.

Arthur pulled a lighter from his pocket and went about flicking it on with his thumb again and again like a tic. For a second, Maggie stood mesmerised by the dancing flame appearing and disappearing, appearing, disappearing.

She blinked. Now! She had to leave now! The heaviness in the air was suffocating her.

"I'll be back soon," she said again as she took off, away from the others, further into the forest and away from the school.

She had no idea where she was going; she was just spurred on by the urgency to get away. She pushed past the sharp twigs and branches of a fallen miro tree. Foliage scattered on the dry earth at her feet, making her slip a little in her haste to get away, and she forced herself to slow down and steady her breathing. What was she running from? If she didn't want to be kissed by JP, she could have just said no. Same went for the weed. What had she been thinking? She couldn't keep blaming everything on Vicky.

A fantail flittered overhead, startling her before settling on a low-lying branch only a few metres ahead of her. She paused as if she were expecting it to give her a message of some sort. In return, it tilted its head to the side, it's small eyes unblinking.

Was it the weed, she wondered, that was making her so paranoid? The feeling had intensified, she realised, the further she got from everyone. Not only that, but the skin on her nape prickled as if she were being watched.

Slowly she pivoted and glanced around, startling the pīwakawaka into flitting away. She was far enough into the woods she couldn't see or hear her little group. Although it was quite likely there was nothing to hear. Not if Arthur and Vicky had gone back to swallowing each other's tongues. Maggie felt sick just thinking about it.

And did that mean JP was just sitting there awkwardly, or maybe ... maybe he'd come after her, and that's why she felt someone was close by.

But even as she thought it, she knew it wasn't him. Whoever this was, it was big energy. Dark energy. Something inexplicably evil.

Or else she was just extremely stoned, she reminded herself, and this really was just the paranoia kicking in.

A sound came from behind her, a rustling in the nearby undergrowth, and she twirled around to catch sight of something small and furry scuttling away.

A peal of laughter rang out, making her heart thunder in her chest.

She had been so sure Gavin had followed them into the forest. Sure she had heard him – and Vicky had too. Arthur had shaken his head, scowling in her direction when she'd mentioned it. And even JP had seemed uninterested. But she had been certain then and was certain now. But why had he followed her so deep into the forest? Wouldn't his mother be worried? Heart pounding, Maggie brushed a palm across her forehead, wiping away the beads of sweat. If Gavin was following her, that still didn't explain the ominous feeling she felt closing in on her.

The air grew thicker, and Maggie inhaled deeply as if she were about to put her head underwater. What now? She had no plan. Being away from the group hadn't exactly calmed her any. Every noise, every rustle in the brush, put her on edge. Despite the sun being high in the sky and dappling the ground through the leaves above, there was little warmth in the air. It should be warmer. It *had* been warmer only minutes ago, she was certain.

Maggie took a step backward, putting some distance between her and whatever was moving towards her.

As she edged further backwards, she darted her eyes one way and the other, searching. For what, she wasn't sure. She squealed when she ran into a tree.

"Hello?" she called, her voice sounding weak and wobbly.

Maybe Vicky had come to check in on her. Oh God, she hoped it was Vicky.

"Hello?" she said again, this time a little louder.

How far had she wandered? With the exception of a fluttering of wings somewhere behind her, all was quiet. If Gavin had been following her, he was awfully silent now.

She was alone.

The thought struck her hard, making her instantly regret having left everyone. Somehow, even with Arthur there, it suddenly seemed safer.

She could have just told JP she wasn't interested. Sure, Vicky would have been annoyed, but who she dated wasn't Vicky's choice, anyway.

Maggie felt behind her, almost wrapping her arms around the tree, as she pressed up against its trunk. Someone was here, with her in the small clearing. Her other senses were on high alert. Her legs threatened to buckle beneath her, and she pressed herself up even harder against the tree trunk until it felt like the bark was tattooing her back through her clothes.

Her ears strained for any signs of Vicky or JP having come to find her. Hell, she'd even take Arthur right now. Maybe.

There was a smell too, something besides the rotting leaves and earth and moss. It was … it couldn't be? Had Arthur actually followed her?

Her breathing shallowed, and she willed herself to count her breaths to slow it down.

The smell: the sickly sweet, woody scent of alcohol. Whiskey. Or Rum. She wasn't sure. She wasn't much of a drinker. But she knew what it was. Almost overpowering, as the invisible presence seemed to be only a mere couple of metres away from her now.

Her insides threatened to shut down. Her limbs felt like lead, and her heart galloped in her chest.

Oh, Christ. She felt it now. The radiating violence of hatred and anger, swirling within an arm's length. It was coming for her. Whoever – whatever – it was, it was angry with her.

But why? What had she done?

"Vicky?" The whisper, almost pleading, fell from her lips as she turned her head to the side and squeezed her eyes tight. She held her breath waiting … waiting.

Foul breath, a mixture of alcohol and tobacco, warmed her cheek whilst simultaneously freezing her blood.

Please. Please, don't hurt me, she silently begged the unknown entity.

"Maggie?!" Vicky's cry broke through the horror, making Maggie's eyes fling open.

"Vicky?" she called in return, the presence suddenly forgotten, weakened by the interruption of a stranger.

"Vicky?" she called again louder. In a moment of bravery, she let go of the tree, propelling herself forward and running towards where she thought Vicky's voice had come from. To her surprise, no ghoul or demon or whatever it was, tried to stop her. She thrashed at the branches in her way and bolted through the bush, unsure of where to go but driven by hunch alone. Even more terrifying than from whence she'd come, was the terror she'd heard in Vicky's voice. Something was very, very wrong.

She pushed on, fighting gnarled tree limbs and prickly podocarp needles, which tore at her skin. She dodged exposed roots and fallen vines until a new smell assaulted her nostrils and clawed her throat raw.

Shit! It was smoke. Smoke like that from a wood fire.

"Maggie? Where are you?" a shrill voice called, followed by a man's booming echo, she recognised at once as being JP's.

"Vicky! Vicky, I'm here!" Maggie called back, hurtling herself past ponga and ferns. Oh God, the smoke was only getting thicker, and for a moment, beyond the beating of her heart, she heard the white noise and crackling of burning wood and brush.

The heat became stiflingly, suffocatingly warm.

She stopped for a moment. The smoke burned her eyes, making them tear up, and she rubbed them angrily with her fists.

What the hell was happening?

When a calloused hand grabbed her arm, she shrieked and tried to break away, remembering immediately who she'd been running from in the first place.

"Maggie. It's me! We've got to get out of here!" It was JP, his eyes wildly darting, scouring their surroundings. He coughed and almost doubled over, clutching his chest.

"Where's Vicky?" Maggie tried again to tear herself from his grasp. She combed the bush for any sign of flaming red hair or the azure blue of Vicky's dress.

"Arthur's got her," JP said, coughing again, and wheezing between breaths. "We need to get out of here!"

A rush of emotions flooded Maggie. Vicky was alright. Arthur wouldn't let anything happen to her. Right?

"This way," JP said, tugging at her arm and nearly dragging Maggie off at an angle from where she had been headed. "It leads to the road," he said between rasping breaths.

The road? Why not the school? But she needn't ask. The crackling of fire. The smoke, thick black-and-grey choking clouds, and what's more the licking of flames amongst the trees in the all-too-close distance.

The woods were on fire.

Oh God, oh God, oh God!

Smoke and heat made her nose run. She tried to swipe at her face with her arm, but JP was tugging her, beating his way through the bush. Though her lungs ached, she followed him, stumbling and falling, slamming into his back at times when he had to quickly change direction to avoid and outrun the fire.

Almost blindly, she put full trust in the man ahead of her, who's hand now grasped hers in a bone-crushing vice.

She couldn't tell how long it took before the trees spaced out and a glimpse of blue sky opened above them. Beyond the trees, she could just make out the tall grasses, the colour of straw, that separated the forest from the road.

"Maggie?" A voice weak in the distance fuelled her. Though her legs ached, she pushed on. Her skin was slick with sweat and pink from heat as if the flames themselves had been licking at her.

Vicky was okay. She'd made it. And there, in the distance she saw them, Vicky and Arthur standing there waving their arms at them. The road. They'd made it to the road.

And then she saw it. Fear made her stumble and crash into JP's back. He turned in surprise and tried to help her regain her balance. All the time, Maggie's eyes were glued to the road.

They weren't alone. Vicky and Arthur weren't alone. The feature-less shadow of hate and anger raged, burning with flares of red as if it too were on fire, sparking behind Arthur's right shoulder. Waiting for her.

"Come on," JP nearly growled through his panic, pulling her along with him.

She spared a glance over her shoulder where big black clouds and the billowing grey wrath of the fire's destruction followed them. She could just make out the blackened earth and trees engulfed in flame.

How? How? she thought, before focusing in on the entity. Why was it waiting for her? It made no sense, and she had no choice but to head straight towards the thing, to where Vicky also waited, tears streaming down her cheeks as she jumped up and down, waving her arms, oblivious to how close to evil she stood.

Could they not see it? Vicky? JP? Even Arthur? Surely, he must see it or at the very least feel it. Because it was becoming clear that for some reason, it had attached itself to him, yet its sights were set on her.

She stumbled the last few paces towards the road, where Vicky laugh-sobbed and rushed at her. After an exuberant embrace, Vicky pulled her even closer to the road. JP stopped and bent in two hacking and gasping, clearing his lungs.

"What …?" Maggie tried to form words, but her throat clenched in protest, raw as it was, sending her into a coughing fit.

"What" wasn't the right word, she realised.

"How did this happen?" she finally managed, her voice cracking.

Vicky bit her lip and her eyes darted in Arthur's direction.

"It's okay," she said, placing her hands on either side of Maggie's face and pressing her forehead against hers. "We're safe now, but we have to go."

"We need to get help," Maggie agreed. There was a local fire service. They needed to get to them and sound the alarm.

She looked once more over her shoulder. With an arm around her, Vicky tried to pull her away.

All Maggie could see were clouds of smoke. And everything, everything seemed to be engulfed in flames.

Maggie turned back to where the men walked ahead, following the road, eager to put distance between themselves and the fire.

"He started it," Maggie said, in a half whisper, not even as a question. Her eyes remained glued on his figure before her.

"It was an accident. Just an accident," Vicky said, eyes wide and imploring.

Was it? Maggie wondered. Because although Vicky was talking about Arthur and it being Arthur's accident, Maggie wasn't sure that *she* was meaning Arthur, more so the figure beside him, glowing red, almost boasting of his victory. It was obvious to her; he had a score to settle though she didn't know what. Even if no one else could see him, she now knew he was no figment of her imagination. As the thought slid across her mind, the figure turned toward her, featureless but for the glowing red embers of what might have been a smile.

CHAPTER 12

Natalie

Riki arrived just as the lunch bell went.

Natalie caught sight of him out the window, walking towards the office. Even from across the court, he made for a striking figure, and Natalie felt a flutter in her chest.

"Remember we have buddy reading after lunch, so you'll need to collect your book boxes when the bell goes," Natalie said to the eager faces waiting expectantly to be released for lunch. She kept her voice even despite the urgency she felt to rush to the office and intercept Riki. She wanted to hear his take on why Cole might be acting out in such a way, beyond what she already knew.

"And remember your hats, tamariki," she called as she waved them to leave. A tidal wave of children scampered for their bags and lunch boxes.

Glad to not be on duty, Natalie followed them out of the class, then quickly strode across the court, hoping she would be able to catch him before Victoria or anyone else could interfere.

She was fortunate; Victoria must be tied up elsewhere, and she arrived at the office door just as Riki and Cole opened it to leave. She took a small step backwards in surprise, and flashed a smile, uncertain of how to proceed. No parent was ever thrilled to be called into school to pick up their child part way through the day. And though he'd taken it calmly when she'd told him over the phone, she'd seen these things play out in a myriad of ways, including accusations being thrown at the teacher.

But looking at Riki now, if anything, he seemed embarrassed and a little downtrodden. He held Cole by the hand, and Cole's bag in the other. Cole's eyes remained focused on the ground.

She attempted a reassuring smile, using the time to calm her pulse as she did so. In her rush to reach him, she hadn't thought through what she wanted to say.

She needn't have worried. He turned towards Cole and crouched at his height. Letting go of his hand to gently turn his son's face towards him.

"Cole, I need you to take your bag and go sit in the ute and wait for me, so I can talk with Miss Sullivan. Understand me?"

Sniffing, Cole turned and ran towards a blue ute parked beside the office.

"I'm so sorry," Riki said, standing up to meet Natalie's gaze.

There it was again. Holy. She couldn't remember the last time someone had had such a visceral impact upon her. She did a quick scan: His pale-yellow T-shirt accentuated his toned, bronze arms and what she imagined were washboard abs. Her imagination had also conjured up a picture of what he looked like sans jeans. She was going to go straight to hell for how unprofessional her thoughts were.

Get a hold of yourself, Natalie scolded, swallowing hard, and focusing back on the situation at hand.

"This isn't like him," Riki continued. "Or it wasn't ..." He left the sentence unfinished, and Natalie felt a pang of pity as she filled in the blanks herself.

She mentally chided herself again. What kind of person lusted after someone who was still grieving the death of his wife? The horrible thought hit her: Was she turning into her mother?

"Is the other boy okay?" Riki asked.

"Yes, he's fine," Natalie said. She'd managed a quick check in with Brittany, and other than a little redness on his back, he'd seemed fine.

"How is Cole's counselling going?" Natalie asked, steering him away from blocking the door with a gentle nod of her head.

He followed her down the stairs and they took a few steps closer to the car park so they were in easy eyesight of Cole, and their conversation wouldn't be overheard as the teachers moved to the breakroom for lunch.

"There's not been much progress, to be honest," Riki said, drawing his palm over his face. "He's started talking about a new friend he's made though?" Riki said, a hint of hopefulness making his lips curve ever so slightly.

Oh, crap! Natalie thought, suspecting she knew where the conversation might be heading.

Natalie smiled, unsure of what to say. The truth was, the students in her class had tried including him in their games and each time he had pushed them way and distanced himself, preferring to be alone ...

"Gavin?" Riki said. "Which one is he?" Riki turned around and gestured towards the steps of her classroom where her students all sat in little groups devouring their lunches.

"We don't have a Gavin in class," Natalie said gently, making Riki face her again, a puzzled expression on his face.

"Oh, maybe he's in a different class?" he asked.

She shook her head.

"I don't understand ..." Riki said, and her heart dropped. The look in his eyes was just too much.

"I think Cole has"—she paused. Was she going to tell him the *whole* truth and risk sounding crazy?—"... an imaginary friend," she said. Close enough, she thought.

Riki's shoulders slumped. "Oh."

"It can be quite common at this age," Natalie hurried to console him. "Particularly with what Cole has been through."

"It just doesn't make sense." Riki shot a worried glance towards Cole, who was sitting in the passenger seat of the ute, eyes locked in the direction of the caretaker's shed.

"Cole said the boy he hurt ... he'd been making fun of Gavin—Oh," he said again, realisation dawning.

If Craig had been teasing Cole about his invisible friend, then of course it could have been upsetting to Cole.

"Has Cole ever lashed out in this way before?" Natalie asked.

Riki shook his head and swallowed. "Honestly"—His voice caught, and he cleared this throat. "His mum would have known what to do.

I just ... I just ... I'm at a loss. Hurting another child. And now an imaginary friend ..."

Riki shot another glance in Cole's direction. Natalie fought off the instinct to touch his arm in comfort as she would do a child. He was hurting, and as much as Natalie wanted to help him, she wasn't sure she knew how. Not without coming across as a complete nutcase. Not everyone was open to the idea of there being a spirit world. Hell, if it hadn't been for the fact that she'd never had a say in the matter, she would have put as much distance between herself and any talk of the *great beyond* too. It wasn't a conversation for people who had their shit together. And it wasn't like she craved any more reminders of how far removed she was from that status quo.

"What has Cole told you about his friend Gavin?" Natalie asked. As reluctant as she was, it might be time for her to intervene. The thought sent chills through her veins. There was enough darkness and secrecy in Te Tapu – she'd learnt a long time ago to leave well enough alone. But, after her encounter a few weeks back with whatever had threatened her behind the school, she suspected some forces were already at work, awoken from their slumber.

Her mind drifted back to the new teacher, Riley. She couldn't place why she thought it, but Natalie felt it in her soul that Riley had had something to do with it. It had been somewhat peaceful around Te Tapu until she arrived. After that, they'd gotten more animated, the shadows. They'd been appearing more frequently. Some were okay. The young man in the cheese cutter cap, he'd never been a threat, so she'd left him be.

However, there was a young woman too, and she was not so easy to dismiss. Her energy was erratic at best. It had made Natalie nauseous, and for whatever reason she seemed to have shown up more and more once Riley started. Things had settled again, for a little while at least. As if those spirits had found their peace ... And then *he* had shown his face. The shadow man she'd seen when she'd last been by the shed. Whoever he was, he'd been worming his way into her nightmares quite a bit lately. He seemed to be growing stronger. Why now? She had no idea. And now there was also the little spirit boy.

For years, she had wondered if there was a young child haunting the school. Shadowy movement in her periphery. Laughter just out of hearing distance. But then again it was a school. So full of life and noise and movement by day, anyone would be forgiven in thinking they might not be alone in the quiet moments. Schools could be eerie places when empty.

"What do I know about his imaginary friend?" Riki asked, dejectedly.

Natalie nodded and followed Riki's gaze towards Cole. What was Cole looking at? she wondered. His line of sight was towards the tool shed. Her skin prickled. Whatever he was seeing, she hoped to God it wasn't the shadow man. For a child as sensitive as Cole, she could only imagine how seeing even half of what she'd seen might fuck him up.

"He hasn't really said a lot. Just that he's made a friend. Gavin. He said the other kids are mean to him, tease him. When you called and told me what happened, I thought maybe he'd been protecting his friend. Maybe Gavin had been teased or something." Riki shrugged a shoulder. "I mean, I could almost give him credit for that."

Natalie tried to stifle a smile but felt her lips twitch anyway. As much as she didn't condone violence, there was something to be said about someone defending an underdog and a bully getting their comeuppance.

"Cole's been through a lot," Natalie reminded him. "I'm sure this is just his settling in period and him trying to process everything he's feeling. When you've got a moment, maybe we can sit down and strategise some ways to help him better deal with his anger when it arises."

Oh, she was bad. And inching closer to crossing a line.

"You know, I'm on classroom release tomorrow afternoon, if you wanted to talk some more?" She felt the thrill of suspense as she waited for his reply.

Home run, she thought, watching something in his demeanour shift. It was subtle, but she'd read things right, she was sure of it.

He nodded slowly. "I'd like that," he said, his eyes smiling. "Maybe over lunch?"

"Perfect," Natalie said, thinking of how it might feel to brush her hand over his chest, run her fingers down his ... Hell! She was going to hell!

"Shall we meet at the tavern, then? I've heard they do a mean burger," he added.

Natalie's mind raced ahead. Helena was off on Friday's. Katrina, Rob's wife, would be there tending the bar but screw her. People would talk regardless. Natalie deserved some fun.

"Sounds good," Natalie said. She was sure she was breaking a million rules right now, but what the fuck? He was cute as hell, and maybe she really could help him.

"Tomorrow, then," Riki said, his posture relaxing a little. He smiled, a real one this time, before nodding goodbye and heading towards where Cole waited.

Natalie watched the ute back out of the car park and turn to head out the school gates. Teachers didn't have parent meetings at pubs. What she was doing was wrong ... but also, she had to admit, exciting.

When she moved to return to the staffroom, she instead caught two eyes narrowed in on her from across the court. Liam. He had his yellow toolbox in one hand, looking like he'd just come out of Brittany's room. His mouth was a thin line, and for a moment she thought she was going to be sick. All remnants of excitement and self-congratulation fled, drowned instead by an intense sense of guilt. She swallowed hard against the rising bile. He shook his head and turned away from her, leaving a shadow in his place. She hadn't noticed it before, but it was him. She was sure of it. The shadow figure. His face twisted, flashing white teeth within a cruel smile, before fading into nothing. Natalie shivered.

She wasn't making it up. Whoever he was, he was getting stronger. And despite her animosity towards Liam, she also felt a sliver of fear for him.

CHAPTER 13

Natalie

Natalie precariously balanced on the small foothold of the shelf she stood on, holding onto one of the metal shelves with one hand and reaching up to shuffle a suitcase closer to the edge of the shelf above her. If she balanced it just right, she'd be able to slide it off towards her and jump off the shelf, catching it in both arms at the same time. Work and Safety would have a field day, she thought.

This wasn't her first time climbing or performing acrobatics to get resources from the lundia sliding shelves of the resource room. And she suspected she wasn't the only one. Everything seemed wedged in or haphazardly balanced. Other than books and journals in accessible book boxes, the resource room was really just a dumping ground for all those things Te Tapu teachers no longer used or had space for in their own classrooms. And Natalie was just as guilty as the rest at stashing boxes of things she no longer needed, but maybe ... maybe someone else would.

As it went, the suitcase came down easily, and she was able to catch it just as she'd planned. Although old and large enough to require two arms to catch, it hadn't been heavy. She used one foot to shift the debris littering the linoleum floor and made space enough to put the suitcase to open it. She had already tried two cardboard boxes, with no luck. She was even more dubious about the suitcase holding what she was wanting, but it was worth a look anyway.

Buckles unclasped, the suitcase sprang open. At first glance, it appeared to be stuffed with old costumes. Despite her low expectations, disappointment still hit with a whoomph. Shit!

She rummaged through the old seventies style shirts, and pink tutus, and the brown velvet bear costume in case beneath them were the records she was searching for.

While there were two less arduous and time-consuming solutions to finding what she wanted, she was reluctant to embark on either. Letting Victoria know she was looking for information on the history of the school and previous students, could lead to a whole lot of questions she didn't want to answer. Especially after what had happened to Newbie. And although she wasn't exactly sure what had happened, Natalie knew enough to know it had been bad.

Earlier in the year, the new teacher, Riley, had decided to investigate the history of the school, and from the whispers Natalie had heard, she found a fair amount. Had Riley brought up her plans in a staff meeting or at any other opportunity, Natalie was sure someone would have persuaded her to choose another inquiry focus. Hell, even Natalie might have said something. She'd lived in Te Tapu her whole life, and she knew all too well how touchy the residents of Te Tapu were about keeping the past in the past, especially around strangers. And Newbie was a stranger.

Te Tapu had a past. Like probably most small rural communities, it was closeknit in the sense that everyone knew each other's business, or at least they thought they did: the good, the bad and the sordid. And when it came to what people didn't know, gossip and rumours tended to link people even tighter than the truth: Natalie had come to know that everyone had something to hide, everyone had an agenda, and everyone was a liar. Even the best of them. Natalie's family included. She wasn't privy to all the details of how her family featured in the saga, but they featured. And she'd heard things. The worst she'd heard was that Grams's own brother had killed one of the O'Regans. Murdered in cold blood if the rumours were to be believed, and then faked his own death. Grams never talked about it. But the townsfolk still remembered.

Even to this day, the O'Regans held an almost royal quality about them. They were the untouchables. The ones who could do no wrong. Hell, even Liam was put on such a pedestal. And it irked Natalie no end. What made him so special? All because his great grandfather, Ol' Man Tom, had founded the village.

But there were others, usually the outsiders, like her, like her family, despite having lived there since the late 1800s, who refused to bow down and worship the O'Regans.

Somehow, Riley had screwed up. Natalie was sure it hadn't been intentional. But had she bothered to do any real research, or even talk to the locals, someone would have told her to let sleeping dogs lie. Sometimes the past was meant to stay buried.

Though Victoria had been tight lipped about the specifics, it hadn't mattered. The community talked, and she heard rumours all the same. Hell, even Helena had come home cursing about it only a night later. Some of the village folk had warned her during her shift in the tavern that the new teacher had made quite the display of Te Tapu in the late 1930s. It was an affront to the community, dredging up the past like that. Making a display spectacle of the time O'Regan's boy wonder, the infamous Jake O'Regan, had been murdered by a simple farm-hand. A time most sought to forget. There were other stories too. Ones where roles were reversed, and it was believed that Jake had actually killed Natalie's great uncle, bringing shame on his family, taking his own life in return. Whatever the truth, no story painted either the O'Regans or the MacKenzies, and by association the Sullivans, in a good light.

Even Helena had been understandably pissed off about it even though she didn't much care for family history. Helena lived much more for the day. But the Sullivans had had enough dirt thrown their way over the years. Whether murderer or victim, you didn't cross the O'Regans. Their name was their everything.

But here Natalie was, dredging up the past again, although her reasoning, she argued, seemed a lot more altruistic. Surely. Somehow a young boy, not much older than Cole, was haunting the school. Because that's what he was. A spirit. A spirit somehow attached to Te Tapu Primary, who now had some kind of connection or fascination with a child in her class. And if she or anyone wanted to help him, it would help to know who he was and – she swallowed hard at the thought – how he had died. She had seen enough of him to know he'd not gone peacefully. Half of his face had melted like a wax candle; his lips had shrivelled so far back on the left side of his face that it had laid his teeth bare almost all the way to his molars. Natalie felt bile rise up again at the thought and she squeezed her eyes shut to will it away.

She wasn't sure she'd find anything in any school archives, but she knew there had been some. She'd seen them once before in the resource room, hence her present hunt: a pile of papers, old-fashioned attendance records and old school photos. She'd stumbled upon them in her first year at Te Tapu. Another casualty of teacher hoarding, they'd spilled out almost on top of her when she had been collecting books for her reading groups one day. She'd stuffed them back into the cardboard box they'd been stored in without paying them too much attention, but they had stayed in her mind regardless. While there was no sign of the box, it didn't mean they hadn't been put into another form of storage container. As she remembered it, the box was old and busting at its seams even all those years ago.

Part of her knew she was wasting time. It was logical those documents were the very ones that Newbie had stumbled upon and used for her ill-fated local history presentation. Maybe she still held them. Even more likely Victoria had them, and if she did, Natalie could wisely assume there would be no getting close to them. Victoria was as tight lipped as the rest of the community on Te Tapu's history.

"Oh!"

The exclamation of surprise made Natalie jump just as she was attempting to fasten the clasp on the suitcase having found nothing of use.

Natalie's eyes shot to the doorway where Newbie stood shifting on her feet like she'd just walked in on something she shouldn't. Natalie narrowed her eyes, her guard going up without reason. What was it with this woman that set her on edge? Was it just her connection with Liam? No, it had started before that although that hadn't endeared her to Natalie either.

"I can come back later," Riley said, her eyes darting behind her. She was ready to dash and leave.

"It's fine," Natalie growled. "I'll be done in a minute." She tried grappling with the second clasp, which was stubbornly refusing to close. "Fuck."

"Can I help?" Riley asked.

Natalie hmphed and shrugged her shoulders in a sort of acquiesce.

Riley tentatively took a step towards her and then kneeled on the other side of the suitcase. "I'll push down and hold it closed if you think it'll help?"

Natalie said nothing but let her do just that. It did help. The clasp connected easily.

"Where does it go?" Riley asked skirting her eyes around the shelves.

"Up there," Natalie pointed to the one free space on the top shelf. Already moving, Natalie climbed back up onto the second shelf as she'd done the first time in getting it down, using one hand to hold onto the metal shelf bracing. She reached one hand out towards the suitcase. Riley picked it up and, with both hands, lifted it as high as she could. When Natalie had enough of a grasp of it with one hand, she was able to oomph it up a little higher above her head to get it back into its position, with a small grunt. She jumped back down and wiped her dusty palms on her thighs.

"What were you looking for?" Riley asked.

Her wavering voice irked Natalie even more than the question. Sure, Natalie hadn't exactly been welcoming, but this woman was acting like she was scared of her. For a moment, Natalie wondered just what it was that the others had said about her. She was sure Liam wouldn't have been singing her praises.

It took Natalie a moment to give in and actually answer. She punctuated it first with a sigh, aware of how rude she was coming across. Internally she scolded herself for being a bitch. Give Newbie a break, she chided herself. She's new. She knows nothing. But another voice, or more a feeling, held her responsible for things being as messed up as they were. Things had been okay, tolerable at least, until she got here, and then things changed. She felt it. There was unrest within the school. Newbie had woken something up. Most people would be oblivious to it. They might sense a little unease every now and then or see an inexplicable shadow. But others, like her – hell, even like Cole – couldn't so easily dismiss things. Grams had called it a gift. Funny, how it had never felt like a gift to Natalie. It was just another thing that made her different.

"Earlier this year you did a presentation on the history of Te Tapu," Natalie said.

Riley flinched and colour rose high on her cheeks. She nodded without speaking. Her eyes were wide like she wanted to put as much distance between her and Natalie as she could. She could hardly blame her. From all accounts, her little stunt had hit like a lead balloon.

"I'm looking for some records – attendance lists, that kind of thing. They might have been in with the stuff you used."

"I don't have them," Riley said. She'd moved back to stand in the doorway. There was very little room to share in between the sliding shelves. She reminded Natalie of a trapped rabbit ready to bolt.

"I think the box is with Victoria," Riley added.

Natalie considered Riley for a moment, trying to intuit what she was thinking right now. Whatever had happened, whatever Riley had found, Natalie knew there had been something of importance. Had she wanted to, she probably could find out, but truth be told, she had no interest in entangling herself too deeply in Te Tapu's drama. Or anybody's drama for that matter, living or dead. What with her grandma's walkabouts, her mother in general and her own struggles keeping a roof over their heads, she had enough to contend with.

And now? a small voice in the recesses of her mind asked. If that was true, why was she on a hunt to find out about a dead boy who may or may not have died near the school and was now haunting one of her students? It wasn't enough just to say it was because his dad was cute. Adding another person to her life would only complicate things.

"What exactly was in the box?" Natalie asked.

Riley paled, her eyes flickering, and Natalie waited expectantly, wondering what Riley's next words would be. Natalie had given her no reason to trust her.

"Old school rolls and photos ... some newspaper clippings ..." Riley hedged. "You'll need to ask Victoria." Quickly, she changed the subject: "I really just wanted to get a few readers for my class. I can come back later."

What was she hiding? Natalie wondered, eyes narrowing again.

"Right. I'll ask Victoria, then!" Natalie snapped. She didn't mean to be so sharp. Maybe it had become a habit. But if she thought Riley was evasive, Victoria was likely going to be even more stoic. Natalie ground her teeth to stifle a growl bubbling up in her chest.

Riley stepped aside as Natalie stormed out of the room, heading towards the office.

God, why was she so angry? She knew this was going to be the outcome. She should have just saved herself time and hit Victoria up about it from the beginning.

It took Natalie a few minutes to find Victoria. She hadn't been in her office though her car was still in the car park. Victoria was almost always one of the last to leave. She finally found her behind the main class block by the small greenhouse, a new addition to the school grounds. Her wiry form bent over a table with hands deep in potted soil, replanting seedlings by the looks of it.

Victoria wouldn't stand for heavy-handedness. She could be pretty sharp if pushed, so Natalie would need to tread carefully. Although Victoria was one of the most caring people Natalie knew, her softness often hid beneath a hard exterior, and with her, no most definitely meant no.

As she approached, Natalie's eyes wandered towards the tool shed standing a mere twenty metres or so away. She shivered, remembering the last time she had been there. For the moment, it looked pretty unassuming. Just a small wooden shed with a corrugated iron roof and a padlocked door, sheltering under the leafy green limbs of an overgrown feijoa tree. She was still curious as to the plaque hidden around the far side. While it might have been hung with good intent, it had certainly upset someone. Natalie shivered remembering the fierce malevolence directed at her.

What would Victoria think if she knew the school harboured a menacing shadow spirit? Or any spirits, for that matter? Like the little boy. How many of the staff even believed in spirits? she wondered.

"How did your conversation go with Mr Lomas?" Victoria asked, standing up to address her and pulling Natalie out of her trance.

Somewhat startled, Natalie sifted through her thoughts trying to remember what she'd come to ask.

Victoria went about removing her gardening gloves and gave her forehead a wipe with the back of her hand.

"Oh, yes," Natalie said, "it went well. Riki's concerned of course. He was worried about the other boy. He was somewhat shocked. It's apparently quite out of character for Cole to act out that way." Natalie needled her bottom lip with her teeth for a moment, wondering if she should tell Victoria the next part. Or a version of it at least.

Victoria eyed Natalie, head slightly tilted, saying nothing. It was a typical Victoria stance when people weren't forthcoming. Her silence was usually enough to get people speaking.

"We're going to get together to talk strategies for supporting Cole to deal with his emotions in more positive ways," Natalie finished. It wasn't a lie. Then, at least, if Katrina or any of the other Te Tapu gossips at the tavern went to Victoria about her schmoozing with a parent, she could genuinely say Victoria was in the know.

Victoria raised an eyebrow at her, and Natalie mentally kicked herself for how perceptive Victoria was. She'd known Natalie and her family forever; lying or leaving out details wouldn't fly with her. To Natalie's relief, Victoria took it no further; instead, she changed the subject.

"So, what is it you needed?" she asked leaning back against the seedling table and crossing her ankles.

Now that the moment was here, Natalie realised she had no good excuse for asking what she was about to ask. Crap!

"I'm trying to find out a bit about the history of Te Tapu School." There it was. Natalie expected it to hit like lead, particularly after Riley's incident earlier in the year.

As it was, Natalie was surprised to see the pinched expression on Victoria's face.

"What *exactly* are you looking for," Victoria asked, her voice strained.

"Student lists. That kind of thing. It's a bit of a personal project," Natalie said nonchalantly, hoping to ease the tension floating in the space between them. "I wanted to see if someone I know went to this school."

"And why don't you just ask them?" Victoria said, her eyes locked on Natalie.

"Well ... actually ... they've passed now." Natalie met her stare.

There it was, a barely perceptible chill in the air despite the sun hanging high in a nearly cloudless sky.

Natalie noticed a quick shift in Victoria's expression, a slight lessening of her guard before returning to a steely stoicism.

Jeez, she hated beating around the bush. It would be so much easier if she could just be upfront and tell her. Hey, Victoria, do you know your school is haunted? By more than one ghost actually. But the one I'm most interested in is a little boy, maybe nine years or so, badly scarred face, maybe he'd been in an accident or something.

Oh, and just so you know, there's also some horrible evil man who is legitimately scary as fuck, popping in time to time too.

Natalie mentally swore. She was going to have to step a little closer to the truth if she was going to get any answers from Victoria.

"Have you ever heard of a kid, first name Gavin, who used to go to this school?" Like ripping a Band-Aid off a cut.

Victoria looked like she was mentally scrolling through attendance lists from the past thirty or so years she'd been principal at the school. For a second, a flash of recognition showed in Victoria's eyes, but with a small shake of her head, Victoria dismissed it.

"I can't recall the name of every student who has attended this school. No one's springing to mind. How long ago was it?"

Well, that was the problem, wasn't it? Natalie really had no idea what year Gavin the ghost had passed. Other than the violent disfigurement to his face, which she wasn't ready to mention just yet, there was nothing remarkable that stood out about the kid. He wore blue corduroy pants and a tan collared shirt. Somewhere between the nineteen sixties and the nineteen eighties, maybe? History and fashion were two topics she had very little interest in generally.

Natalie shrugged in response. Hell, if Victoria would just hand over the box of documents and photos that Riley had seen, she could search herself.

"I wouldn't mind going through the records myself if I could?" Natalie asked.

"I'm sorry, Natalie, but they're in storage and not easily accessible at the moment," she said with a smile at odds with her narrowed eyes and the small line etched between her brows.

Natalie was losing patience. Small warning bells sounded in the back of her mind. She was about to do something stupid. Remember you need this job; the voice reminded her. No school wants to hire a teacher who sees invisible people.

But it was too late. Her self-restraint was thinning, and she wanted to get back home to check in on Grams.

"Victoria," Natalie said, her voice gaining acerbity again, no longer caring how crazy it made her sound. "Do you know of anyone who might have died here? At this school?" she said bracing herself, for what, she wasn't sure.

Victoria looked like she'd been sucker punched. The colour drained from her face, and her jaw slackened. She clung tighter to the shelf she leaned on.

Natalie kept her eyes homed in on Victoria, so there was no room for her to lie her way out of it. Every fibre of Natalie's being made her believe Victoria knew something.

"Te Tapu's an old school," Victoria said.

Natalie was sure her voice quavered.

"I'm sure you've heard the stories the same as everyone." Victoria seemed to be regaining her composure, her voice returning to its usual directness. She wiped her palms on her pant legs and faced off against Natalie. Despite being at least a head shorter, Victoria had an aura about her that gave her a much bigger presence.

"You're talking about my great uncle?" Natalie asked. Until that moment, she'd forgotten about Grams's brother. Those who believed he'd been murdered also believed it had happened at the school. The skin on her arms prickled and her hairs stood up on end. Liquid ice replaced the blood in her veins. A sudden change in light made her look up. Sure enough, the sun had passed behind a cloud, and the once-blue sky was now a water colour painting of moodiness. A breeze picked up, and the rustle of feijoa leaves on the shed's iron roof made her skin crawl. She darted her eyes towards the shed, then to the classrooms. She half expected to see a dark figure standing there, just like before. While no one was present, she had the unsettling feeling that someone *was* listening. Someone she couldn't see.

Victoria also stood at full attention. Her eyes followed Natalie's. For a second Natalie wondered if whatever was causing this was her uncle. Had he been the man she'd seen? Angry about his murder or angry because he was a murderer? She shook her head. No, it didn't feel right. From the few pictures she'd seen and the small amount she'd learnt from Grams, Billy hadn't been like that. He wouldn't have hurt anyone.

Victoria rubbed her arms.

"Anyone else?" Natalie asked, refusing to be beat in what was beginning to feel like a show down. "A young boy, maybe?"

The tall pine trees along the fence line of the drive behind them swayed in an uneasy dance. Something Natalie said was upsetting someone.

Victoria shook her head, but her eyes darted towards the treeline too.

"Maybe eight or nine?" Natalie continued. "And ... and ..." She swallowed hard, unsure how to word it; even thinking about it made her feel ill. "Something happened to him, and I think it was here at school. He was badly hurt ... like ... like ..." How to describe it? "Like part of his face had been burnt away."

This time, Victoria swayed, one hand covering her open mouth.

The wind picked up more, and Natalie swiped at her hair lashing at her cheeks and whipping her eyes. What the hell was going on?

The words she needed came from nowhere. "Victoria," she said, her voice rising to be heard over the blustery symphony of wind versus trees. "Was there ever a fire at the school?"

Like the weather had been sucked away by a giant, invisible vacuum, everything stopped. The wind – gone. Disappeared. The trees, straight and stoic sentinels again. The sky: blue. Cloudless. Eerily unblighted by clouds. And the sun high in the sky once again. Natalie inhaled sharply. When her eyes met Victoria's, a new fear hit her.

Victoria looked older, paler, frailer. And she was trembling all over. Whoever stood before her was no longer Natalie's once-formidable principal, the woman who took no prisoner when it came to angry and disrespectful parents. Hell, Natalie had even seen her put Arthur O'Regan in his place before, and no one messed with Arthur. Or an O'Regan, for that matter.

Tears welled in this other Victoria's eyes. One loosened and rolled down her cheek, and Victoria swiped at it with the palm of her hand.

"Victoria?" Natalie said, her voice small.

Victoria's eyes widened. "Yes," she whispered. "There was a fire. And it was all our fault. We killed Gavin Jenkins."

CHAPTER 14

Maggie

1964

It had been bad. A roaring inferno like Maggie could never have imagined. Clouds of suffocating black, grey and white billowed into the sky. Cracking and popping and an orchestra of white noise filled her senses as she watched the bush alight with flame. It had been a weird sort of kismet that Arthur's dad, Hugh O'Regan, had been driving back from Riccarston. He stopped immediately on seeing the four of them standing in shock on the road. Four, because Maggie was sure she was the only one who saw the other, the dark shadow wavering in and out of eyesight, sometimes even dissolving into Arthur.

The ute pulled to a skid in the gravel. Hugh rolled down the window and leaned out.

"What the heck happened? You kids, okay?" Eyes wide, he stared beyond them at the fire.

Turning, Maggie faced the destruction. Victoria tugged on her arm, mumbling and crying, but Maggie tuned her out – her voice like the hum of static. Like fire. Maggie was entranced. Or drugged, she thought, remembering the weed. Maybe this was all a bad dream. The heat added to the ethereal quality of her surroundings. Her skin was slick with sweat – the warmth from the fire was maddening on top of the already hot summer's day, adding to the out-of-body feeling.

Though she could hear voices behind her, her brain refused to translate. She knew they belonged to Mr O'Regan and Arthur. Just as she knew Mr O'Regan was angry. Had Arthur told him that he'd started it?

The fire was nearing them at a stampeding pace, and Maggie coughed, her lungs filling with the harsh woody smoke of the forest. How long before it reached the school? Would it travel so far in the other direction that it would reach her house?

Victoria tugged harder, frantic. Male hands on her arms, twisting her away from the fire and pulling her towards the ute, broke the spell.

"We need to get out of here. Sound the alarm," JP said.

Arthur jumped up on the deck. Victoria waved her on to the other side of the cab, yelling at her. Just words. She didn't want to hear Victoria's words. How had she been so stupid? JP shoved her to Victoria, who went about pushing her into the cab and squeezing in beside her. A thumping from the back window, and Maggie twisted to see JP crouching on the deck beside Arthur. He banged on the window again, and Mr O'Regan pressed his foot to the ground. The ute fishtailed on the gravel before gaining traction.

Victoria had stopped crying, resigning herself to whimpering instead. Eyes wide, Maggie peered past Mr O'Regan out his window to the school.

Her stomach lurched, and she flung her fist to her mouth. Oh God, it had reached the school. She could see it licking at the back wall of the classrooms closest to the reserve. Mr O'Regan swore under his breath, and they picked up speed. It was only a few minutes before a sharp left turn sent Maggie sliding into Victoria, who whined as she hit the passenger door. Mr O'Regan slammed on the brakes and brought the ute to a stop alongside the fire station. He shoved open the door and leapt from the cab, shouting. Maggie turned in her seat to look behind her. JP had jumped from the deck and was racing towards the bell tower. Arthur threw himself into the driver seat and slammed the door. Maggie's first instinct was to recoil from him, but then the tolling of the bells, the fire alarm, stole her attention.

"We need to help!" Maggie called out as Arthur threw the shift into gear and tore away from the fire station back onto the main road.

"Stop the car!" she cried out in panic when Arthur ignored her.

"I'm to take you back to the house," was all he said, his monotone voice at odds with the panicked situation around them.

"But we can help!" Maggie protested.

"No, we can't!" Vicky had found her voice again. It was raspy and hollow. "We'd just get in the way."

"We'll tell them the truth. It was an accident?" Even as Maggie said it, she cringed at how it came out as a question. Vicky's look had suggested Arthur had started it. Had some stupid joke gotten out of hand? She shuddered and shifted in her seat to try and put a little more distance between her and Arthur, which was nearly impossible in the cramped space.

She could still hear the bells in the background, and they tore into the driveway just as a blue truck sped past towards the fire station. More volunteer firefighters, Maggie thought. It wouldn't be enough though, would it? They'd need more than the one small truck. They'd need the fire service from Maramanui, maybe even from further out, like Riccarston. And even then ... Maggie's stomach rolled again as they came to a stop outside of Arthur's house.

Arthur killed the engine, and Vicky went to open the door beside her. Arthur lunged across, grabbing her arm and eliciting a squeal from Vicky. Maggie flattened herself the best she could against the seat.

"We don't tell *anyone*," Arthur growled, his voice low. His eyes were steely and unblinking, yet even so, they flicked back and forth between Maggie and Vicky.

"But it was an accident," Victoria whispered, her eyes wide.

Maggie couldn't remember a time she'd ever seen her look so scared.

"You think anyone's gonna care if it's an accident if it takes down the school?"

Maggie shrank back. The shadowy presence she'd seen was back – like a dark haze behind his eyes, perceptible in a way that didn't make sense.

Maggie caught movement by the front door of the house. Mrs O'Regan stood on the steps, a tea towel in her hands as if she were finishing up drying dishes.

"Tell no one!" Arthur whispered out the corner of his mouth before swinging the cab door open and dropping down out of the cab. He started towards his mother who was now walking towards them, genuine confusion marring her features. Maggie sat there, frozen, her thoughts in turmoil.

"Please, Maggie," Victoria pleaded. "It *was* an accident. The fire department's on to it. Everything will be okay."

Maggie turned to her. Who was this woman?

Vicky's attention moved towards the window, and Maggie followed her eyes. Arthur was standing in front of his mother, waving a hand for the two of them to join them. Vicky slipped out of the cab, dropping on to the gravel below. Maggie took a deep breath and followed suit. What else could she do?

CHAPTER 15

Maggie

1964

Mrs O'Regan was gracious in offering them fresh orange juice. Maggie, parched, took it gratefully despite the pang of guilt. Mrs O'Regan had asked all the expected questions, and Arthur had answered them all convincingly, Maggie thought, and yet she had the distinct feeling Mrs O'Regan wasn't buying it.

The story was close enough to the truth. Mr O'Regan had been driving back from Riccarston when he saw the fire and their little group. Arthur told his mother they'd had no proximity to the fire. They had already been on their way back to the house when his dad pulled over giving them the warning. On the way, they'd stopped at the fire station to raise the alarm so his dad and JP could help with the efforts to put it out, and Arthur had been tasked with driving the girls home.

Maggie could smell the smoke clinging to her hair and wafting around her every time she moved. Surely Mrs O'Regan could smell it too. The fire had nearly licked her skin. She had no idea what state she looked like, but there was something about Mrs O'Regan's demeanour that led Maggie to believe she didn't fool easily.

"Why were you near the school anyway?" she asked, refilling Vicky's glass with more juice from the carafe sitting on the table between them. Vicky, for the most part, kept her eyes downcast on the table, but now she shot Maggie a warning glance, and Maggie's blood boiled. Of course Vicky didn't trust her. Goody-two shoes Maggie. Was she really just waiting for her to screw up?

"We weren't there long, Ma. I told you. We walked through it on the way to the Harrison's orchard. Juliet said we could help ourselves, remember?"

"The orchard? Really?" Mrs O'Regan sighed heavily and pushed herself up from the table.

She was a striking woman, Maggie thought. And she wore her age well. She also had a reputation. She was involved in too many local charities to count, and almost without exception people in Te Tapu sung her praises. They did the same of Mr O'Regan. Maggie's eyes wandered to a framed picture on the side table. A marriage portrait by the looks of it. They were a particularly handsome couple.

"Well, whatever the real story," Mrs O'Regan said, a tightness in her voice, "I'm glad you're all safe. Girls, I want you both to stay here until we have confirmation the fire's under control. You can use the telephone to let your parents know. Arthur, take your dad's ute. We'll load it with as many buckets of water as we can find and drinks for the lads, and you can find a way to be useful." Her voice was stern.

Arthur's eyes narrowed and he scowled, but Mrs O'Regan held her ground.

"You help your father and bring him back here safely!"

Arthur turned on his heel and stormed out the front door, making it swing shut with a slam. Mrs O'Regan closed her eyes for a moment. When she opened them again, she gave a forced smile. "Let's help load the ute with what we can."

The four of them made quick work of it, gathering buckets and anything similar from the sheds, filling them with water, and lifting them onto the ute's deck. Maggie wasn't convinced much water would arrive there. Arthur was not a gentle driver; the likelihood of his precious cargo spilling was high. Maggie and Vicky went about making jam and cheese sandwiches and filling a box with cups and carafes with drinks for the fire fighters. It wouldn't be much, but who knew how long it would take to calm the fire. And doing something felt better than the prospect of doing nothing.

It was somewhat with relief when Arthur and his dad's ute receded down the driveway.

There had been a number of sirens whizzing past the end of their drive, meaning help had likely arrived from nearby towns. Still, it made Maggie sick to think how much was being destroyed in the blaze. How? How had it happened at all? The questions kept rolling around in her head, but she knew she needed to be alone with Vicky, without any chance of being interrupted, before she could ask anything.

With her son gone, Mrs O'Regan also seemed to breathe freer, or else it was Maggie's imagination.

Both girls called home. Maggie's house was closest to the blaze, and she was relieved to hear it didn't look like it, or her family, were in immediate risk. Yet. Her parents went about wetting down the outside of the house anyway and had filled buckets with whatever water they could get.

To get to her house, she'd need to follow the road past the fire, and she didn't want to get in the way of the firefighters doing their job. And if she were honest, she wasn't sure she'd be able to stomach the sight of what was going on right now. All because four young adults, who should have known better, went out for a snog and a smoke in the woods.

The guilt sat heavily in the pit of her stomach.

Vicky had no reason to stick around. Her house was on the other side of town and nowhere near the action. Maggie assumed Vicky stayed because she was there. Despite that, Maggie could barely stand to look at her. She was still angry with her. Her stupid immature crush had led to this. She swallowed hard and bit back tears thinking about the school, then went about busying herself with putting the kitchen back to how it was before she and Vicky had torn it apart gathering supplies.

Mrs O'Regan had been calling around the town, checking in on those she could who were close to the fire or who might be adversely affected. She'd just put the phone receiver on the hook and sighed heavily, massaging her brow with one hand, when the phone rang, making them all jump.

"Hello, O'Regan residence, this is Peggy," Mrs O'Regan said. After a pause, her jaw fell open, and she turned her back on them. As she nodded and made small, horrified sounds, Maggie tensed and she let Vicky grab her hand and give it a squeeze.

"I'm so sorry, Judith," Mrs O'Regan said, her voice pained. "I haven't seen him, but I have Miss Carrie and Miss Stone here with me. I'll ask them?"

Mrs O'Regan pulled the receiver away from her ear and covered the mouthpiece with her hand. She swallowed and blinked again holding her eyes closed a second too long.

"Girls," she said, her voice barely more than a whisper. "Judith Jenkins is on the phone. She says she saw the four of you earlier in the day at the school. The thing is"—she paused, her voice frayed—"Gavin's gone missing. Judith wants to know if either of you have seen him since them. Or maybe ... maybe he followed you?"

Black dots danced in front of Maggie's eyes, and bile burnt a path up her oesophagus.

No. It couldn't be. Surely not. Dear Lord. Could Gavin be caught in the fire? Could they be the reason a nine-year-old child was missing?

CHAPTER 16

Natalie

After pulling into the driveway, Natalie sat for a moment in her car. Her legs felt leaden. She killed the ignition and sat there staring at the peeled siding of her Grams's house. Helena's car was missing from the carport, which Natalie was thankful for. She couldn't deal with Helena's drama right now. She had too much she needed to figure out. Her emotions too raw. She had too many questions. All of which, she suspected could be answered once she made a move to actually leave the car and go inside. Then again, she doubted she'd be able to get any answers from Grams. Besides, if she asked her grandmother outright, she risked the chance of upsetting her.

She unclenched her fingers from the steering wheel and dropped her hands into her lap, letting her mind float for a moment more.

Victoria's confession had left Natalie reeling. If it had even been a confession. Had she really meant it when she said she'd killed Gavin? For her whole life, she'd known Victoria. Not once had she suspected her of being a murderer. It just didn't add up. Damn it! If she'd only had a few more minutes, Victoria might have told her more. How did the fire start? Why was Gavin there?

But just as Natalie had regained her composure, Newbie had interrupted them.

Victoria's countenance changed with the skill of years of performing in front of a class, an art most teachers were accomplished at.

"I'm sorry, Victoria," Riley's broke in, and Natalie gritted her teeth against another surge of anger boiling in her abdomen. Why was this woman always there messing things up?

"There's a phone call for you in the office. I was in the staffroom. Sandra's already left for the day, so I answered it."

Natalie held back a low growl.

"They said they were from the Ministry. I asked to take a message, but they said they'd been playing phone tag with you all day."

Victoria gave Riley a thank you smile, and Natalie balled her hands into fists at her side. She glared at Riley. Goddam her! Riley looked nervous, her eyes sweeping backwards and forwards from Natalie to Victoria.

"Tell them I'll be there in a moment," Victoria said, her voice even and kind, the one she reserved for the children.

"O-kay ..." Riley said, her voice trailing off. She seemed reluctant to go, but after a moment, she turned heel and left.

"What do you mean, you killed Gavin?" Natalie asked, returning to their conversation. Her voice was strained. Victoria couldn't drop a bombshell like that and then walk away.

"It was a horrible accident." Victoria shook her head, eyes downcast for a moment, before lifting her chin and squaring off with Natalie. "We'll talk about it more another time." Principal Victoria was back.

"Victoria!" She could hear her own indignation. Natalie was in no mind to be so easily dismissed! "Victoria! We're talking *now*!" She held back from stomping her foot in exasperation.

Victoria raised an eyebrow as if sensing her brewing tantrum. She jutted her chin out even further, and stalked off after Riley towards the staffroom, leaving Natalie reeling in her wake.

"Victoria!" she called after her once more. Principal or not, no call from the Ministry of Education could be more important than completing a murder confession. But she had also said it was an accident. Which was it, then?

Natalie wanted to call after her: Murder or accident? Why was it that deaths in Te Tapu never seemed clear cut? Her great uncle. Murder? Accident? Suicide? Depending on who told the story deemed which way the verdict bent. Jake O'Regan – was he a killer, a victim, or just misunderstood? And was his death murder, accident, or suicide?

And then there was Anna.

Murder or accident? Murder or accident?

No! Natalie's mind fought back at her. Don't think of Anna!

Natalie could taste blood.

Screw this town and its secrets and its lies. They couldn't stay buried forever.

CHAPTER 17

Natalie

Natalie felt a headache coming on again. A faint pounding behind her left eye. She was pissed at Victoria. For a moment, she'd let her guard down and had been so hopeful she was about to get answers. But bloody Newbie had interfered again, creating an excuse for Victoria to hold her secrets closer for another day. Maybe, just maybe, she could get some answers from Grams if she was careful. But why was she struggling to leave the bloody car? Why did her legs feel so bloody tired and leaden?

Come on, Natalie, she cajoled herself. You can confront Victoria tomorrow. Just get your ass up and get inside, before Helena gets home and ruins everything. As she was apt to do.

Natalie pried open her eyes she hadn't realised she'd closed. The first thing she noticed was the front door. Oh God, why hadn't she seen it before? The door was slightly ajar. Shit, had she forgotten to lock it? Or was Helena the last to leave that morning? Natalie couldn't remember. Oh please, let this be Helena's fault.

As realisation hit, it was replaced with a new prayer, one her head screamed as she flung open the door and raced for the front steps. Oh God, please let Grams be home, better yet, watching game shows in her favourite chair or safe in bed resting. Please, please don't let her be gone.

She took the steps two at a time, her heart in her throat.

"Grams?"

She pushed open her grandmother's bedroom door, the first on the right, too urgent to care if she woke her, but she knew even as she did so, what she'd find. The room was empty, bed unmade, sheets pushed back in a dishevelled heap.

"Grams?" she called again, aware of the way her voice hitched at the end. Fuck! Oh fuck! Not again!

The thought tumbled around her mind making circles until the words became gibberish as she dashed down the hall pushing every door open as she went.

"God damn it, Grams! Where are you?" Tears prickled her eyes. The onslaught of emotions made ribbons of her insides.

The kitchen. It was all there was left. On hearing the quiet chatter from the television, a hint of relief washed over her, but on seeing Grams's armchair empty, she knew without a doubt. Grams wasn't here. She'd gone. Again. Walkabout. Which meant she was in the woods. She always went to the woods.

Maybe she hadn't been gone that long, Natalie consoled herself. Maybe she could find her before any trouble came from it.

Or maybe you'll find her dead in a ditch. The thought brought bile to the back of her throat.

God she was stupid. She should have taken Victoria up on her offer years ago. Grams should be in a home; assisted living. Being looked after. Even if it was paid for by a possible murderer.

She rushed to the kitchen window and scoured the back of the section. Nothing.

It was usually at night she went wandering. What had changed?

Swearing again in fear and frustration, Natalie sped back down the hallway. She flew out the front door, slamming it shut behind her. On reaching her car, she wrenched open the driver's side door and threw herself behind the wheel. It was possible Grams was still close by, and fortunately the first part of Grams's usual escape route was gravelled enough that she could drive it. Better to drive. There was no knowing what mental or physical state she'd find Grams in.

If you find her, the voice in her head reminded her. Natalie gritted her teeth against the threatening tears.

She turned on the ignition and slammed the gearshift into reverse. The wheels of her car screamed in protest on the gravel. Then, after forcing the gearshift back into drive, she made her way around the side of the house.

Slow down. Breathe. Common sense reminded her. She'd need to proceed slowly, scan her surroundings so as not to miss anything, regardless of how fast her heart raced in her chest.

Around the back of the house, a metal gate led to the neighbouring paddocks. Fingers fumbling, Natalie unhooked the clasp on the gate and swung it open then jumped back into her car. There was no point closing it again. No sheep were in the paddock at this time, and it was obviously doing a useless job of keeping anyone in or out anyway. Grams must have climbed it. Despite looking anything like, Grams was spry when she wanted to be.

Natalie forced herself to stay in the lowest gear. Window down she called out every few seconds for Grams. It was ridiculous really. She'd never answered when Natalie had done this before. She was usually too lost in her own world.

Please be safe. Please be safe. Where the hell are you, Grams?!

Natalie continued scanning her surroundings. The gravel trail was meant for farm vehicles. To her right paddocks ran towards the road. To her left was a ravine with brush. Further beyond this lay the woods, which continued up the hills and circled back around the house towards the town, stopping near the school.

The brush to her left was where she kept most of her attention for anything out of place. Grams's clothing, maybe? Please don't let there be a body ...

There was nothing.

The road eventually ended. She could off-road it, but from past experience, this was usually where Grams left off to go towards the woods anyway.

Natalie killed the engine, grabbed her phone from the dashboard and slipped it into her back pocket before setting off. The brush lined the edge of a bank, which Natalie negotiated her way down using the branches and trunks from the beech trees for balance. It wasn't the first time Natalie had wondered how her grandmother managed this same trek. The bank dipped off to a ravine, and she followed the dirt path worn now by previous excursions.

"Grams?"

No answer. Natalie hurried as fast as she could, striking out at the branches that clawed at her arms, at the midges hovering around her face and in front of her eyes.

"Grams?" Where was she?

Natalie made fast work of following Grams's usual trek ... where was she?

She was halfway between the house and the school now. Why did Grams always come this way? What kept drawing her back time and time again?

"Grams?" Natalie paused, surveying her surroundings, senses heightened.

For a second, she thought she heard something, something at odds to the usual sounds of nature. Not birds. Not footsteps. Not breaking twigs or rustling undergrowth. Breathing. It sounded like breathing, heavy breathing.

Oh God. Someone was right there. An oppressive weight pushed against her, and she quickly turned her head away from the onslaught of foul, warm breath blowing into her face. The smell of whiskey made her nose crinkle. She took a step backwards. No one was there, no one physical anyway, yet someone *was* there. The air around her had grown thick and had her eyes not told her otherwise, she could swear a man stood in front of her. The thought brought an image right to her mind. The angry shadow figure from school. He was here. Though she couldn't see him, she could feel him. Too scared to turn around, she took another step back, her breath caught in her throat, her hands stretched out, feeling her way.

Her fingers felt the rough bark of a tree trunk before her body and she pressed herself against it, the heavy energy moving with her. In her mind's eye, she could see his face almost touching hers. His breath, moist on her face, and she turned her head again, wanting to escape.

"Whore!" A voice, thick with malice whispered in her ear. "Another fucking paddy."

His words stung, making her limbs turn to ice while her mind reeled trying to make sense of the assault. Whoever this person was, he'd been no fan of the Irish. But how had he known of her Irish ancestry? Grams was Irish, but she'd married a Māori man, and as for Natalie's father, Helena had never told her.

"Even in death, he and his whore thought they could better me. Fuck me over. Ruin me. Ruin my family. It's only fair ... only fair I ruin his ..." The last word came out as a hiss.

Natalie fought against a darkness threatening to buckle her knees. Her mind was melting into unconsciousness. She closed her eyes tight, trying again to envision a ball of white light surrounding her, protecting her, trying to block out his attack upon her, like pins probing for a spot to enter, to take over.

Was that what he wanted? To possess her? Was he the reason Grams went wandering at night?

Oh God! Grams?!

Natalie fought to hold on; she needed to find her grandmother. Needed to make sure she was okay. Whoever this spirit was, that was all he was – a spirit.

A hand slowly rode up her leg, fingers digging deep as they crawled their way further and further up. Her heart plummeted in her chest, shocking her eyes open. Holy fuck, spirit or not, she could feel him touching her.

"Get. Off. Me," her voice was low. She forced herself to move her head to face him.

His eyes blazed red, his face more shadow that human, an ugly swirling mass of anger and malice with jeering white teeth in a crooked smile.

His lust and hate licked at her skin like flames, fuelling her anger. No man was going to force himself on her like this. Certainly not a dead man.

"Get. Off. Me!" she said again, this time with the full force of her fury aimed at the entity. Her hands automatically sought to push him off her. They touched nothing, yet the monster vanished.

Heat ran up Natalie's body, and whether from fear, relief or a mixture of both, her stomach roiled and she retched onto the ground in front of her, hands on knees to steady herself. When her heaving had passed, she wiped her hand across her mouth and used the corner of her shirt to wipe the tears running down her cheeks.

What the hell was that?

And where the hell was Grams?

"Grams," Natalie yelled, louder this time, desperation and fear that whoever had been there would return or had gone after Grams.

Nothing. There was no sound.

"Maggie!" she yelled, hoping her first name might provoke an answer.

There it was. A whimper, not too far away. She was sure of it.

"Maggie?" she called out again.

Again came a light whispering of motion; a small, human-like sound, further amongst the trees. Hope gave Natalie energy, and she crashed through the undergrowth, beating back branches and limbs that created a wall against reaching the woman's form lying face down in the dirt.

"Grams!" Natalie called out in fright.

Her yellow sundress exposed pale legs and bare feet. A white cardigan hung lopsided off one shoulder. She lay with her head turned to one side, her white hair knotted and dirty, hiding her face. Despite the shock, Natalie couldn't help thinking how young she appeared.

Natalie flung herself down beside her unconscious form. "Grams? Grams? Can you hear me?" She bent so her ear almost touched the side of her face, one hand resting lightly on her back. She was breathing. Natalies's hand moved with each shallow breath, and Grams let out a small whistling sound as she did. But she wouldn't rouse.

While nothing presented as broken, that wasn't to say there wasn't internal injury. Broken ribs, hips. The list could be endless.

Natalie's eyes darted around trying to make sense of what had happened. With no immediate sign of what had taken place, no signs of struggle or anything prominent to trip over, she didn't know what to think. Oh God! How could Natalie have been so stupid? This was all her fault.

Blind panic rushed to the surface and her eyes welled. She used her last reserves of inner strength to beat them down. Think, Natalie. What do you need to do?

In a Eureka moment, Natalie remembered her phone in her back pocket. Doubt hit her whether there would be reception, but with relief, full bars showed. They weren't so deep into the bush, then; surely the road was not so far away. She still needed help though. For a second, her brain went blank, who to call. What to do? Her fingers found the buttons before her brain could comprehend what she was doing.

111.

"Hello. Emergency services. What's your emergency ..."

Natalie answered the questions as instructed, frustration settling in as she tried to give details as to where in the bush they were, in more detail than between her house and the school. While the phone's GPS would help, what she really needed, she realised with a start, was Troy. He'd been out this way enough. He'd know where to go. She told the operator as much. They needed to get hold of Troy. She gave the operator his details and all the other details she could, remembering nothing of the actual conversation.

The operator offered to stay on the line with her, but her phone showed an incoming call from Troy, and she told the operator to get emergency services to hurry before hanging up.

"Sullivan! What's happened?"

Hearing his voice threatened a new overwhelm of emotion.

"It's Grams," Natalie said, hearing her voice crack and not caring. "We're in the woods, a good ten minutes from the road off from the house. My car's there. Troy ..." Words failed her, eyes glued to the back of Grams's head. She'd brushed her hair away from her face. Grams looked like she was sleeping. Only she wasn't. She was hurt. And despite no obvious signs of bleeding or anything of that nature, something was very, very wrong. She wasn't moving and her breath was so shallow Natalie's hand barely moved from where it rested on her back.

"Please hurry," Natalie pleaded into the phone, tears now running rivers down her cheeks. "She's not moving, Troy."

"I'm on my way, and we've an ambulance following. She'll be okay," he said calmly. "Just stay with her. Keep her comfortable. I'll call you when I'm at your car."

Sobbing, Natalie nodded, aware he wouldn't be able to see.

She had royally fucked up this time. If something happened to Grams, if she was seriously hurt … She'd never forgive herself. She knew Grams couldn't be left alone. Her walkabouts had been happening more and more often. And if they didn't bolt the outside of the door when they left … An imperfect solution but all they had …

An eternity passed before she heard the distant wail of sirens. She'd spent the whole time, stroking Grams's hair and talking to her, apologising mainly. She'd do better. She promised. She'd get her the care she needed, one way or another, even if it meant selling the house and getting a smaller apartment. Whatever it took. Family first, she promised.

Her phone rang seconds after the sirens.

"We're here and we're heading in," Troy said. "Keep talking to me, tell me where to go. Did you keep to her usual trail?"

"Yes," Natalie replied trying to visualise the route she'd taken to get to where she was now. The thing was, although she'd started off on her usual route, she'd lost all consciousness of where she was once that thing attacked her. Oh God, what if he was still hanging around here somewhere, ready to attack again. Could she really protect them against such an invisible evil?

"Keep talking to me, Sullivan," Troy said, a no-nonsense steel in his voice.

"I went off track," Natalie said. "When I got to the clearing, I got all turned around, I … I don't know which way I went." The edge of panic seeped into her voice again. Every second that passed seemed far too long. "Please, please hurry," she whispered into the phone. At last, she heard them, the trampling of brush underfoot, voices, Troy.

"Here! We're over here!" she yelled out, waving her arms and choking with emotion. And then they were there, Troy and another officer and three paramedics hustling towards her with an orange stretcher carried between them.

They went to action right away, dropping to their knees beside Grams, while Natalie scrambled to move out the way and let them do their jobs. Then, without knowing how she got there, she was in Troy's arms, face pressed into his chest. Uncontrolled sobs erupted, a deep grief exploding out of her. And Troy held her. His arms wrapped around her tight.

"It's okay. Maggie will be okay. She's a tough bird. It's okay," he soothed, and somehow it worked.

Natalie sniffed, her tears drying on his chest. Embarrassed, she pulled away slightly.

He kept his grip on her arms. "Can you tell me what happened?"

"She did it again," Natalie said. "I got home. The door was open. She did it again ..."

Two of the paramedics and the other police officer lifted her grandmother onto the stretcher. Her eyes were still closed, an oxygen mask covered her face. She was breathing at least.

"I can help," Troy said, instantly joining to take a grip of the stretcher.

"We've got this," one of the paramedics said. "Light as a feather."

"Any health problems we need to know about?" one of the paramedics jumped upon Natalie. "Does she take any medications?

Names? When did she last eat? Drink? How long has she been here? Did you move her?" The questions kept coming, methodically, with pauses to take notes, as they made their way back towards the gravel road.

"Is she going to be okay?" Natalie asked, still in shock. She had to be okay. She had to!

"We'll know more once she's been checked over at the hospital," one of the paramedics answered.

Hospital. Her wanderings had never landed her in hospital before. A heavy arm wrapped itself around her shoulder, and Troy pulled her close to him again as they walked.

"She'll be okay, Sullivan. Wait and see."

Natalie sniffed back tears. He couldn't know that. Hell, she didn't even know what had happened. Had that monster gotten to Grams like he'd tried getting to her? Touched her? Hurt her? Possessed her? Had he succeeded? Was he right now inside her, sucking off her life force like a fucking parasite?

A new wave of nausea rose inside her, and she pushed Troy away, lunging for the nearest tree where she retched again.

"Sullivan?" a concerned voice echoed through the roaring in her head.

"Is she okay?" another voice asked, sounding like they were underwater.

"Shock?" someone else said.

And then Troy was there again, hand on her shoulder.

"Sullivan? Talk to me," he said quietly.

"I'm fine," she said choking on the words as she did so. She was fine. And she really wasn't. Wasn't sure if she would ever be, in fact.

If Grams died it would be all her fault. Hers and hers alone. What would people believe then? Accident or manslaughter by neglect?

CHAPTER 18

Natalie

The ambulance made good time, fifteen minutes to the closest hospital in Maramanui, forgoing the extra distance to the larger facility in Riccarston. Maybe Grams was going to be okay, Natalie thought. Still, Natalie's anxiety made it feel like an eternity, sitting in the back of the ambulance, holding Grams's hand.

They'd fixed Grams up with a drip and oxygen, taken her vitals and done the best they could. She'd need a thorough assessment and a slew of tests at the hospital. The paramedic concurred that nothing looked broken, but it didn't necessarily account for internal injuries or whatever had caused her loss of consciousness.

Troy followed in Natalie's car, so she'd have it for travelling back home. It was a favour. He was still technically on duty and would need to leave again after dropping off the car. Crime didn't stop just because Natalie's grandmother had gone walking again. He'd also promised to give Helena a call.

Worst case scenarios crashed together in Natalie's mind. If Grams didn't survive this …

Her stomach pitched.

She could still feel the foul breath of the man who held her hostage against the tree. Who the hell was he? Was he the one enticing Grams out into the woods? If so, why? Was he someone from her past, maybe? It had to be more than him not liking the Irish.

There were too many questions. Too many unknowns.

Thank God, Troy had been there. He'd come when she needed him and was now helping her out with her car. He'd stay with her at the hospital too if she asked. She knew he would. He'd call it in as a family emergency. They'd been in each other's lives for so long they were basically family.

The faint wave of embarrassment intermingled with affection grew as she remembered how tightly she'd clung to him crying, and he'd just held her.

She knew he wanted more. He'd said as much on multiple occasions, and yet the idea of anything more … just wasn't for her. They were supposed to have a no-strings-attached arrangement.

It took Troy longer to find her, due to having to park her car. When he did, she was in the waiting room sitting on a hard plastic chair, leg nervously bouncing up and down and foot tapping with anxiety as she waited to hear Grams's condition. She had been taken away for tests, and as these things went, there could be a long wait ahead.

Natalie's fingers tapped on the arm rest trying to self-soothe from the threat of the memories from the last time she'd been there. She tried to focus on the posters on the wall around her, willing the memories away. The posters were depressing and did nothing to calm her;

the words bled together. The large television screen on the wall was turned all the way down but was playing a show about cats from hell or something by the way it depicted cat owners being terrorised by their feline family members, requiring some tattoo covered cat expert to come in and save the day. It would have been something Grams or Anna would have loved. Anna ...

She couldn't. Now was not the time to go reliving the past. Right now, Grams was the only one who mattered. The past was the past. Dead. Buried. Gone.

Her phone buzzed. A text message: *Where are u?*

She replied with directions for Troy to find her, and he made fast time of it.

On seeing her, he came to an almost immediate stand still. Gauging how to proceed, Natalie thought. It was like déjà vu. A replay of three years ago. Slightly different characters but the same setting. Her stomach pitched again, and she swallowed hard to fight against the rising bile in her chest.

She held Troy's gaze. Did he remember too?

He walked towards her, rummaging in his pocket with one hand as he did so. When he got to her, he pulled out her car keys and held them out to her.

"How is she?" he asked, a sudden distance between them that hadn't been there before.

Natalie shifted awkwardly. Him standing over her while she sat was suddenly unsettling. She wasn't sure if she was supposed to stand as well or not. She held her hand out and took the keys from him.

"Thanks," she said pocketing them.

Concern showed in his eyes, but the rest of his face was all serious-ness, his lips pressed together forming a thin line.

"I'm still waiting to hear," Natalie said in response to his original question. "They're taking her for an MRI." She tried to return his stoicism but felt her bottom lip tremble and glanced away.

When she turned back, Troys fingers twitched, closing into fists and then releasing again. Drawing her eyes up his face he looked conflicted. Like he wanted to say something but wasn't sure how or what to say.

"Nat ..." he said, his voice not much more than a whisper.

Nat. He called her Nat. Somewhere in the depths of her mind alarm bells sounded. He rarely called her Nat.

"I know what you're gonna say," she answered, feeling a rebuke coming on. She already felt like shit. Him telling her off wasn't going to make her feel any worse than she already felt. "I fucked up. I should have double checked the door—"

"That wasn't what I was going to say," Troy said, his jaw tight.

She narrowed her eyes his way. She didn't believe him.

He sucked in a deep breath.

"I can't keep coming to your rescue," he said, and Natalie's hackles rose.

"I care about you. I care about Maggie. But you're stubborn as hell, and we both know that's not going to change anytime soon."

Fire flared in Natalie's cheeks. Was he really telling her she couldn't change? Giving her a character critique, right here, while she waited for news about her grandmother who had just been found uncon-scious in the woods?

Natalie dug her fingers into the plastic arm rests.

"You know how I feel about you," he said, his voice low, eyes never leaving hers. "And you've made it clear how you feel. I'm a distraction or a convenience—"

Natalie went to protest, but Troy put his hand up to stop her and shook his head. She bit down on her lip. Anger and frustration threatening to swamp her.

"Maggie needs proper care, Nat. Care you can't give her. She needs to be in a care facility. We've talked about this, but nothing's changed. Whatever you're trying to prove, thinking you can do it on your own, just know that next time, if there even *is* a next time—"

Natalie's eyes welled. His words hit low. She swallowed hard.

"Next time this happens, you can't call me. I'm out. I've tried to be your friend. I've tried to be more. But I'm done. I can't keep watching you destroy yourself like this and taking Maggie down with you ..."

Natalie's heart threatened to tear apart her rib cage. She had so much she wanted to say. She wanted to yell and swear at him and call him a coward. She wanted to stomp her foot in frustration. She wanted to scream at him to just bloody leave, if he really believed her to be so selfish! And another part of her wanted to jump up and hold him to her and tell him he couldn't leave. She needed him. It didn't matter she wasn't in love with him. Where had love gotten her before? Instead, she just glowered at him, and she saw his resolve waver for a moment.

"I'm sorry, Nat," he whispered. "I hope Maggie's okay." His voice cracked ever so slightly, and his slip of emotion felt like a dagger to her chest.

Then, just like that, he straightened his shoulders, lifted his chin and turned around to leave, coming to a quick halt as he almost slammed into Helena.

"Officer," she said in the haughty tone she often gave Troy, flicking her hair over her shoulder like someone half her age.

"Helena," he said in reply, before sidestepping around her and disappearing down the hall.

"Well, lover-boy's in a bit of a mood, isn't he?" Helena said with a raised eyebrow. "Where's Mum?" She scoured the waiting room as if Grams was going to magically appear.

Natalie gripped the plastic armrests of the chair tighter. It was impossible to separate the hurricane of emotions that were colliding and tangling together, made worse by the fact she was here. Back in the same bloody waiting room from three years ago ...

"She's in with the doctor," Nat said, through gritted teeth.

Helena flung herself into the chair next to her. "Well, when does she get out?" She had her phone in her hand and was scrolling through messages.

Natalie glared at her.

"Well?" Helena repeated. "Oh, don't look at me like that," she said lifting her eyes to meet Natalie's.

How? How could she be so callous. They were at the hospital for *her* mother!

Something must have clicked for Helena, her face fell ever so slightly, and for a second Natalie thought she saw real concern in her face. "Lover-boy told me she went wandering again and I should meet you here. She is okay, isn't she?" Helena clicked her phone off and turned it face down on her knee.

"You did lock the door when you left this morning? Right?" Natalie's voice came out like a low growl. She knew the answer, and she dared her mother to say it. It was becoming harder and harder to contain her anger.

"I haven't been home." Helena's face went stony.

Realisation hit, momentarily winding her. That meant Natalie had been the last one to leave the house.

She rewound her thoughts back to leaving the house in the morning. Could she really have been so careless?

She remembered she had slept in after a restless night. Dreams crashing together. Twisted and dark. She'd been running late. She'd gotten Grams up. Washed and dressed her. Made her breakfast. Set her up in her favourite chair with the TV on. Rushing out the door, she'd nearly tripped over Poe who thought it the perfect time to weave around her legs. Then she'd rushed back in, having forgotten her phone, lying on her unmade bed. It was more than possible that in her haste, she'd forgotten to bolt the door.

Anger drained away, and Natalie covered her face with her hands. Oh God! It *was* her fault. Troy had been right, even if he hadn't said it outright. It was always her fault.

"You left the door unlocked?" Helena said an edge of accusation in her voice.

"It was an accident," Natalie whispered. An accident. Always an accident ... where was the accountability?

"Would it have been an accident if I had been the one to screw up?" Helena spat.

She had a point. Natalie never gave her mother much leeway, why should she expect the same? Natalie pulled her hands away from her face.

"I got home, and the front door was open," Natalie started. "I found her in the woods. She wasn't moving." She needled her bottom lip with her teeth, biting back tears, remembering how small and frail Grams had looked. Almost like a hatchling having fallen out of a tree. "The paramedics didn't think anything was broken but they couldn't rouse her."

"What do you mean couldn't rouse her?" Helena said, her voice pitching.

"Miss Sullivan?" A voice cut in, saving Natalie from trying to find the words.

"Yes," both Natalie and her mother answered at the same time.

"I'm Maggie's daughter, Helena, and this is her granddaughter, Natalie," Helena said, taking charge. She'd already jumped out of her seat and was standing close to the white-coated man addressing them, her head in line with his chest.

He was an older man with a sinewy, leathery face and grey hair. Natalie recognised him instantly, and her arms wound around her stomach as the wind went out of her for a second time. Panic bubbled to a bursting point. He was asking Helena questions, and she was answering them, turning now and again to Natalie for her input, but Natalie couldn't hear anything beyond the blood rushing in her ears. It was happening again. The thought kept swirling around and around, crashing into past memories:

I'm very sorry Mr O'Regan ... internal bleeding ... we did everything we could ...

Then a wailing like she'd never heard before. Hers. Natalie's anguish, bleeding into the roaring white noise in her ears.

"Natalie! He asked you a question!" the edge in Helena's voice pulled her back to the here and now.

"I ... I don't know ..." Nataile managed to fumble out the words. She had no idea what the question had been. She was lucid enough to know that her worst fears hadn't come to pass; even Helena would have been broken up if she'd learnt there was no hope for her mother. But right now, all Natalie wanted was to get out – to get far, far away from the grey linoleum floors, the lemony-white walls and the hospital smells. Those damn hospital smells.

She needed to get away from the memories.

It took her a moment to realise she was standing, pushing past Helena and the doctor, sprinting down the hall towards the exit, gasping for breath as she did so. She nearly fell out the sliding doors, stumbling down to the pavement where she stood hunched over gasping for breath. Tears streamed despite clenched eyes. She'd lost the battle as the memories flooded back. She was being ripped apart all over again.

She's dead. Anna's dead. The words ricocheted around her head. Grams might be alive, but Anna was dead.

CHAPTER 19

Natalie

THREE YEARS AGO

She was beautiful. The sun hit her long auburn hair in such a way as to shimmer with copper. The breeze made a few flyaway strands escape from behind her ear. She swiped at them with one hand whilst awkwardly holding the other end of the picnic blanket.

"What?" she said in mock admonishment.

"Nothing," Natalie said, smiling.

Between them, they gave the blanket a shake and laid it on the ground.

She'd chosen right, bringing Anna up here, faraway from prying eyes. Anna's car was hidden behind a toetoe bush off the side of the gravel road, the same offering them cover from the main road. From there, they took a fair walk to get to where they were now. Anna plonked herself down on the tartan blanket, her legs swept up to her side as she went about pulling out homemade sandwiches wrapped in beeswax wraps, and a couple of bottles of sparkling water. Nothing stronger. Anna didn't drink.

A dappling of clouds marred an otherwise blue sky, and the breeze was warm. The sun filtered through the weeping willow tendrils hanging above them, marbling Anna with light and shadow.

Light and shadow. A perfect description of what they were doing.

They were on private land belonging to the O'Regans, but it wasn't like that had stopped anyone before. Heck, most of Te Tapu belonged, or had once belonged, to the O'Regans. There were hidden pieces of utopia scattered all around this area. Places that were passed down through generations as make-out spots or swimming holes. Like everything in Te Tapu, each place had a history with myths and stories connected to them: the good, the bad and the ugly. These locations were hoarded by each new generation of teenagers. Not as much anymore, though. Not with the allure of Maramanui or even Riccarston on their doorstep. It seemed everyone over sixteen had a car nowadays and better things to do than stay in Te Tapu.

The hill they were picnicking on gave them an almost three-sixty view of the countryside surrounding them. Green hills and valleys blended into the horizon. A quilt of paddocks was dotted with sheep, and the winding main road, visible in the distance, could be followed with the eye almost to the centre of Te Tapu. Natalie could even see the sprawl of the woods between her house and the school. She regarded the view with an almost superstitious sense of awe.

"Well? Are you going to join me?" Anna asked. Her head was tilted to the side, a hint of colour high on her cheeks, the smallest of smiles playing on her lips, and warmth flooded Natalie's body.

She was mesmerised by this woman. They'd know each other for a mere nine months, and yet ... Natalie couldn't remember life before her and couldn't dare imagine life without.

Natalie kneeled down opposite her, and Anna held a wrapped sandwich to her. The sun hit the diamond-surrounded sapphire on Anna's ring finger, making it sparkle. Though Natalie felt a pinch in her chest that she was still wearing it, she shook it aside, gently pushing Anna's hand away. Instead, she crept closer to Anna on hands and knees, leaning over the rest of the food. She brushed a strand of hair behind Anna's ear, before leaning in to skim her lips with her own. She tasted her fruity lip gloss, and Natalie shuffled further forward, pushing the food and drink bottles out of the way blindly with one hand, her other hand making its way around the back of Anna's neck, fingers beneath her hair, pulling her closer. Anna shimmied closer too, and Natalie felt a trail of fire where Anna explored Natalie's curves with her fingers before pulling her to her. Natalie moved her mouth along Anna's jaw line, leaving small kisses all the way to her ear lobe and then down her neck. Anna smelt like summer, Natalie thought. Fruit, and freshly cut grass, star-filled nights, and new beginnings. God, she wanted her.

Anna let out a soft moan, one hand caressing Natalie's back, the other between them, gently touching, squeezing, massaging Natalie's breast.

Every fibre of Natalie's body throbbed with desire. Anna gently pulled Natalie down with her until they were lying face to face on the picnic blanket. Natalie's mouth found Anna's again, her tongue meeting hers with a deepening urgency. Anna's hand slid between Natalie's legs, making her shudder with pleasure, her body aching to be closer still. It was never enough: this magnetism between them. They could devour each other, live inside each other's skin, and it would still never be enough.

Their hands fervently explored each other's bodies. Natalie maneuvered herself on top of Anna, trying to eliminate all space between them, and Anna embraced her tighter, moving and grinding her pelvis into Natalie's, hungry for release.

She was hers; Natalie knew. The ring on Anna's finger meant nothing.

Anna O'Regan belonged to her.

CHAPTER 20

Maggie

1964

"It's not possible!" Victoria whispered, an edge in her voice, as she rinsed the potato under the tap. She positioned it on the cutting board and went about slicing it in half and then half again.

Maggie paused peeling the potato she held. She couldn't believe how adamant Vicky was being that this wasn't because of them. She'd insinuated herself that the fire had started because of Arthur.

Peggy was down the hall in one of the spare rooms, making up the beds for them. She'd insisted they stay the night, and with the fire between them and Maggie's house, Maggie wasn't going to argue. It seemed Vicky wasn't going to either.

"A boy is *missing*, Vicky! And we were likely the last to see him!" Maggie hissed back. Her stomach swirled, and she bit her lip to hold back the ever-present tears.

Vicky huffed and reached for the potato Maggie had been peeling. Maggie drew the peeler around its circumference one more time before dropping the potato into her hand.

Vicky held it for a moment as if weighing up whether to say aloud what she was thinking.

"Last time we saw him, he was with his mum and sister. If he ran away after that ..." Vicky's cheeks flushed, and Maggie thought she knew exactly what she was going to say. If he ran away after that it wasn't their problem. Except it was! Particularly, if Arthur had started the fire.

And the thing was, Maggie couldn't shake the feeling she'd heard someone else out there with them. A child maybe ... It had crossed her mind at the time that maybe Gavin *had* followed them!

She dropped the peeler and it clattered to the ground at her feet.

Vicky rushed to bend down and pick it up for her.

"Look, I'm sorry," she said, standing up and handing Maggie the peeler. She took Maggie by the shoulders to peer at her. "I really do hope they find the child. If he saw the fire, surely he'd be scared enough to go somewhere safe away from it."

It was a weak hope. Poor Gavin was mentally challenged. He could barely talk. Would he even be able to call for help if he was in trouble? The truth was, Maggie had no idea how he might act if he saw fire.

Vicky seemed to take Maggie's quietness as an acquiesce, so she pulled her in for a quick hug, before turning back to the chopping the potatoes. Maggie watched her for a moment. How was she handling things so well?

"Vicky?" Maggie probed. She couldn't bite her tongue any longer. "How did the fire start?"

Vicky stiffened, back to Maggie. Vicky slowly put the knife down on the chopping board and turned to face her.

"He was just playing around," she said. "Flicking the lighter. Setting the grass on fire and stomping on it to put it out. He was just goofing around or bored or something." Vicky's cheeks flushed again but she held Maggie's gaze.

"Bored?" Maggie couldn't keep the sharp sarcasm from her voice. He hadn't looked bored when her tongue was down his throat.

"Yes!" Vicky huffed again. "Maybe he was bored. I don't know. But it *was* an accident! I guess one of us hadn't put the cap on the flask properly, and it had leaked. And everything was so dry. We tried! Arthur and JP jumped all over it trying to smother it, but it caught. Next thing I know, they're running, and I'm being pulled along behind them, and I'm in a panic because I had no idea where you were!" Her voice cracked and she chewed on her bottom lip. "It happened so fast," she whispered. "There wasn't even a breeze, and it just ... took off."

A noise came from the doorway, making both Maggie and Vicky start. Maggie dropped the peeler again and rushed to retrieve it.

"Girls?" Mrs O'Regan's voice was strained. She stood in the doorway to the kitchen, her eyes moving slowly back and forth from Vicky to Maggie. "What do you know about the fire?" she asked, her voice tightly controlled.

Mrs O'Regan's eyes landed on Maggie's.

Maggie squirmed. She turned away and was relieved when Vicky answered.

"Nothing," Vicky said, with an air of innocence. "We were lucky to have noticed the smoke and to cross paths with Mr O'Regan when we did." She smiled at Mrs O'Regan.

So that was it, Maggie thought. Vicky was intent on covering for Arthur.

"Where were you exactly?" Mrs O'Regan's eyes narrowed.

"At the school, heading towards the orchard," Vicky answered matter-of-factly. The Harrison's Orchard lay behind the school on the edges of the wood. It wasn't unheard of for people to cut through the school to get there.

Maggie clamped her teeth together to stop her jaw dropping and scrutinised Vicky's face. The slightest hint of colour showed high on her cheek bones. Guilt, Maggie thought. It wouldn't be noticeable to anyone else, but Maggie had known Vicky long enough to know at least a small part of her was not comfortable with lying.

"You cut through the school?" Mrs O'Regan asked, her eyes unsmiling.

She knew. She knew Maggie and Vicky were lying.

"It's the weekend," Vicky said. "So we knew no one would be there." She paused for a moment, and Maggie was somewhat comforted by the fact she actually appeared a little abashed. "It was partly nostalgic."

Maggie's cheeks heated up. She'd never be able to look Mrs O'Regan in the face again.

Mrs O'Regan was eerily quiet for a moment.

"I do remember what it was like to be young," she said softly, almost wistfully, Maggie thought. "You were at the school, but you didn't see anyone?"

Of course, they had seen someone. Three someone's in fact. But Arthur had started the lie, so Vicky was dutifully continuing with it, yet even to Maggie, it reeked of dishonesty.

"And neither of you know anything about how the fire started?" Mrs O'Regan asked again.

"Nope," Vicky said quickly, at least trying to appear a little downcast about things.

Maggie could feel Mrs O'Regan's eyes on her, two hot pokers scouring her mind, Maggie thought. Maggie shook her head, still unable to meet her eyes, despite knowing her flushed face was giving her away all the same.

"Right. Well, the spare room is made up for you both. Let's finish dinner, and maybe the men will be home by the time it's finished cooking," she said.

It had been wishful thinking.

Maggie had no sense of how long she'd been lying in bed, sheets pulled up to her chin, listening to Vicky's soft breathing in the bed beside hers. An hour. Two. Maybe longer. The room was nearly pitch black but for the shadowy forms of the furniture in the room. Maggie's brain had been unable to stop dissecting the day. Why had she had given in and gone with Vicky? She'd felt so uncomfortable the whole time. The smoking, the drinking, JP's attention. The darkness around Arthur, which she'd always known was there, had made her skin crawl, and then there was the shadow man who attacked her in the woods. The shadow man that had somehow linked himself to Arthur. Maybe it hadn't been Arthur that made her skin crawl, maybe it was whoever had attached itself to him.

Maggie was too wired to sleep. She tried her hardest to not let her mind wander towards thoughts of little Gavin Jenkins, but her brain refused to listen. She had been sure she had heard a young boy's laughter out there in the woods with her right before she was attacked. With Gavin's history of running off, Mrs Jenkins always had her hands full. It must have been hard, having a child so lost in his own head. A child who saw the world in such a different way that it led to him being misunderstood by children and adults alike. Kids were especially cruel, and Maggie had heard the teasing many times before. They called him freak. Retard. And so many other slurs. Even Arthur had contributed! The thought made her nauseated. The poor boy; he was still a child. A child without a dad and with a mother with her hands already full with another little one.

A sliver of light from the hall leached under the doorway.

Senses alert, Maggie heard a distant door open and heavy footsteps coming from the direction of the front entrance. There were muffled voices too, although Maggie couldn't make out what was being said.

The men must have arrived home. Maggie strained to hear what was being said. Did this mean the fire was out? Was everyone okay? Did they find Gavin?

Questions for the morning though. It wouldn't be right for her to ambush them right now, as they must be exhausted. She could only imagine how tiring the whole ordeal must have been.

Yet, with a sudden urgency, Maggie realised she needed to pee. The bathroom was down the other end of the hall, closer to the front door. The more she told herself just to wait until it sounded like everyone had gone to bed, the more the urgency increased.

Cursing her body's needs, Maggie gave in and quietly climbed out of bed. She grabbed a cardigan Mrs O'Regan had loaned her and pulled it over top of her also-loaned nightie. The voices hadn't seemed to have moved much from the entrance way. She could probably get to the bathroom and back without bumping into anyone. She'd just be super quiet so as to not attract any attention. She felt like an imposter being in someone else's house, wearing someone else's clothes.

Maggie spared a glance at Vicky, whose hair formed dark snake-like shadows around her head on the pillow. The gentle undulation of her breaths had Maggie believing that Vicky probably didn't spare a single thought for the terror they'd caused today. They could have been killed. The way the fire made a beeline for Maggie in particular, Vicky had been right to have been scared at the time, and that was without her knowing that Maggie had also been fighting off an invisible attacker.

And then there was Gavin. Had Vicky any conscience about the poor child? Any concern for him at all? Not for the first time, Maggie wondered if she really knew Vicky at all.

Tiptoeing on the wooden floor, Maggie crept across the room to where the hallway light illuminated the floorboards under the door. Pausing to find the door handle, she listened for any change in sounds from beyond the bedroom. When all seemed well, she twisted the doorknob and pulled the door open, just enough to slip through. She walked close to the wall down the hall, heading closer to where the muffled voices became more discernible. As she tiptoed closer, she recognised one as Mrs O'Regan's. The other, male, belonged to neither Arthur nor JP.

Maggie stopped, hugging the wall opposite the door to the bathroom. The voices were much more audible from here, and she guessed the other voice was Mr O'Regan's. His voice was husky, and every now and then he coughed. The heavy scent of smoke and ash hung in the air. She shouldn't eavesdrop, but Mrs O'Regan's voice held her captive. A jolt of shock coursed through her body as she realised what Mrs O'Regan was saying.

"How long, Hugh? How long do we have to keep covering for him?" Her voice was shrill.

"We don't know that he did it." Mr O'Regan heaved a deep sigh.

Maggie cautiously leant forward to peer around the corner. Mr O'Regan's face was blackened from soot, his white hair stood out at various angles, and all of him was filthy and tired looking. He gently held his wife's arms. Despite the drama of the moment, Maggie could see a bubbling of deep love between them. Or maybe it was more that she felt it. Regardless, it was with a wistful stab of envy that Maggie found herself wishing for a love like theirs.

"We do know. We may not have evidence, but we know!" Mrs O'Regan said, her voice higher than when she'd spoken to them during the day. "He's always involved. Always, Hugh! And now he's getting others involved." She waved a hand in the direction of the hall, and Maggie ducked back behind the corner in case either turned in her direction.

"Maggie, one of the girls with Arthur today is Billy's sister." Mrs O'Regan's voice cracked.

A silence drew out, and Maggie struggled to make sense of why that mattered. What did Billy have to do with anything?

"Billy?" Mr O'Regan's reply was weak.

Maggie imagined Mrs O'Regan nodding her head.

"And Judith rang," Mrs O'Regan said, her voice breaking again. "Gavin's gone missing."

"I know," Mr O'Regan said. "We kept our eyes open. We'll know more in the morning when the cleanup begins."

The silence was heavy, and Maggie's stomach dropped. Did that mean Mr O'Regan expected to find the poor boy dead? A cold sweat broke out across her chest and the back of her neck, and she rubbed her arms to dispel the goosebumps that had risen there. She felt sick and faint and a whole manner of things all at once.

A muffled sob came from around the corner, and Maggie peered through again. Mrs O'Regan was covering her face and Mr O'Regan had pulled her close to his chest. She pushed him away momentarily.

"I want him gone," she said, barely above a whisper.

Maggie inhaled sharply. Was Mrs O'Regan talking about Arthur? Did she really think so little of her own son that she wanted him gone?

Mr O'Regan was shaking his head. "It's going to be okay. We'll work things out."

"No, Hugh. I want him gone. Every day I see more and more of Jake in him. He's more Jake's son than he'll ever be yours. And if that little boy turns up dead ..." she choked back a sob.

Mr O'Regan pulled her closer to him again, and Maggie shrunk back behind the corner again.

Words and alarm bells crashed together. Were they talking about Arthur? She had thought so? But would Mrs O'Regan really disown her son like that? Nothing was making sense and yet somewhere in the recess of her mind she thought the answer lay with Jake. Jake O'Regan. It was the only Jake she knew. The one who haunted her family. The one no one talked about because they were just rumours. Just rumours ... weren't they? Te Tapu's secret. The infamous prodigal son of the town's founder Ol' Man Tom. Mr O'Regan's brother. The man who might have killed her brother.

Maggie covered her mouth with her palm trying to stifle the sob threatening to escape and give away her hiding place. She turned around to make her way back to the bathroom, then slapped a hand over her mouth to stop from screaming as she came face to face with Vicky.

"Sshhh!" Vicky pleaded, finger pressed to her lips and eyes wide.

"What are you doing here?" Maggie hissed at her, the fright near making her pee herself.

"Looking for you," Vicky whispered in reply, fear lighting up her eyes.

"How long?"

"I heard it all," Vicky replied, her eyes locked on Maggie's. "We need to talk."

They did. They really did. Vicky was her friend, and Maggie would do almost anything for her, but she knew, with every ounce of her being, that Arthur was bad news. Heck, even his own mother saw it. Which meant Maggie had no choice. She had to make Vicky see it too. Otherwise, she knew, it would be the end of them.

She believed it now; the whispered war cry of the MacKenzies: The O'Regans were cursed.

CHAPTER 21

Natalie

"What the hell was that about?"

Helena's voice grated on Natalie's nerves, and she squeezed her closed eyes tighter.

Natalie had found a bench across from the entrance way under a tall totara tree. She was bent forward, folded, as if her heart had caved in again just as it had three years ago. She was focusing on her breathing to quell the nausea sitting heavy in her stomach whilst also trying to black out the swirl of pictures swimming through her mind.

And the last person she wanted to be anywhere near right now was Helena.

Helena sat down beside her. Natalie heard the tell-tale noises of her fumbling for a cigarette in her purse and then lighting it. The harsh smoke made her nose crinkle. It had been Anna who had encouraged

Natalie to quit. Her mother smoking around her was just another insult to injury.

"She's going to be okay, you know," Helena said, before exhaling noisily.

For a second, Natalie thought she meant Anna, then like a tonne of bricks hitting her, she remembered. Anna was never going to be okay. Anna was dead.

Resigning herself to having to face Helena, Natalie opened her eyes and sat up.

"She's still in and out of consciousness, but they can't find anything really wrong with her." Helena took another puff of her ciggie, and Natalie felt both a craving and repulsion.

"Want one?" Helena asked, as if reading her mind, and holding the packet out to her.

Natalie narrowed her eyes and shook her head.

"Be like that, then," Helena said haughtily. She took another long drag before throwing the butt on the ground. She smushed it with her shoe, then slouched backwards on the bench.

"Can I see her?" Natalie asked, finally finding her voice.

Helena shrugged. "They want her to rest. They're keeping her in overnight at least. You'll have to ask them."

Natalie felt another flare of irritation. Doctors or not, they couldn't keep her from her grandmother.

Except they could, she remembered. Just like she wasn't allowed in to see Anna. But this was different. This time she was family.

"Are you gonna tell me what all that was about? You look like you'd seen a ghost."

Helena had no idea.

"Don't tell me this is because of your little girlfriend?" Helena continued.

Surprise made Natalie shift in her seat. Helena wasn't naturally so observant. But with that ... the tone ... the way Helena said it ... A fire grew inside Natalie's gut, and she balled her hands into fists to restrain her temper.

"She. Wasn't. My. Girlfriend!" Natalie growled.

"You're right," Helena said, her own temper ignited. She sat up and her eyes sparked at Natalie. "She wasn't your girlfriend. She was married to an O'Regan. Whatever fling you might've had, it was never gonna amount to anything. You don't go fucking around with O'Regans, Nat."

Natalie felt like she'd been slapped.

"She was leaving him!" Nat said indignantly.

Helena raised an eyebrow. "Really? That's what she told you? Ha!" She shook her head in pity. "The only way you leave an O'Regan is in a body bag." Helena's jaw dropped, realisation hitting her.

Natalie saw red as all her fears, her anger, the ideas floating around her mind, infiltrating her nightmares, for three years, flooded back.

"Shit, I'm sorry, Nat," Helena whispered, reaching out to pat her knee. "I didn't mean that—"

"Yes, you did!" Natalie jumped up from her spot on the bench. "You mean everything you say," she spat at her mother. "Do you even care your mother is right now in the hospital? She was found wandering again! And Troy's not gonna help us!" Everything, everything tumbled out at once. Her words lashing at her mother, while hot tears rolled down her cheeks.

"And it's all my fault! Mine! Everything!" She wanted to hit something. Hurt someone. Make the pain stop. Her sobs came in belly-aching waves, and try as she might, she couldn't rein them in. "Troy left because of me. Grams is in the hospital because of me." She hiccoughed another sob. And then to her surprise Helena was standing before her, wrapping her arms around her and holding her tight. Natalie tried to push her away, but despite her mother's small frame she held Natalie in an iron grip.

"Sshhh," Helena whispered trying to soothe her.

Natalie's body convulsed with sobs, fighting against the words rising up she was powerless to hold back. "It's my fault Anna's dead," she said, before dissolving completely into her grief.

Helena surprised her. Natalie could count on one hand the number of times her mother had comforted or been there for her, and yet here she was. She held Natalie until she was able to stop crying. Then she guided her back to the bench and sat her down, where she pulled out another ciggie and offered Natalie one as well.

"So it was serious?" Helena asked.

This time Natalie nodded.

"Shit." Helena shook her head, appearing like she actually felt for Natalie. Like she actually cared. She lit the end of her cigarette and took a long drag.

They sat in silence while Helena finished her smoke.

"What are we gonna do?" Helena finally said.

Natalie shot her a puzzled look. Was she meaning about Anna? It wasn't like they could go back in time or bring her back from the dead. In fact, that was one of the things that hurt the most. She could see spirits. She never asked for it, but they were there all the same, and yet, not once had she ever seen Anna. Maybe she had been wrong. Maybe Anna didn't love her as much as she did.

Grams had known. Back then, her mind had been with them more often, and Natalie had shared almost everything with her.

"Not everyone who dies comes back," she said in one of her more lucid moments. "But that's a good thing. It means they're at peace." Then she'd squeezed Natalie's hand. It didn't make the pain any less.

Right now, she'd give anything for Grams to squeeze her hand, to tell her everything was going to be okay. Her mother was trying her best, but being twenty-four years out of practice, in Natalie's life at least, was asking a lot.

Helena was still looking at Natalie, waiting for her to answer about what they should do. The thought rose up. Was she meaning about Grams's wanderings or something to do with the O'Regans? Like getting revenge on them? Anna's death was Natalie's fault because she loved her. Anna was leaving Liam for her, and although she'd always suspected him of killing her, she had never had any proof. But who else would be angry enough to hurt her? Gossip in Te Tapu had a habit of spreading like wildfire, and despite their best attempts at keeping their relationship quiet, it didn't mean they had succeeded. Especially since her mother in all her oblivion had apparently known.

"We're gonna have to make a plan," Helena said, interrupting Natalie's thoughts. "Mum's gonna need someone watching her. Full-time." With a sigh, she threw her cigarette butt down by the other.

Of course. It had been on her mind too, but how? Getting in a carer was expensive, and she doubted Helena would be willing to give up her freedom to stay home and watch her mother. And despite Helena's moment of motherliness, Natalie wasn't so naïve as to think she could be trusted to look after Grams. A moment of niceness couldn't make up for a lifetime of selfishness. And Natalie couldn't look after Grams. It was mostly her income keeping a roof over their heads and bills paid. So what next?

"Maybe I can cut back a few hours," Natalie said, doing the maths in her head. It would mean making even more sacrifices.

"What about that woman you work with? Didn't she offer once to help out?"

"You mean Victoria?" Natalie said. The thought left a bad taste in her mouth, made worse by their last encounter.

"Weren't they friends or something? Mum and what's-her-face, once upon a time?"

"Victoria," Natalie repeated.

They had been friends, but after today Natalie thought she might now have a better idea of why they'd become estranged. Maybe Grams had known Victoria was responsible for a child's death. A child whom Natalie now had to help find a way to move on.

Oh God, why was her life so complicated?!

"I'm not asking Victoria," Natalie said, an edge of sharpness creeping back into her voice.

"Why the hell not?" Helena asked, picking up on Natalie's tone. "If she's asked to help in the past, why not take her up on it? Jeez, Nat," she said, falling back into the tempestuous mood Natalie was most familiar with. "I can't do it!" Helena said, shuffling in her seat to face Natalie. "I'm not good with that kind of stuff."

At least she wasn't under any illusions otherwise.

"And you've got your job," she continued. "I'm not stupid. Without your income we lose the house."

"Have you ever thought of stepping in to help?" Natalie snarled. And just like that, they were back to the same old argument.

"I'm doing my best!"

Natalie snickered. Oh, she had so much to say in response, but then they'd just keep going in circles.

"If you don't talk to that woman, the one you work with, then I will!" Helena said, standing up and stomping a foot.

"Victoria! Her name's Victoria."

"Right, well, talk to Victoria. Whatever stupid delusion you have of thinking things can stay the same, lose it! We need help. This isn't about you and your bloody pride anymore, Nat. So ..." She huffed, her lips moving as if willing them forward. "So get over yourself!" She flicked her hair over her shoulder as part of her typical-Helena dramatic exit and stormed away.

There it was again. For the second time that day she'd been called selfish. She bit her lip, fighting back another deluge of tears. They didn't get it. None of them did. She wasn't being selfish; she was trying to keep everyone safe. Who could she trust? Before Anna died, never in a million years would she have believed Liam would have killed Anna or that the O'Regans would have a hand in covering it up, ruling it an accident. And yet, it was the only thing that had made sense at the time. Still did. All the clues were there. And yet no one cared. The investigation was closed after barely being opened.

Yet Natalie had known. She'd always known. It hadn't been an accident. It had been a murder. A murder people in Te Tapu were willing to cover up, to push under a rock. Like they'd done before with her family. And now Victoria had confessed to killing a child. She wasn't going to be the reason her grandmother died. She would come up with something. She always had. She'd find a way to look after Grams, to stop her wandering alone in the woods. She'd take care of it. Like she always had. She only had herself.

CHAPTER 22

Natalie

After Helena stormed off, Natalie took some time to pull herself together and will herself to return to the hospital, pushing down every reminder of Anna. The doctor was so busy, she managed to avoid him. One of the nurses at the nurses' station told her Grams had awoken. Other than being mildly dehydrated, they couldn't find anything wrong beyond her dementia. They were keeping her in overnight to be safe.

Natalie was allowed to visit, although only for a short time.

Seeing her grandmother so small and frail in the hospital bed sucked the air from Natalie's lungs. More childlike than ever, Grams's wispy white hair haloed her head on the pillow. Her face was grey and drawn, but on seeing Natalie the corners of her mouth curved.

"My moko," she whispered.

Natalie swallowed hard as a torrent of emotion welled up in her chest again. Not the time, she reminded herself. She needed to be strong. Grams needed her.

Natalie pulled a chair closer to the side of the bed, then sat. Leaning in, she gave her grandmother a small kiss on her forehead, then took Grams's hand between her own.

"How are you feeling?" Natalie asked smiling gently.

"You need to stop him," Grams said, her voice cracking and tears welling.

A stab of alarm froze Natalie's blood. "Stop who?"

Grams's mouth moved but no sound came out, and Natalie leant closer.

"Who, Grammy? Who?"

"He's cursed us, my moko. Our family … No one hurts an O'Regan and gets away with it." Her eyes grew wide and darted around the room as if she were expecting someone else to be there.

"The O'Regans?" Natalie asked, confusion breaking down the walls she'd just put in place. It was always the O'Regans. Always.

"He says he didn't kill my brother, but I know he did. I've seen his eyes. The devil lives there."

Natalie shivered. The mention of his eyes made Nataile instantly think of the figure she'd seen standing beside Liam. Could they have seen the same thing. She knew her grandmother was sensitive like her, saw things others didn't, but …

Grams started sobbing. It took Natalie a moment to fully home in on what Grams has said. "Your brother?" she whispered. Dementia confused the brain, but rumour had it he'd supposedly been killed by an O'Regan. Or else had killed one, depending upon who you listened to. If he had been killed, no justice had been given. Just like with Anna.

"Why were you in the woods, Grams?" Natalie asked, her voice thick with emotion. She hated seeing her grandmother like this. Trapped inside her mind and in so much pain.

"The little boy. I was looking for the little boy, but then *he* comes. He always comes. Stay away from him, Vicky. Stay away. He's just like his father!" Grams pulled her hand from Natalie's and hit the bed, her eyes darting around the room.

Vicky? Why had her grammy called her Vicky?

Dementia, Nat, common sense argued. Nothing her grandmother said right now could be trusted. She was mixing things up. She must think she was her teenage friend, Victoria. Natalie bristled, reconciling that with her principal who had just admitted to being involved with a young boy's death. Was this the same boy her grandmother was talking about? Maybe. If Victoria and Grams had been somehow involved in whatever happened to him, then maybe she was relieving those moments. Guilt made a person do stranger things. But it pained her to think her grandmother might be involved somehow, that she'd have reason to feel guilty.

The ice trickling through her veins refocused her on what she'd been ignoring: Grams had said *he comes*. A man comes when she's in the woods. Was it possible she was talking of the same man who had attacked her? The thought filled her with dread. She'd hoped her grandmother had been safe from that at least.

And who was he? Jake O'Regan, the one who killed Great Uncle Billy? But then who was she telling Vicky to stay away from? Jake O'Regan didn't have any sons.

A nurse knocked before entering the room.

"Everything okay in here?" she asked.

Grams was still squirming in her bed.

"She's a little agitated," Natalie said, not knowing what else to say.

"Well, I've brought her something to help her sleep a bit better."

"When will she be able to come home?" Natalie asked.

"We need to keep her in overnight, but if everything goes well, someone will be in touch tomorrow to let you know when you can collect her."

Natalie nodded. She hated to leave her alone but there was so much she needed to attend too.

The nurse made some cooing sounds and inserted the shot into her drip. Grams calmed almost immediately, her eyelids flickering with heaviness before closing.

Natalie wiped a tear that escaped unbidden from her eye. Then, giving her grandmother's hand a small squeeze, leant over and kissed her once more on the forehead.

"Sweet dreams," she whispered, before leaving the room.

Sleep didn't come so easily for Natalie. Too much was on her mind. Her grandmother's words about their family being cursed mixed with those of the entity in the woods, calling her a whore. It wasn't a stretch to believe they were cursed. Whatever Natalie's great uncle had done to upset Jake O'Regan, it hadn't ended with her uncle's death. Natalie tried to push away the memories of stale whiskey breath on her cheek and the overbearing weight of an invisible man pressing up against her. Her stomach turned, and she rolled over in bed, hugging the duvet closer to her chest. Images of finding her grandmother sprawled on the ground mingled with memories of Anna and their last picnic together before the accident. No, *murder*. And then there were images of her grandmother in hospital, superimposed with those moments where she'd rushed to the hospital to be with Anna, only to be pushed aside by Liam and his father. The anger, the hatred. She couldn't even go to the funeral. God, her head hurt and her heart ached. Nothing made sense.

And then there was Victoria, her principal. Bad guy? Good guy? Natalie didn't know anymore. When Grams came home, Natalie would need to put a plan in place for her care, and that would likely impact upon her teaching job. And she needed the job. It was what kept a roof over their heads and food on the table. Yet, she wasn't sure how she could face Victoria right now. Victoria, who had been best friends with her grandmother ... before she wasn't. Victoria who had offered to pay for Grams's care, no strings attached, and yet had just admitted being involved in the death of a little boy.

Though she ached to be with her grandmother, to stay by her bedside, not only had the hospital not allowed it, but Natalie had also made up her mind to go to work. It was one day, and a half day at that. Not only did she need the money, but she still had a meeting with Riki to talk about Cole, which suddenly seemed more important now she knew he was likely being haunted by a child Victoria might have been complicit in killing.

One big, ugly, tangled web was what it was.

In the end she must have gotten a couple of hours of sleep because the alarm on her bedside table woke her with a start. Her head throbbed and eyes felt swollen equally from the tears she had shed and the tears she hadn't. Though every part of her yearned to just spend the day in the bed and ignore all of her responsibilities, Natalie forced herself up. Her limbs were leaden, but her sense of obligation outweighed her physical exhaustion.

Helena was nowhere to be found, and Natalie was both irked and relieved by it. Part of her still had things to get off her chest and was partially craving a fight, the other half wanted to avoid an argument she knew wouldn't see any resolution.

She gave the hospital a call before heading to work. Grams had slept through the night without any issue. They were going to do a few more tests today, then be in touch in the afternoon to organise Grams's discharge.

Victoria ambushed her as soon as she got to school. "I heard about Maggie," she said.

Natalie continued to go about writing the day's schedule on the board. She knew she'd have to face Victoria at some point, but it didn't have to be now. Her mind was still groggy, and her emotions were on edge.

"How is she?" Victoria asked.

Natalie finished what she was writing, and then with a loud sigh turned around her face her. She tightened her face so as not to show any emotion.

"She's fine. I'll pick her up later." Natalie's eyes narrowed. This woman only pretended to care. "Let me guess? Troy told you?" One of Victoria's granddaughters worked at the police station. Confidentiality, it seemed, was more of a guideline than a rule in Te Tapu.

Victoria nodded, and Natalie noticed her wringing her hands. She seemed nervous, which threw Natalie for a moment. Victoria was almost always in control.

"I owe you a bit of an explanation," she said.

Natalie watched her, trying to intuit what was coming.

Victoria pulled a chair out from behind a desk and sat down, gesturing for Natalie to do the same. Natalie hesitated before giving in. If she was wanting answers, she was going to have to play nice.

"There was a fire. In the summer of 1964. It started in the woods between your place and the school," she gestured towards the back wall with the whiteboard, behind which was the woods.

Natalie swallowed. A sadness dragged on Victoria's features. It was hard being angry at a woman who suffered her own demons.

"I was with your grandmother at the time."

Natalie swallowed hard.

"There were four of us. It was stupid really. There was a clearing people went to sometimes, out of eyeshot of the adults," Victoria's face changed, a hint of a wistful smile showing in her eyes. "We were young ..."

"A make out spot?" Natalie said

The smile reached Victoria's lips. "You could say that. There were four of us, and we were just playing around. We never meant for it to happen. Your grandmother, Maggie, she'd gone for a bit of a walk, and in the meantime, the rest of us were drinking, and smoking, and everything was just so very dry that summer." Her jaw stiffened.

"One of the boys was playing with his lighter, flicking it on and off, and I guess some of the home-brew whiskey had spilled from the flask ... I've never seen anything like it." Her eyes widened with the memories.

"It was a force unto itself. And suddenly, everything was alight. We panicked. Maggie hadn't come back. The boys wanted to get to the road out of the fire's reach, and I wanted to find Maggie. I could see it heading towards the school, but there was nothing we could do about it."

Victoria's eyes had welled.

"But you found Maggie?"

"We did, or JP did. The boy she was with," she offered by explanation. "We didn't know that Gavin had followed us into the woods. If we'd known ..."

Victoria's voice trailed off and Natalie wondered how she planned on finishing that sentence.

"They found him the next day," she said, and a chill ran down Natalie's spine. "He'd somehow found a way under the classroom. The classroom that had once stood here. It was a relatively new build too, only ten years old or so. They found him huddled in the far back corner of where the building once stood. The coroner ruled he'd probably seen the fire and tried hiding from it, as by his mother's accounts he was apt to do when scared: hide himself in a small space. We didn't know it back then, but I suspect had he been alive today he would have been diagnosed as having autism." Victoria's face completely fell. "He couldn't communicate very well and became overwhelmed easily and acted out. Children and adults called the poor boy horrible names, and many blamed his mother." Victoria's voice cracked. "People can be so awful. And back then ... we just didn't know how to deal with anyone ... different."

"What happened to his family?" Natalie asked, her voice small.

"It was just his mum and his little sister. They left not long after. Some people can be particularly cruel in the face of tragedy."

Natalie felt sick. Had they really blamed the mother? Why not blame the people responsible for causing the fire to begin with?

"Why didn't *you* leave?" Natalie asked, and Victoria for a second looked taken back like she'd been slapped.

"It had been an accident," she said, her face betraying her uncertainty. "We hadn't meant it to happen."

"But everyone knew you were involved, didn't they?" Something wasn't sitting right. Victoria had been the principal of Te Tapu school for thirty plus years, and Te Tapu was not a community that forgot and forgave easily. The only people who tended to get away with things were O'Regans. Like with what really happened between Jake O'Regan and her great uncle. And though rumours sometimes seeped out into the open, they were treated as urban myths. How had she not heard of the school fire before?

"They knew you were involved, right, Victoria?" Natalie kept her eyes fixed on Victoria's face.

"It was an accident," she whispered.

A knowing crept over Natalie. She had to ask. "You said there were four people, you, Grams, and a guy called JP. Who was the fourth person?"

Natalie knew before Victoria even opened her mouth, yet it still sent a chill shooting up her spine.

"Arthur. Arthur O'Regan," she said.

CHAPTER 23

Natalie

Always. It always came back to the O'Regans. And although she couldn't bring herself to ask, Natalie would have bet her house it had been Arthur who started the fire. Regardless, it answered the question why it had remained a secret.

"It was a very long time ago. You understand that, right, Natalie?" Victoria found her voice again. Her principal voice. "I'm sharing it with you because I've always wondered if that was why Maggie always takes off for the woods. If she is somehow replaying that day. Beyond that, no good can come from sharing what I've just told you."

Victoria stood up, her composure fully back in place, a steel rod through her spine. Though a head shorter than Natalie, Victoria had a presence about her that, if riled, could knock most people on their ass.

But so did Natalie.

"I don't think you get to make those decisions," Natalie said, an edge in her voice. If what had happened that day was now putting her grandmother at risk, she would tell whoever the damn she needed to make it stop. Not to mention, it made Natalie even more certain that the boy haunting young Cole was Gavin Jenkins.

A rush of chatter and laughter and children with backpacks signalled the bus had arrived. Through her sliding doors, Natalie saw the students swarm onto the school grounds, peeling off in different directions towards their classrooms.

"I'll be off site during my classroom release this afternoon to meet with a parent," Natalie said, her eyes holding Victoria's. Normally she'd ask. Right now, she didn't feel she had the capacity to do so. She was telling rather than negotiating.

Victoria's eyes sparked for a moment, not used to her staff speaking in such a manner, then they softened. This time she wasn't going to argue.

"Is it regarding anything I need to know about?" Victoria asked, falling back into principal mode.

Natalie saw some of her students hanging up their bags on the hooks outside the classroom; they'd be upon them in seconds.

To hell with it. She knew she shouldn't. Somethings were always better off unsaid, particularly when they put into question your mental faculties, but she couldn't resist. She needed to see Victoria's expression, needed to see her hurt. If she had been complicit in protecting an O'Regan ...

"I'm meeting with Mr Lomas about the incident with his son the other day, remember? We're discussing putting a plan in place to help support him at school. You know? Since his mother died. And to discuss his *imaginary friend*." Natalie did air quotes around "imaginary friend," internally scowling at how sarcastic she sounded yet also enjoying the moment.

"His imaginary friend?" Victoria asked almost cautiously.

"Yeah. The young boy with his face half burnt off, who follows him around school."

A flurry of emotions starting with confusion and ending with what Natalie translated as fear, flew across Victoria's face. A rush of students flooded into the room, leaving no space for further conversation, and Natalie did her best not to smile. She didn't like hurting people. But, even more, she didn't like people getting away with murder and hurting others. Whether the fire was set intentionally or not, it had killed a boy. Her grandmother, by Victoria's own admission, was not with them when the fire started. And Natalie refused to think right now that maybe Grams had helped protect an O'Regan. She doubted it. Not if she believed an O'Regan had killed her brother. And Natalie couldn't bring herself to think of it now, especially not while she lay in a hospital bed. But if Victoria *had* kept this secret, *had* protected an O'Regan, *and* had stood back and let an innocent woman and her young daughter be run out of town while grieving the death of her son, then in her books, Victoria deserved all the pain she got. And Natalie wondered again if maybe she knew now why Grams and Victoria's friendship had ended.

Victoria looked like she had more to say, but with students tugging on Natalie's arm for attention, there was no opportunity to do so. Natalie turned away from her, and after a sullen moment, from the corner of her eye, she saw Victoria walk out the sliding doors, across the courts towards her office.

CHAPTER 24

Maggie

1964

"It's our fault he's dead!" Maggie turned her back on her friend, a rush of emotions, anger, guilt, grief and fear, threatening to drown her. She scrunched her eyes tight, trying to hold back the tears. It was weird that she had any more tears left to cry. It had been four days since the fire. They'd found the little boy's body the next day, huddled beneath the classroom closest to the woods. Most of the classroom had been devoured by the fire. Miraculously the small part standing was where they found little Gavin Jenkin's body. He didn't survive. His blood was on their hands.

"It's not our fault! It was an accident!" Vicky argued, her voice pitching. She'd said it so many times now, but it made no difference. Accident or not, Arthur had been playing with his lighter starting mini fires. With the summer being as dry as it was, it was a recipe for disaster.

The fact that their involvement was not yet out in the community, ate Maggie away. Surely, the police should be interviewing them. People should be asking questions. From what she'd overheard a few nights back, Mrs O'Regan had already jumped ahead to blaming her son. It made no sense. And it made even less that Vicky was fighting her so hard on not going to the police.

"If we go to the police, they might think we did it on purpose. Then what?" Vicky's voice had lowered a little. She touched Maggie's shoulder. Maggie shrugged it off and turned to face her.

"Even if we don't get jail time, you can kiss any college or job prospects goodbye."

"But what about Mrs Jenkins?" Maggie said, slumping down onto the edge of the bed. "People are talking. Mam told me she overheard people at the garage yesterday blaming her for not having a tighter rein on her child." Maggie's voice cracked. It wasn't fair. Everyone knew Gavin was a law unto himself, as were most nine-year-old boys. Add a disability into the mix, and Mrs Jenkins having her hands full with a pre-schooler ... it wasn't fair they were questioning her parenting in the wake of such a tragedy.

Vicky looked downcast. She was hurting too, Maggie knew it, but she was also stubborn, and Maggie suspected it had more to do with her new crush than it had to do with their reputations.

"I thought I heard him," Maggie said. "I told you I thought some-one was following us."

"It was an accident," Vicky said again, her voice weak. She slumped onto the bed beside Maggie.

"Have you talked to Arthur?" Maggie asked, gritting her teeth against saying his name. Despite seeing the dark figure beside him and knowing he might have been influenced in setting things alight – even the firefighters said it was uncanny how fast and purposefully it had spread – she didn't like him. And she loathed the idea that Vicky might still be involved with him even after everything that had happened.

"What do you want me to say?" Vicky sighed, exasperated. "He made a mistake. Of course I've talked to him."

"Even though you heard what Mrs O'Regan said?" Maggie felt her temper rising. "Even she wanted him gone from the house. His own *mother* thinks he's bad news!"

Neither of them said what else was on their minds. Mrs O'Regan had also said he was more Jake's son than her husband's. The question was whether she meant it figuratively or literally. Jake who was rumoured to have murdered her own brother. A chill shot through her at the thought.

Vicky's eyes flashed. "She might have said it, but she didn't mean it. We all know the O'Regans don't out each other. You've heard the stories, Maggie. For all the rumours that an O'Regan killed your brother, there are just as many, if not more, that he was framed. Mr and Mrs O'Regan are well liked in Te Tapu. Regardless of what they say behind closed doors, they wouldn't put their reputation at risk like that by drawing attention to Arthur. And I bet anyone who does draw attention to him won't be looked upon favourably either."

Maggie hated to admit it, but she knew Vicky was right. She remembered hearing her older sisters talking when she was a kid. Mam had nearly been run out of town after Billy's death. As it was, for a time she had to travel to the next town for supplies to avoid run-ins with the locals. People refused to believe an O'Regan could be responsible. They thought the MacKenzies' were just stirring up trouble. Despite

Maggie not technically being a MacKenzie, the rumours had followed her through school. You couldn't escape your family's history, certainly not in a small village like Te Tapu.

So that was that then. They did nothing. They kept the secret, and Mrs Jenkins suffered alone while no one else was held accountable. And they swallowed their guilt because implicating themselves implicated an O'Regan. And Vicky, her best friend since primary school, was okay with it.

The thought sat heavy in the pit of Maggie's stomach. This wasn't like Vicky. She was a good person. What had Arthur done to her to make her this way? Maggie felt another flare of anger build.

"What do you see in him?" Maggie asked through clenched teeth.

Vicky narrowed her eyes and then, obviously seeing something else in Maggie's expression, she answered the question.

"I can't explain it," she said softly. "'Whatever our souls are made of, his and mine are the same.'"

Maggie scanned Vicky's face. She was quoting *Wuthering Heights*. Surely, she was joking? Victoria and Arthur were no Catherine and Heathcliff. When Victoria fell, she always fell hard.

Ice flooded Maggie's veins. She could see Victoria wasn't joking.

A shudder ran through her. Even though she knew the words to be from *Wuthering Heights*, it was as if she'd heard them before. Like they meant something more.

But Victoria would never convince Maggie that she and Arthur had the same souls. She'd seen the evil on Arthur's shoulder, the monkey on his back. She'd never seen that in her friend. Until maybe now. That Vicky had chosen Arthur over a grieving woman, had chosen the darkness, had chosen to lie, and had pleaded with her to do the same, came with a realisation that hurt more than anything Maggie had ever felt before: she wasn't a friend. Vicky couldn't be. She'd chosen. She'd lived out her own argument. When sides were called for, people always chose the O'Regans. And Vicky had made her choice.

"You need to leave now," Maggie said, unable to look Vicky in the eyes.

"What do you mean?" Vicky's voice pitched with confusion.

"I mean, you need to leave. As long as you choose an O'Regan there's no place for me in your life."

"You're being ridiculous!" Vicky reached out for Maggie's hands, and Maggie pulled away.

"No! As long as we stay silent about what really happened, the fire, the burning down of the school—"

"One classroom!" Vicky interjected!

"—the death of Gavin Jenkins—"

"It was an accident!" Vicky was standing in front of Maggie now, her face flushed, eyes welling, pleading.

"—we are *guilty*!" Maggie stood to square off with Vicky. Adrenalin pumped through her limbs with a fury almost foreign to her. "I'll keep it secret," Maggie said, the words like acid on her tongue. "In honour of the friendship *we had*. Not for Arthur, and not for anyone else!"

"Had?!" Vicky squealed.

"You need to leave." Maggie clenched her teeth, willing back the deluge of tears she felt coming.

"Maggie?" Vicky's voice was small, giving Maggie the last iota of strength she needed.

"Now!" she spat, before turning her back on her friend. She bit down hard on her lip, her heart pounded in her chest, and she waited for what seemed like an eternity, but would have been mere seconds, until she heard Vicky's footsteps moving away from her.

Maggie heard her bedroom door open, and Vicky pause. "I'm so sorry," she whispered, her voice pained.

Maggie bit down harder on her bottom lip but the tears fell anyway. She waited for the sound of the bedroom door closing, Vicky's footsteps disappearing down the hall, and then the tell-tale sound of the Bug's engine bursting into life, before she allowed herself to dissolve completely into the grief that overwhelmed her.

She'd keep the secret of the fire until she died. For Vicky. And for her family. No matter the cost to her. She'd take it to her deathbed if it meant those she cared about never had to suffer at the hands of the O'Regans again.

CHAPTER 25

Natalie

Natalie managed to avoid Victoria for the rest of the day. She stayed away from the staffroom, which was easy enough to do with being on playground duty at morning tea. And Victoria never sought her out either, much to Natalie's relief. She didn't fancy going round two with her. And with what usually happened when Natalie got too surly, there was an edge of embarrassment and regret that she wasn't yet ready to make amends for.

She'd watched Cole carefully while on playground duty. In class he stayed to himself as much as possible. He quietly did his work, and though Natalie hated to admit it, it was easy to forget he was there as other more loud and needy students monopolised Natalie's attention. Funny how it was often the quiet, on-task students who fell through the cracks of a teacher's focus.

Morning tea provided more of an opportunity to observe Cole. He'd eaten fast before slipping away from her sight. After a good ten minutes of walking around the school and electing a few of his classmates to search for him and report to her, she found him sitting on the ground, up against the caretaker's shed. She studied him from a distance for a while, just watching. Gavin was sitting beside him. From where Natalie stood, the side of his face, burnt, blistered and scarred was turned away from her. And had anyone else been watching, they would have just seen two little boys, one slightly older than the other, sitting side by side in animated conversation, interrupted time to time by Paper, Scissors, Rock and hysterical laughter. Except, had anyone else been standing where Natalie was, they would have only seen the one boy: Cole.

The fact they sat by the caretaker's shed made Natalie uneasy. Above them hung the plaque. She still hadn't learnt the story behind it, it having fallen from her mind what with everything else going on in her life.

But the last time she had been there had been the first time she'd seen the shadow man. The realisation hit her. In fact, he'd been standing right where she was now.

Natalie spun on the balls of her feet, half expecting him to be there, right within touching distance, his sour whiskey breath filling her nostrils. His smile stretched into cavernous mocking.

But he wasn't there. No one was. Children played on the nearby playground, and the odd few children ran past the back of the classroom block, laughing and yelling and chasing, oblivious to the little boy and his invisible friend in the corner by the shed.

Natalie glanced down at her watch. She had about five minutes before the bell went and everyone returned to class. Pretending to not be interested in the two boys by the shed, Natalie walked past them in the direction of the greenhouse and circled around a little closer to them. The boys wouldn't see her from this angle, but she was hoping she might overhear anything that might be said. Other than giggles and laughter and Cole chanting "Paper. Scissors. Rock!" there was nothing more than two little boys enjoying each other's company.

Taking a gentle breath and making just enough noise for them to notice her approaching and not be startled, Natalie made her way to where the boys sat. Rounding the corner, she got a small glimpse of Gavin before he disappeared leaving a startled Cole calling out in surprise.

"Hi, Cole," Natalie said, her voice warm.

Despite her best intentions Cole still jumped in his spot. He looked at her, his mouth slightly open and his eyes wide, his hand still held out towards where his invisible partner had been, his fingers in the scissors pose. He dropped his hand to his lap.

"Where did Gavin go to?" Natalie kept her voice light. She was taking a gamble.

Cole said nothing, his jaw still hanging open. Then he took a deep breath and swallowed. "You can see him?" he half whispered.

"I did see him, but now it looks like he's disappeared."

Cole glanced around him before sitting dumbly. Colour flushed high on his cheeks, his usual shyness settling in.

"This is an interesting place to play," Natalie said, not wanting to overwhelm him with questions about his ghostly playmate.

"Gavin likes to play here. He says the bad man can't get him here."

Natalie's blood ran cold, not least because it was more words than Cole had ever spoken to her at one time, but also because the *bad man* was a phrase that spoke to her nightmares.

"What bad man, Cole?"

He shrugged and peered down onto his lap. Trying another tact, Natalie tried again. "Why can't the bad man get him here?"

Cole gaped up at her, his eyes wide, pupils large, and he slowly lifted a finger to point above him at the plaque hanging on the wall of the shed.

It didn't make any sense.

"It's very pretty," Natalie said. "How does it keep you safe?"

Cole shrugged and kept his lips sealed. Sharing time was over, Natalie concluded. But she still had questions.

"Did Gavin ever tell you anything about himself? About how he … got hurt?"

There were probably ethical rules she was breaking right now. Just like you weren't allowed to question a child you suspected was being hurt or abused in any way, asking a child about his dead playmate probably carried its own dire complications if anyone were to find out.

Remembering back to Cole's altercation with the young boy in Brittany's class the other day, Natalie had to ask.

"Did Gavin have something to do with why you and Craig were fighting the other day?"

Cole continued to watch her blankly for a moment, then obviously feeling he could trust her with a little more sharing, he spoke again. "That boy saw me talking to Gavin, so he called me a freak. And Gavin doesn't like it when people call other people names."

"I understand," Natalie said, crouching down to Cole's height. "It doesn't feel very good to be called names, does it?"

Cole shook his head.

"Is that why you hit him?"

Cole's eyes welled up and his bottom lip trembled.

"It's okay, Cole, you're not in trouble."

"I don't know why I hit him," Cole said, his voice shaking. "It was like Gavin was inside of me, and I could feel how upset he was. He doesn't like being called a freak. People used to call him that a lot. I didn't know I was going to hit him. But then I did."

Cole bit down on his bottom lip and wiped away a stray tear from his cheek.

From the other side of the school, the bell chimed out, signalling a return to class. All across the playground, children scurried off in different directions to their classes.

"Thanks for telling me, Cole," Natalie said, keeping her voice even, despite the many thoughts swirling through her mind. Had Gavin really possessed Cole for a moment?

"Shall we go back to class?" Natalie stood up, holding out her hand to him.

Though Cole got to his feet, he held his hands close to his stomach and walked ahead of her towards the class. Natalie went to follow then stopped and turned around again to look at the plaque. A Claddagh ring. Irish. Like her. She reached out to touch it, closing her eyes for a moment.

There was something special about it, greater than the fact it bore her great uncle's name: a story she still needed to find out more about. There was a lightness to it, as if it were infused with love. No wonder the boys felt safe here. Yet ... for them to feel safe here, they had to feel unsafe elsewhere.

Natalie surreptitiously glanced around her again, expecting to see a shadowy grey form watching her from afar or, more hopeful, a young nine-year-old boy ready to move on to the other side.

But if she was being watched, they were well hidden. But for the few stragglers late in making their way to class, it was just her: Natalie. Alone. Always doing it alone.

CHAPTER 26

Natalie

THREE YEARS AGO

"**I** 've meet with a lawyer," Anna said.

Natalie rolled over to face her. She reached out and pushed a strand of auburn hair from her face, letting her fingers gently trace the side of Anna's face.

"I'm going to tell Liam tonight." She chewed on her bottom lip, and Natalie's heart swelled.

"You're really doing this, then?" Natalie asked. It all felt too good to be true. It had been a whirlwind of a relationship: nine months. And yet, Natalie had never felt this way about anyone before. It had taken her by surprise.

Every February a fishing competition was celebrated at the local tavern, with fundraising going to the school. The turnout was always huge, and although Natalie would have given anything to get out of going, as a teacher she had no choice. It ended up being one of the best days of her life. From the moment Natalie first laid eyes on Anna, she knew. There was something special about her. So much so that she could ignore the fact she hung on the arm of an O'Regan.

Somehow, they had ended up at the same table and had begun talking. From there, they were inseparable, much to the annoyance of the likes of Katrina. Katrina and Rob and Liam and Anna had been an inseparable foursome for a year or so, and then along came Natalie.

It had all started off innocently enough. A friendship of sorts. Shopping, getting coffee together. But all the time, Natalie knew by the way Anna looked at her that the feeling was mutual. One evening after too many drinks on Natalie's part at the tavern, she'd walked Anna to her car and Anna had offered her a ride home. It was the beginning of the end. Like two teenagers, they sat outside Natalie's house, and Natalie leaned in to kiss Anna. Her whole life changed when Anna returned the kiss.

And now here they were, eight months later, lying in each other's arms under a weeping willow, with panoramic views of Te Tapu, talking about spending the rest of their lives together.

Anna smiled, her eyes shiny. "I'm really doing this!" she said.

Natalie's heart felt like it would burst. Anna giggled, and Natalie pulled her up to a sitting position. Cross-legged, she gripped her hands within her own.

"How do you think Liam will take it?" Natalie asked. While they'd tried their best to keep things undercover, with Te Tapu being as small as it was, there was always a possibility of rumours, sightings, and even of Liam already knowing.

A shadow passed over Anna's face, and her mood turned sombre.

"He's going to be hurt," she said, sadness changing her voice. "He doesn't deserve this."

Natalie's heart ached for her. Anna loved him. Had loved him. And she was right; whatever Natalie's feelings towards the O'Regans, she couldn't imagine loving Anna and then losing her.

"He'll be okay," Natalie said.

"He will," Anna agreed. "Over time."

Natalie massaged the top of one of Anna's hands with her thumb.

"It's not so much him whom I'm worried about," Anna said. "It's his dad. It's the community. The O'Regans are held on such a high pedestal. Their reputation is everything ..."

A cool breeze made the willow tendrils whisper above them, and goosebumps rose on Natalie's arms.

"A divorce is one thing. Leaving him for another woman ..."

Natalie knew what she was saying, but it still struck her with fear. Was she having second thoughts about their relationship?

As if reading her mind, Anna answered her. "No, no. We're in this together, and everyone who has a problem with it will just have to get over it. Only ..."

Only? Natalie waited, resisting the urge to pull her hands from Anna's.

"It might be best if we keep things under wraps for a little while longer. One bombshell at a time."

Natalie did pull her hands away, then, though Anna was quick to grab them.

"I just mean, let's not go shouting it from the roof tops right away. Let's keep our relationship on the down-low for a little bit longer.

I'm not going anywhere," she told Natalie, smiling at her. "We belong together."

A wave of relief washed over Natalie. They would be okay. The next few months might be a bit ugly, but they would get through it. She knew it.

Natalie looked down at the ring on Anna's finger. Anna followed her gaze and released Natalie's hand, going about twisting the ring off her finger. She held it up between her thumb and forefinger for Natalie to see. The sun still hit the diamonds around the sapphire, making it sparkle.

"It's just you and me," she whispered holding Natalie's eyes, before slipping the ring into her skirt pocket. She pulled Natalie towards her, and once again they were the only two people in the world. Everything outside of them vanished.

With both excitement and reluctance, Natalie dropped Anna off outside the Te Tapu Garage. This was it. Their beginning. When Natalie next saw Anna, she'd be single. The path would be that much clearer for them. Just the two of them.

Natalie parked across the road from the garage. Anna's car had been getting its brakes done, but it was ready for pick up. Afterwards, she was heading into her lawyers in Maramanui to pick up the paperwork to give to Liam that night. Natalie wanted to go with her, but Anna insisted on going alone. Their relationship had been hard enough to keep secret, and divorcing an O'Regan was always going to come with some fall out. Even being seen as a friend at this time could be a dangerous thing. Not that Natalie cared. She'd agreed to not sing about their relationship from the rooftops only because Anna had asked her. Being bad mouthed in the community didn't bother her.

Between her family's history with the O'Regans and her mother's drunken promiscuousness, not much could be said that she hadn't heard before. When things settled down a bit, Natalie would suggest to Anna that they leave Te Tapu. Anna's family had never been thrilled she moved here, and Te Tapu had done little good for her own family. Helena could stay if she wanted. She doubted her mother had any ambition outside of Te Tapu. Or any ambition at all, to be honest. Grams would be another matter. Despite her family's history, she was reluctant to leave. But then again, Grams's mind had been getting worse and worse lately. Natalie hated to admit it, but there might come a time when Grams would need to go into care. The thought sat heavily in the pit of her stomach.

She looked over at Anna, who sat in the passenger seat.

Whatever the future held; they'd get through it together.

Anna grabbed Natalie's hand and held it in hers for a moment. Natalie ached to kiss her, to hug her, but it was Te Tapu, the most public part of the village, and the garage, as it had always been, was owned and run by O'Regans, so she restrained herself with a simple hand squeeze.

"Call me later?" she said.

Anna nodded, and a smile reserved just for Natalie reflected in her lips and eyes.

"I love you," Natalie mouthed at Anna as she opened the car door and stepped out onto the pavement.

Before turning away, Anna locked eyes with Natalie and mouthed back, "Love you too."

Natalie watched her as she walked across the road and disappeared into the shop. When Anna was no longer visible, Natalie spun a U-turn and headed along the main drag, back home.

CHAPTER 27

Natalie

THREE YEARS AGO

It was Helena who told her, in one of the rare moments where she was thinking beyond herself.

For a moment, Natalie considered declining the call when she saw her mother's name pop up on the incoming call screen. Something stayed her hand though, and she accepted it and put her phone to her ear.

4:01pm. Funny how a time could stay in your mind as your world came crashing down. While her mother was telling her, Natalie glanced at the digital clock on her bedside table in her room, where only moments before she had been deep in the process of writing student reports for school.

Helena was at work at the tavern. Troy had been in to get a statement for some theft that had happened the night before, when he got the call. Helena overheard. Car accident on the stretch between Te Tapu and Maramanui. Single occupant, female. And then the part that put Helena on the phone to Natalie. "It's the O'Regan girl," the dispatcher had said.

It wasn't a secret that Natalie and Anna were friends, that they spent a lot of time together. Still, even at the moment when Natalie's world crashed down, she had to wonder what had caused her mother to call her.

The next fifteen minutes were a blur. Speed limits ceased to exist until Natalie had no choice but to slow down at the crash site. An ambulance was there, lights flashing, paramedics lifting a stretcher into the back of the vehicle.

To her left a blue Subaru was upside down in a ditch. A police car was parked horizontally across the road, and Troy was standing there waving cars to slow and pull over, allowing for the ambulance to do what it needed to do. On the other side of the accident, two more police cars blocked the road, lights flashing.

Natalie ignored Troy's hand signals and drove closer. His face was pinched as he stormed over to the car.

"What are you doing, Sullivan?" His face dropped on meeting her eye.

"Is that Anna?" Natalie asked her voice choking, already knowing without a doubt. It was Anna's car in the ditch. "I need to get through." Panic raced through her veins, stripping her nerves bare.

Troy softened his tone, his expression pained. "You can't be here," he said. "Go home, Sullivan."

Natalie shook her head, sobs choking her voice. "You don't understand! I need to get through. I need to be there."

Troy looked over his shoulder, then back to her, closing his eyes briefly. When he opened them, he waved her through to the right just as the ambulance took off towards the next town.

"Thank you," Natalie said, knowing he wouldn't have heard; she had already turned her car to drive on the opposite side of the road.

"Let her through!" Troy yelled to his colleagues, who with some confusion did as he ordered.

Natalie kept the ambulance in her sights although it had a good start ahead of her. The whole time her internal dialogue went mad. How had this happened? Please, please, please be okay, she begged to anyone who might be listening.

Arriving at the hospital, parking, racing through the hospital entrance, it was all a blur, jumbled colours and sounds disassociated from reality.

"Where is she? Where is Anna?" she demanded of the woman at the reception desk.

"Calm down," the woman said. "Who are you looking for?"

"Anna O'Regan," Natalie shouted at her. Why was everyone acting so calm?

"If you're going to shout, you're going to have to leave," the woman said in a no-nonsense tone. "Tell me again, who are you looking for?"

"Anna O'Regan," Natalie said, trying her best to steady her voice but getting a glare from the woman as her attempt failed. "I followed the ambulance here." God, why weren't they helping her?

"Are you family?" the woman asked, ignoring Natalie's urgency.

"What do you mean family?" She wanted to reach over the counter and throttle the woman. "Just tell me where she is!"

The woman scowled at her. "If you keep raising your voice at me, I'm going to have to call security."

Footsteps hurried behind her.

"I'm family," a male's voice said out of breath.

Natalie turned around to come face to face with Liam. His brow scrunched at seeing her and he looked Natalie up and down before quickly turning back to the receptionist. "I'm Liam O'Regan. I just got a call that my wife, Anna O'Regan, was brought in following a car crash."

Natalie's jaw dropped a little.

"Right, Mr O'Regan, take a seat, and someone will be out to see you as soon as there is any information."

"Thanks," Liam said, weakly, before turning away.

All sorts of emotion had welled up in Natalie, not least fury. No one knew. They might not be married, but Anna was hers. Not his.

The receptionist, remembering Natalie was still standing there, looked back up at her with a smile, and Natalie did everything possible to resist slapping her smugness.

Liam positioned himself on one of the hard plastic chairs. He bent forwards with his elbows on his knees, rubbing his hands together, head hanging. How was he able to just sit there?

Natalie paced. No one was going to tell her anything because in their eyes she was no one. She needed to see her. Needed to know she'd be okay.

Resigning herself to being stuck in the reception area, she filled a paper cup with water from the water dispenser and sipped it.

"Why are you here?" Liam asked, barely looking at her.

She stared at him for a moment and took another sip. They had never warmed to each other, and it wasn't likely they would now. From the positioning of the car and the timing, Anna must have been on the way to the lawyers; she wouldn't have even had the divorce papers yet.

"Whatever was between the two of you, she was *my* wife," he said, his voice strained.

All the oxygen left her body. Did he know? Had they not kept it as hidden as they'd thought?

"She's my *wife*," he repeated, his voice catching, and he swallowed back a sob before closing his eyes for a second.

Almost simultaneously, Arthur O'Regan walked past the reception desk to join them, followed by Troy as if he'd escorted him here to the hospital himself. From the corridor, a white-coated doctor and a young woman with a clipboard appeared before them.

"Mr O'Regan," the doctor inquired, his eyes roaming over the waiting area.

"Here," Liam said, jumping from his seat and striding towards the doctor. Natalie couldn't help it; she joined his side.

The doctor looked at her, and when Liam said nothing, took the clipboard from his intern's hands, flicked through a couple of the pages and sighed before meeting Liam squarely in the eyes.

"I'm very sorry, Mr O'Regan. Your wife came to us with serious injuries, including internal bleeding. We did everything we could ..."

The doctor's voice petered out, replaced by a growing roaring white noise that turned into a scream. Strong hands grabbed at her, linked around her waist and tried to pull her away, as her fists pounded at the doctor's chest, and he backed away trying to cover his face. There was yelling. Wailing. Her name. Anna's name. All colliding into each other. Flashes of Liam's face broken, one of the nurses, holding him as if his legs were going to give away. Arthur, standing there, unmoving, his face expressionless. A dark figure, standing there behind him. Laughing. Why was he laughing at her?

Someone was yelling for security. Someone else was saying her name over and over. Troy. He was the one who had wrapped his arms around her waist and was trying to pull her away from the doctor. She fought. She bit and punched and kicked and then yelped as a sharp pain stabbed her arm, and then the noises faded, except for the laughing. Who was laughing?

Stupid Paddy whore, a voice said. *You don't fuck with an O'Regan.*

CHAPTER 28

Natalie

Natalie pulled into the gravel car park and killed the engine. She was a little early, having left straight after the lunch bell. Although in walking distance, Natalie had no intention of returning to school to pick up her car after her meeting with Riki in case she bumped into Victoria. Her plan was instead to head up to the hospital to collect Grams.

One drama at a time, and right now she needed to focus on her meeting with Riki.

The tavern was a weathered old building with a gravel car park and double doors at its entrance. The car park already had five or so cars, farmers likely, having called it quits early.

It was the only social hangout in Te Tapu. It some ways, it might have been wiser meeting Riki in Maramanui. It would have potentially saved on the gossip at least, but Riki would need to pick Cole up from school afterwards, and as it was, the community could gossip all they pleased.

She gave her appearance a quick once over in the rearview mirror and drew her fingers through her hair in lieu of a comb.

There was a slight trill in her chest. Nervousness? Excitement? She could kill for a whiskey and coke but would have to settle for something non-alcoholic. Despite any ulterior motives that might have crossed her mind, she needed to remain somewhat professional, particularly as they were meeting to discuss a student of hers.

A mixture of stale booze and musky BO hit her as she entered through the glass doors into the tavern. She recognised three farmers sitting at one of the bar tables, pints of beer laid before them. Hairy legs stuck out from gumboots and grubby shorts. Their scruffy checkered flannel shirts rolled up to the elbows. Arms bronzed and muscular despite their beer belly bods. If Te Tapu farmers had a uniform, this was it.

"Ah, Natalie," one of them, Trevor, who lived only a few blocks from them, waved at her. "Ya mum working today?"

"Nah, she's got the night off," Natalie said, dismissing him and turning towards the bar.

"Maybe you could fill in until her shift?" another one of the men called out, gaining a round of raucous laughter from his group. She'd learnt long ago to ignore the jeering, but she automatically spun around to scowl at them anyway. Balding, obese, twice divorced, Bob Tucker slapped his knee as an invitation for her to come sit on it.

"Grow up," she retorted, then turned back to the counter.

Katrina was there, displeasure painted on strong.

"Shouldn't you be at school?" Her husband was Rob, the Year Three and Year Four teacher. She wiped up a spill on the counter while keeping her eyes glued on Natalie.

"I'm meeting someone," Natalie retorted. "And I'd like a lemon, lime, bitters, thanks."

Their dislike for each other was mutual. She wasn't even sure how it started, only that it got worse as Anna and Natalie got closer. Jealousy, maybe? She guessed Katrina saw her as Yoko Ono, no doubt made worse by the rumours after Anna's death. Natalie had gotten it wrong about how well they had hidden their relationship. Despite the O'Regans best efforts at stomping down any lewd gossip that painted them in a bad light, there had still been whispers that Anna had been seeking a divorce, which Natalie was in part responsible for.

Little was said about how the accident had happened. There were murmurings that a drunk driver had driven Anna off the road. But Troy had let it slip one day, when she'd let him back into her bed, that brake failure had caused the crash. Natalie had no idea if it made it to the final report because it certainly didn't make it to the newspapers, even when she pushed for a proper investigation. Around this time the rumour about a drunk driver intensified.

Prior to the accident, Anna had just picked up her car from Ol' Tom's garage, the garage run by Liam and his father, after having her brakes looked at. When Natalie pressed Troy on it, he'd gotten cagey, like she'd accused him of screwing up his job. He said he'd checked the paperwork. The car had gone in for an oil change, nothing more, but Natalie remembered what Anna had said. It hadn't been an oil change. If Liam had caught wind of Anna wanting a divorce, that she was leaving him for another woman, then maybe he saw her death as a way to keep the O'Regan reputation intact. A drunk driver was a more convenient story than mechanical issues that could be traced back to the garage. It made her feel sick. Worse were the people like Katrina, who treated her as if she had been the one to kill Anna.

Katrina pushed the drink across the counter to Natalie and gestured to the Eftpos machine.

"Whose life are you planning to wreck this time?" Katrina said, gripping the edge of the bar with her hands. Natalie gritted her teeth and swiped her card.

"Don't worry, Katrina," Natalie said in the sweetest voice she could muster. "You can keep Rob. Been there. Done that." She picked up her glass and spun away from the counter, making a beeline for one of the tables at the back of the room.

She didn't know why she'd said it. She liked Rob, but there had never been anything between them. She'd just said it to wind Katrina up. And by the way Katrina glared at Natalie from across the room, it appeared it had worked.

It was true that Natalie had a bit of a reputation. Relationships had never been her thing, which had been what had made her relationship with Anna all that much different. She'd never been against sleepovers, particularly in her teens. She was not her mother though, with a different man for different days of the week. But her mother's escapades hadn't helped Natalie's reputation any either.

And everyone knew about her and Troy. On again, off again. But it had never been serious. Not for her anyway. She felt a pang of guilt thinking about Troy, as she always did. He had felt differently, and she'd taken advantage of that. Somehow, she needed to find a way to make it up to him.

And now here she was with Te Tapu's most eligible bachelor. Just as she thought it, Riki walked through the door. He took a moment to scan the room. Natalie caught his eye and waved to him, and he made a beeline for her. She desperately wanted to catch Katrina's eye and smirk, but restrained herself, all eyes on the man walking towards her. It wasn't too hard to do. On seeing him, her stomach flip-flopped, and the same thoughts she always had on seeing him raced through her mind. Goddamn, he was hot!

"Miss Sullivan," he said by way of greeting. Natalie stood up, suddenly feeling lighter.

"Nat. Please call me Nat," she said gesturing for him to take a seat opposite her.

"Can I get you a drink?" he asked and then noticed her glass.

"No, I'm fine. Thanks." The top two buttons of his shirt were unbuttoned, but despite the heat of the day he wore jeans. His hair still had a shine to it like he'd not long gotten out of the shower, and his cologne made her want to swoon like a heroine in an old-fashioned gothic novel.

"Right. Let me get a drink, then I'll come and join you."

He smiled, and Natalie couldn't stop her own face lighting up. There was something intoxicating about him. Despite the conversation she knew laid ahead, she was pleased he had said yes to meeting her.

He walked up to the bar and chatted with Katrina before ordering a drink. Katrina sent a glance Natalie's way, and Natalie made sure to keep her face neutral. She was tired of being judged by Katrina, by everyone. She probably thought Natalie saw him as just another personal conquest. Which got her wondering: was that what people were to her? Troy, for instance? Anna hadn't been. Anna was different. Just thinking of her made her heart drop. No one could compare to Anna.

Riki came back with what looked like a coke and took up the seat opposite her.

"A bit of an unusual place to have a parent meeting," he said. His tone was gently teasing.

Natalie shrugged and took a sip of her drink before asking, "How is Cole doing at home?" Best to jump right to the point.

Riki's composure sagged. "I don't think there's a cure for missing your mum," he said. A heaviness lay between them for a moment. "He's okay. I think he's enjoying school. He doesn't talk about it much besides mentioning his new friend a few times. Gavin. His imaginary friend, I guess." Riki cringed as he said it.

Natalie held her composure.

"What I don't understand is why he hit the other boy?" he finished.

"Cole said he was standing up for his friend. The other boy had been teasing Cole about him, and I guess it just got too much. Has he hit out at others before?"

Riki shook his head, his face strained. "I don't think so. Not that I know of anyway." He massaged his forehead with his hand, and Natalie genuinely felt her heart go out to him. She hated that he was hurting, but she honestly couldn't think of anything she could say to make things better. In fact, what she did have to say was likely only going to make things worse. She'd weighed it up all day. Be honest or not. She was risking a lot. Her reputation was already pretty shot, so that wasn't really of concern. Yet she did need to do what she could to stay employed, and claiming to not only believe in ghosts but also to see them might not be in her best interests. Except, the only way she could think of to really help Cole meant she had to tell the truth.

"Has Cole told you anything about his imaginary friend?" Riki asked.

His eyes locked on hers, and Natalie forced herself to not look away. Though she wanted to. All of a sudden, she regretted calling the meeting. But what other choice did she have?

Riki waited expectantly while Natalie fumbled for the words.

"Is there something I should know?" he asked quietly.

"I told you how Gavin's not a student at our school, right?" Natalie said softly. There was no way of wording what she wanted to tell him without exponential fall out.

"Of course ... He's imaginary," Riki wore his confusion plain.

"Well, there was a student at our school once, called Gavin," Natalie said.

"I'm really not understanding ..."

Natalie was losing him.

"You said Cole sometimes talks to his mum?" Natalie continued.

Riki let out a deep sigh. "Yeah. He talks to his mum. Less and less lately. The psychiatrist said it's normal when a child's grieving. It's a way to self-soothe." His voice trailed off and Natalie could almost see the inner debate going on inside his mind. There was something he was torn about sharing; she could see it in his eyes.

"His mother believed in ghosts," he said quietly, his eyes fixed on his drink. He picked up the straw and stirred. "She always said that when she died, she'd come back, let us know she was still around. It's funny because for those first few weeks, I thought I saw her everywhere. Sometimes it would be out of the corner of my eye; other times, I would see someone who looked just like her when I was at the super-market. And other times, I'd smell her perfume. I even thought I heard her say my name once." He stopped stirring, lifted his drink and took a sip before facing Natalie. "They call it bereavement hallucination. I guess it's not so different than having an imaginary friend."

"I'm so sorry," Natalie said, meaning it. She knew what it was like to lose someone you love. But she also knew it hurt more when you didn't see those who had passed. Natalie could see the dead. Not by choice. But she could. And yet, not once had she seen Anna, and that hurt almost more than her death. She knew the spirit world existed, and yet Anna had never visited her. And then the question lay heavy – did Anna ever visit Liam?

"Do you believe in ghosts?" Riki asked, suddenly putting Natalie in the hot chair.

She paused, trying to infer what answer he was wanting, but she really couldn't tell. Finally, she nodded slowly. It *was* why she had called the meeting.

"I want to believe," he said slowly. "I just don't know."

His sadness was like a blanket. Natalie wanted to reach across the table and take his hand in his. The lust she'd felt on first seeing him was replaced with a deeper yearning to help, though she wasn't sure that what she was about to tell him would help.

"Anyway," he said, shaking himself from his reverie and sitting a little straighter in his chair. "We've already determined Cole's friend, Gavin, is imaginary, right?"

"Not exactly," Natalie said.

"I don't understand."

"In 1964 there was a fire at the school. It started in the woods nearby and took out a classroom where mine now stands. A young boy was killed in the fire." The words rolled out so fast. She wasn't sure whether to keep going or to give him time to digest. She braced herself for whatever his reaction would be.

He sat frozen, so Natalie continued.

"His name was Gavin Jenkins. He was nine years old and was likely autistic. He hid under the building to escape the fire."

Riki's eyes were wide, glued to Natalie's face, and heat rose in her cheeks. Any moment now, he was going to get up, storm off, maybe yell insults. God, Katrina was going to love that. And then he'd tell Victoria his son's teacher was a nutcase.

"You think this Gavin is the same one my son is friends with?"

It took Natalie a moment to realise what was happening, and a surge of hope filled her. Was it possible he believed her?

"I know how this sounds," she said, deliberately slowing her voice, trying to keep her composure. "But I've seen him." She pictured the young boy with his half-melted face and shivered in both pity and fear. "I think ... no, I *know* your son can see him too."

Any moment now. She braced herself again for the storm she knew was about to come.

Riki closed his eyes and slowly dragged his hand down his face as if to calm himself.

"You've really seen him?" he said, his face more drawn than before. Over his shoulder Katrina was staring at them, watching. What had Natalie been thinking meeting at the tavern?

Natalie nodded.

Riki took a deep breath.

"I think your son can see spirits."

"My wife?" Riki asked.

"I don't know," Natalie said. How could she? Just because she hadn't seen a woman hanging around Cole or Riki didn't mean there wasn't one. She had yet to figure out any rhyme or reason to what she could see.

"This little boy, Gavin ... is he hurting Cole? What do we do?" Riki's voice took on an edge of panic, and to Natalie's surprise she realised he actually did believe her.

"I don't think so. I think they're just friends. It's just that the boy from the other day had been teasing Cole, calling him a freak. Maybe he saw him talking to Gavin. I've seen it myself. And some kids are just cruel. But Gavin got upset; it was triggering for him. I think Cole lashing out was in part his own anger as he tried to protect his friend, and maybe it was in part Cole feeding off Gavin's anger."

"So what do we do?" he asked, and she let the question hang there.

He had said *we*. In any parent meeting, getting a parent to come to the realisation it was a team effort was cause for celebration. She felt another tingle of hope. He was on her side.

"Maybe you could talk to Cole. Ask him about Gavin. Find out why he's here. Let Cole know that ... you believe him."

She'd had Grams. Her whole life, Grams had believed her. Grams, who claimed she could also see spirits. She couldn't imagine what it would have been like to be a child and to see people who passed without having anyone believe her. It's the life she would have had if Helena had raised her alone. Helena was so grounded in the material she could barely see beyond her own nose.

"And then we what ... send the ghost to the light?" The corner of his mouth quirked upwards trying to make light of things, and Natalie felt that magnetic attraction all over again.

"I guess so," Natalie said cracking a full smile. "I have to be honest, Mr Lomas—"

"Riki," he interrupted.

"Riki. Ghost busting isn't really something we learn at teachers' college."

He guffawed at her joke and the tension between them lightened.

"You're definitely not like any of the teachers I remember having as a child, Nat." His eyes again fixed on hers, and she let hers wander to his lips, just for a second, and felt herself blush.

"Thank you for believing me," she said softly. "I know this is a lot."

"If Cole really can see Gavin, it means there's every possibility he saw his mum too. And I like to think his mum has been helping out where she can."

Natalie noticed the smallest of cracks in his voice as he spoke.

"I'm sure she is," Natalie said. And for the millionth time, the question hung over her: why hadn't she see Anna?

CHAPTER 29

Natalie

Time slipped away much too fast, and before Natalie knew, it was just past three. They'd discussed further how they could both support Cole. Riki promised he would find out more about Gavin and from there the two of them, Natalie and Riki, would come up with a plan to help Gavin. Surely there was somewhere better he could be. In Natalie's experience, most primary-aged children enjoyed school, yet she couldn't be certain that given a choice they'd want to spend eternity there.

And although she didn't share it with Riki, it concerned her that Cole had talked about there being a bad man that Gavin was afraid of. It was hard to imagine ghosts being afraid of anything.

But she had a pretty good idea of who they were talking about when Cole mentioned the bad man. Natalie had seen him too. She'd seen him when she was alone by the shed. Seen him standing by Arthur and Liam in the hospital when Anna passed, seen him since then around

Liam, and then, of course, felt him in ways that still made her skin crawl and turn to ice, when she'd come across her grandmother in the woods.

Te Tapu School seemed to attract the dead. But not once had she been as unnerved as by that shadow man. There was also one connection that was glaringly obvious. Whoever the man was, he had an affinity for the O'Regans, which confirmed all her bad thoughts about that family. Didn't like attract like? Whatever good Anna had seen in the O'Regans Natalie was blind to it.

Riki had to leave to pick up Cole from school, and Natalie was due to pick up Grams. They both had to leave and yet … something pulled in her chest at the thought as they walked together towards the door. She felt Katrina's eyes on her the whole time and stepped a little closer to Riki as they walked. It was meant in spite, and yet, she couldn't deny the closeness felt good.

He walked her to her car, and Natalie felt a tingle of anticipation that something was coming. Was he going to kiss her? God, she hoped so, and yet, no! She couldn't. Despite what Katrina believed, she wasn't Helena. And it would certainly blur boundaries pretty fast, kissing a parent in the tavern's car park. Although, she realised, even coming to the tavern had blurred the boundaries plenty.

"Thank you," Riki said as Natalie fumbled in her pocket for the car key. One day she'd upgrade to a car where you didn't need a physical key to unlock the door.

Natalie smiled at him.

"For watching out for Cole," he said. "And … for being honest." He shuffled awkwardly, hands in pockets. "You took a big chance telling me you thought my son was haunted." The corner of his mouth quirked upward, teasing.

"To be honest, it surprised me you took it so well." Natalie paused before opening the car door. Grams was expecting her, yet she really was having too much fun with the flirting or whatever it was going on between them. It had been a long time since she'd … three years in fact.

"Look, I have to go and pick up Cole, but maybe you'd consider joining us for dinner one night? I'll cook. No pressure or anything," he said holding his palms up. "I know there's probably rules against these things …"

"Like hosting a parent teacher meeting at the local pub?" Natalie said, grinning.

"Right. Yeah, that was definitely a little unorthodox," he said.

"I'd love to." Natalie replied. A small alarm bell rang in the back of her mind. What was she doing? Flirting was one thing. It was much harder to keep boundaries in place when you were in their house!

"Great. How about Monday, then?"

Good call, she thought. A weekday. Weekday dinners were on a different, much more casual, level than weekend dinners.

"Oh shoot!" Natalie said, remembering. "Could we maybe do Tuesday instead?" She still had no idea how she was going to get around working and keeping an eye on Grams, but at least Helena didn't work Tuesday evening, she'd rope her in to staying home. And if she didn't like it, tough!

"Tuesday it is!" he said, grinning.

"Tuesday it is," Natalie repeated, opening the car door, and then sliding in behind the wheel.

CHAPTER 30

Natalie

Natalie called ahead to the hospital to let them know she was on the way. She still felt giddy, school-girl-crush giddy, from her conversation with Riki. She had enjoyed herself. Really enjoyed herself. He was funny and cute, and he had believed her. Somehow that had meant more than she could reconcile. She had so whole-heartedly expected him to think her crazy, or to get angry, when she brought up ghosts. But he hadn't. He'd remained open minded.

There were few people she had ever shared this side of her with. Grams, of course, knew. Grams who had recognised her ability right away because she too suffered from the affliction. Natalie had always found it annoying how every TV show, every movie, labelled seeing spirits as a "gift". How? How was it a gift? Sure, maybe if you were able to say your final goodbyes to a loved one, but her experience had started much like Cole's: playground teasing and bullying. Being called a freak and a weirdo. And those she did see; it wasn't like they came to her so she could help them "go into the light". Hell, she wasn't sure some of them would recognise a light if they saw one. Creepy shadow guy for one. Natalie shivered despite the car's AC being on the fritz and it being stifling hot. From Natalie's experience so far, he seemed to enjoy being dead, creeping people out, the living, and the dead if little Gavin was to be believed.

Gavin. A little nine-year-old boy, for reasons beyond her understanding, had decided to stick around Te Tapu Primary School instead of carrying on to whatever waited for him on the other side of alive. Strange choice. But he was only a child. And she was a teacher. Which meant it was sort of her role to help him out. How? She had no idea. But if she could somehow help Gavin move on to wherever souls were supposed to go when they died, then maybe that would give Cole a chance to make some living friends. And help Riki out as well.

Her mind replayed their time together, and she realised she was smiling. For one of the first times she could think of, she'd driven past the worn wooden cross that memorialised the day she lost part of herself, without feeling a heaviness.

She'd told Anna her secret once. That sometimes she saw people who had passed. She'd told her she'd seen someone hanging around Liam, a dark figure, someone she should be wary of.

Anna had thought her kidding, teasing Natalie that she was just jealous. She'd placed her hands on either side of Natalie's face, and looked her straight in the eyes, all teasing gone.

"Liam's not the bad guy," she said. "None of this is his fault. You are the one who has my heart, and soon ..." She gently stroked the side of Natalie's face then pressed one finger against Natalie's lips. "And soon, it'll be just you and me. No more sneaking around. No more hiding or lying. Just you and me."

She moved her finger away and then leant in to brush her lips over Natalie's. And for a moment, all had been forgotten. It wasn't until much later Natalie thought about that conversation. Was she jealous of Liam? Had she concocted some mysterious dark entity around him as a weird sort of way of alleviating her guilt? Because if he were a horrible person, well, he'd deserve the pain she knew she'd be inflicting on him, once he found out. And she could sleep a little better without the word "homewrecker" echoing in her head at three o'clock in the morning.

Some of the orderlies had Grams up and in a wheelchair, ready to leave when Natalie arrived. Natalie felt a huge weight lift on seeing her. She was obviously having one of her good moments. Colour had returned to her cheeks, and she was laughing with one of the nurses who seemed to be teasing her. If it wasn't for the dressing wrapped around her left forearm where a nurse had told her she'd been scratched during her accident, and the blaring hospital setting, Natalie could have almost believed that the day before had all been just a hideous dream.

She stood in the doorway to the room for a moment just watching her grandmother. The curtains had been drawn back and a ray of sunshine sliced the bed and illuminated the top of her head like a halo. Grams was smiling and giggling, and all Natalie wanted was to hold onto this memory forever. To pretend it was just like how things used to be, where it was just her and Grams making caramel scrolls in the kitchen or taking turns to read an Edgar Allan Poe story curled up in her bed, trying to scare each other with ridiculous spooky voices.

A dull ache grew in her chest, and Natalie had to shake it off. No matter how it might appear right at this moment, Grams's moments of lucidity were becoming fewer and fewer.

"I think you have someone here to see you," the orderly said to Grams, before turning the wheelchair so Grams could see Natalie better.

"Aww, my moko!" Grams said. "This is my Natalie." She beamed up at the orderly. "She's a good girl." She tapped the woman's hand resting on her shoulder.

"I'm sure she is," the orderly replied, smiling at Natalie.

"Hello, Grams." Natalie moved in front of the wheelchair and crouched down and took Grams hands in her own. "How are you feeling today?"

She'd already checked in briefly with the doctor, whom she'd managed to catch passing at reception. Grams had had a bit of a rough night to begin with, waking in the early hours, mumbling and thrashing as if trapped in a nightmare. But by the time she fully woke in the morning, she was a changed person. She didn't recall a lot from the afternoon or evening before. She was eating, and all her vitals were fine. Besides her dementia and the scratch on her arm, which would need to be redressed at the local clinic every few days until it healed, she had a clean bill of health.

"Oh, I'm good, sweetheart. You know not to worry about me." Grams smiled, her blue eyes wide and innocent.

Natalie wished it were as easy as that.

After checking out and signing some papers at the reception desk, they made their way across the car park to Natalie's car, one of the orderlies walking beside them to take the wheelchair back once Grams had been loaded into the vehicle. Grams could still walk; this was just one of the added benefits of a small-town hospital. Staff weren't run off their feet, car parks were always free, and staff had the time and inclination to go that little bit further like wheeling an elderly woman out to her car.

The orderly made small talk, asking questions about what Grams was looking forward to most about being home but, Natalie noticed, either Gram's energy was beginning to wane, she was slipping back into her mind, or she was waiting until Natalie and her were alone to indulge in real conversation.

It turned out to be the latter.

When they were leaving the hospital car park, Grams found her voice again.

"Sweetheart ..." she said, and Natalie shot her a smile, before returning her eyes to the road. "Thank you."

"Thank you for what?" Natalie said, taken by surprise. "You know I'd never leave you at the hospital," she teased. "Helena maybe ..." She chuckled, but stopped abruptly. Normally, when Grams was in a good state, that would have made her laugh, and then she would have followed up with a gentle reminder that Helena was doing her best and Natalie should be kind to her, she was, after all, her mother. But this time there was nothing, and Natalie felt a coolness settle on her skin.

"You look different," Grams said instead.

And from the corner of her eye, Natalie saw her puzzled expression. "Really?" Natalie asked, unsure where the conversation was heading, and scared it was heading back to Nonsense-ville.

"Ohh ..." She breathed out in a long exhale. "Ohh ... you've found someone?!" It was both a question and a statement. With the saying of it, the energy between the two of them seemed to relax.

"Has Anna come home?" Grams asked, and Natalie's relief was over.

She was slipping back, Natalie thought. Her lucidity fading again, and yet Natalie had so many questions she needed answers to.

"Grammy," Natalie said softly as she steered the car around the windy corners. "Anna's dead. Remember? She'd not coming home." Natalie's voice threatened to crack, yet somehow she made it through.

"I know she'd dead," Grams said, with an edge to her voice.

Did she though? Or had she forgotten? Natalie couldn't be sure.

"Then there's someone else," she said matter-of-factly.

"What do you mean?" Natalie asked, her eyes locked on the road so as not to betray the emotions boiling underneath.

"Your energy's softer, moko. Just like when Anna was alive."

Natalie said nothing. Strange how, on the drive to pick up Grams, that was exactly how she'd felt. But now, hearing it from another's lips, a jolt of guilt shot through her, just as they were coming up to Anna's death spot. To feel that way about anyone seemed like cheating or dishonouring Anna's memory.

"You know, it's okay to move on." It was said more as a statement than a question.

And Natalie was reminded how well her grandmother could read her. At times, even knowing how she was feeling before she did.

"Love is the strongest force there is, my child. You don't shut your-self off from it."

"You really believe that, don't you?" Natalie said, her eyes briefly drifting over to the wooden white cross on the fence, a reminder of her loss, before locking back on the road.

If that were true, Anna wouldn't have died, Natalie reasoned. If the love Natalie felt for Anna couldn't bring her back from the dead, then it didn't seem like love was much of a potent force at all.

"Grams, did you ever see Grandpa after he died?" Natalie asked. Grandpa had died before Natalie was born, when Helena was still a toddler, but Grams used to talk about him a lot. They'd met during her first year at university. And the way she told it, it was love at first sight. It had broken her heart when cancer took him so young. She still kept pictures of the two of them around the house. Grams didn't often talk about him now, but when she did her affection was evident.

"Aww, honey," Grams said, taking Natalie's hand and giving it a squeeze. "Not everyone who's dead comes back."

Natalie swallowed hard. It wasn't the first time Grams had said this.

"And it's a good thing," she continued. "If they don't come back, it means they're at peace. Isn't that what we all want for our loved ones?"

Natalie blinked back the tears suddenly blurring her vision. Grams had told her this before too, but she still found it hard to comprehend. Anna had loved her; she'd promised her life to her. They were going to grow old together. So how could Anna be a peace? Unless of course, it had all been a lie. The ache in her chest came back with a fury, and Natalie clenched her teeth together and batted back the tears with her eyelashes, refusing to give in to more emotion, particularly when there were more important things to contend with.

They travelled the rest of the way in silence despite the millions of questions Natalie had for Grams. They would have to wait until they got home, when her emotions were better under control.

Pulling up the drive, Natalie eyed the two cars parked in the drive-way. Her stomach dropped. Helena was home, which was surprising in itself. Although she rarely worked, she was also very rarely home. The other car, a rusty red hatchback, was Victoria's. What the hell was she doing here?

Natalie killed the engine and sat for a moment staring at the house. She couldn't remember the last time Victoria had been to the house – if ever. Inside, her two worlds had collided: school and family. Part of her wanted to start the car and reverse, go somewhere, anywhere, far away from whatever drama awaited her inside.

"That's not the Bug," Grams said beside her. "Why hasn't Vicky brought the Bug?"

Natalie stared at her grandmother, slack-jawed. She wasn't sure exactly what Grams meant, but by the way she was focused in the direction of the red car, she had assumed it was Victoria's vehicle. How did she know it was Victoria's, though? Had they had more to do with each other than Natalie was aware of? She couldn't imagine how.

Swearing under her breath, Natalie unlatched her seatbelt, and stepped out onto the gravel driveway. As she walked around to Grams's door to help her out, she kept her eyes on the house, looking for any clues as to what might await inside. She had to half walk, half carry Grams towards the house, as she was still a bit wobbly on her feet. Poe made it more difficult, weaving himself around her legs and mewing, obviously excited to see Grams.

On reaching the door, Natalie hesitated. She almost considered knocking, in order to give Helena and Victoria time to ready themselves for whatever ambush they had planned. Instead, she sucked in a deep breath and turned the doorknob. Sure enough, it wasn't locked.

Helena greeted them, making her way from the furthest end of the hallway. "You took your time," she said to Natalie.

Natalie narrowed her eyes. Straight into it, then. "I told you I'd be picking Grams up after work." She helped Grams over the small lip of the door jamb.

Helena ignored Natalie's comment and proceeded to wrap her arm around Grams's other side. "I've got the bedroom prepared; we can put her in there," Helena said, trying to guide the two of them towards the doorway on the right.

Stifling a growl, Natalie asked, "Grams, where would you like to go? Do you need the toilet? Did you want to watch TV?"

Helena shot daggers at her.

"Come on, Mum," she said. "I've got fresh sheets put on and have even moved the TV in for you so you can watch it from bed."

"Thank you, honey."

Natalie felt her temper rise. When she saw who waited for them in Grams's bedroom, she saw red.

"Hello, Maggie."

Victoria stepped out, half shielded by the door. As petite as she was, somehow she managed to appear even smaller.

"Vicky?" Grams said in a tiny voice, hesitating for a moment and wobbling slightly on her legs

"What are you doing here?!" Natalie growled. She glared at Helena then back at Victoria.

"We all need to talk," Victoria said, a slight tremor in her voice, which in itself unnerved Natalie.

"I don't think so," Natalie said, the last of her good mood dissolving.

"Vicky?" Grams said again. "Where's the Bug?"

Her mind was slipping again.

Natalie and Helena guided Grams over to the bed, where she sat down and pulled her legs up under the covers. Natalie quickly took in her surroundings. Helena had done a good job. She'd tidied and cleaned. There were fresh flowers in a vase on the dresser, beside the small television that usually lived on the kitchen counter. A carafe of water and a glass sat on one of the bedside tables. The used tissues were gone, and Grams's books were stacked in a neat pile and placed on a shelf nearby.

"There's no Bug anymore," Victoria replied with a smile.

Choosing to ignore Natalie's hostility, she moved closer to the side of the bed and poured Grams a glass of water, holding it out for her to take. Which she did.

"What is she doing here?" Natalie asked, glaring at her mother.

"I asked her," Helena said, chin jutting out and hand on her hip. "You don't get to decide everything around here. She might be your grandmother, but she was my mother first!"

Natalie's jaw tightened.

"I have a proposal," Victoria said, her voice reverting back to her principal tone.

"I'm not interested," Natalie said, automatically. She was still angry at Victoria. She'd kept her role, and the role of Arthur O'Regan, in

Gavin's death a secret, and now Natalie was left trying to make things right.

"Sit down, Natalie, and hear me out," Victoria said, her voice growing sterner. Natalie went to argue, how dare she tell her what to do in her own house, but Grams and Helena jumped in.

"Sit down!" her mother ordered.

And more gently, "Please, sweetheart. Let's hear Vicky out," her grandmother said, patting a spot beside her on the bed for Natalie to join. Natalie stood there for a moment, her arms crossed over her body, fight and flight vying for dominance. With a sigh and a gritting of teeth, she went and perched on the bed beside her grandmother.

Victoria exhaled, visibly relaxing, and pulled a chair closer to the other side of the bed. Helena, still beside Natalie, leant back against the windowsill.

"Right. Well, I'll just dive in, shall I?" Victoria said, wringing her hands.

She was nervous. Good. Natalie could guess what she wanted to say. It would be the only reason for Helena to call her, and Natalie had no intention of making it easy for her or anyone else. She didn't want their help. She didn't want Victoria's charity. This was her problem to solve, and she'd solve it. Somehow, she'd make things work; they just needed to get off her case!

"When your grandmother first started getting sick, she reached out to me." Victoria bent down and pulled a canvas tote onto her lap. From it, she pulled a stack of six journals and placed them on her knees.

"My journals!" Grams said, excitement in her voice. "Oh, I remember now. You were going to hold on to them for me, and then give them to Natalie when the time was right," she said. A dark cloud suddenly passed over Grams's face as if she were remembering something else.

Natalie's jaw slackened. This wasn't what she'd been expecting, and something in Grams's expression made Natalie grow cold all over.

"Oh no. No, no, no ... Vicky?" Grams implored, her eyes wide and round.

"It's okay, Mags. You're safe. We'll work it out together."

Natalie didn't understand. Victoria stood up and, leaning over the bed, held the journals out for Natalie. Hesitantly, Natalie took them from her, stacking them beside Grams's legs.

"What are these?" she asked.

"Oh, sweetheart. These are my diaries. It means he's back." Her voice caught.

"Hold up a second," Helena butted in. "This isn't what we talked about. Victoria?" she locked eyes on Victoria, confusion marring her face.

"Yes, it is," Victoria said. "Part of it anyway. When Maggie was first diagnosed, she reached out to me. She was worried about what would happen to the two of you when her health really deteriorated." Victoria shot a look at Helena, and then Natalie. "She thought that after all these years, I might finally believe her." Victoria's eyes welled as she sent a small smile Grams's way. "Well, I do believe you, Maggie. I think I always did. But you were wrong about some things. Arthur wasn't evil. Troubled yes. Bad not evil."

Arthur? Arthur O'Regan? How was it that all conversations led back to the O'Regans? Natalie fidgeted in her spot but stayed where she was. Grams had taken one of Natalie's hands in her own. She would hear Victoria out for her grandmother's sake.

"She left me her journals and said maybe by now they would make sense to me, and once I had read them, when the time was right, I was to pass them on to Natalie because by then Natalie might be the only one who could do anything with them."

Natalie picked up the first journal. It had a pale blue, once maybe-egg-shell coloured cover, now faded with age, dog eared and well-thumbed.

"I didn't get it at first. Not any of it. But gradually, things began to make more sense."

Natalie opened it to a random page.

He was there again. Like Arthur's shadow only heavier, darker, taunting me, knowing only I could see him, and getting satisfaction from it. Vicky was there too. It's been two weeks since we last spoke. I tried telling her. I'd do anything to get her to believe me. I just don't understand how she can't feel him ...

Natalie's mouth went dry. The entry was dated February 2nd 1964. So Grams *had* seen the shadow man. But that had been so long ago.

"And after our recent conversations, Natalie ... I understood ... you could probably see them too."

Them?

"This wasn't what we talked about," Helena said. She was getting antsy, confusion bunching her eyebrows together. "Tell her about Mum's money."

"Money?" Natalie repeated, now as equally as confused as her mother had been seconds before. Helena had referred to Grams having money, and that wasn't the case. Natalie knew because she oversaw her grandmother's bank accounts. There had been next to no savings when Grams had set her up with access to help with the household bills. Grams got the pension, which didn't equate to a lot, not when it came to the deteriorating state of their house. It didn't equate to getting a carer or putting Grams in a home, even with Natalie working fulltime and Helena part time at the tavern.

"A few years back, Peggy O'Regan died," Victoria said, and Natalie winced again at hearing the O'Regan name. "Peggy was Arthur's mother," Victoria added for clarification.

"In her will, she left money to Maggie."

Natalie stole a glance at her grandmother, whose mind seemed to have drifted off elsewhere. She didn't appear to be listening.

"Why would she do that?" Natalie asked. Her shock was tempered by the fact that so much of what she had thought she'd known suddenly seemed wrong. The elements of surprise were fading.

"Tell her!" Helena said. "She'd not going to give in if you don't tell her the details."

Helena was right. All of Natalie's senses were on high alert that some trick was coming.

Victoria took a deep breath. "It didn't make sense to me at the beginning either. Why Peggy would leave money for Maggie and why Maggie didn't let either of you know." She bounced a look between Helena and Natalie.

Natalie felt something shrink inside herself. Grams didn't keep secrets from her. It didn't make sense.

"Earlier this year, I started to understand. And later," Victoria said, looking directly at Natalie, "you can maybe thank Riley for that."

Riley? Newbie? Natalie's mind was reeling. Get to the point, she wanted to rage at Victoria.

"It seems that Peggy believed the rumours around Maggie's brother's death at the hands of an O'Regan were true. Peggy believed that Jake O'Regan killed Billy MacKenzie. Over a girl, nonetheless. A girl, from Peggy's account, who was deeply, madly in love with Billy, and he with her. Peggy was friends with her, Gwen Davies, and yet not even Peggy knew all the details about what had happened, only that Gwen was raped by Jake. Billy found out. And for that part, Peggy blamed herself. She thinks Billy must have confronted him, and ..." Victoria swallowed hard, her expression pained. "And Jake killed him."

Natalie's head swam. How was it no one was more upset about this? Helena did nothing but tap her foot impatiently at Victoria to get on with her story. Grams silently stared into space. And although Natalie could see Victoria's emotions were closer to the surface, she couldn't understand why no one was furious right now. Peggy had known her brother-in-law had killed Grams's brother, Natalie's own great-uncle, and yet, no one had done anything. There had been rumours that Jake had been found dead – murder or suicide – Te Tapu was divided, and yet it was her family who were treated like the outcasts, not the O'Regans. No one aimed a disparaging eye towards them.

"So, Peggy felt guilty for her cover up? For allowing the O'Regans good name to remain. For not speaking out and condemning her own brother-in-law?!" Natalie's voice got louder. "And yet, screw the MacKenzies!"

"Peggy wrote a note to Maggie in her will explaining it. She said she and her husband had loved Billy and the girl who Jake had ruined. There was no compensation in the world that could bring Billy back, but she wanted to do something. And Maggie ... she reminded Peggy of Billy. And I guess she felt sorry for her. While Maggie's other siblings had escaped Te Tapu, built their lives elsewhere, Maggie was still here. Still living with the ghosts of the past – much like Peggy. And she knew there was no chance of any of you accepting money while she was still alive. Too much animosity existed between your families."

"We could have decided that," sparked Helena, and Natalie bristled.

"She was right!" Natalie spat, choosing for the moment to ignore her mother. "We wouldn't have accepted it!"

Helena growled and Victoria held up her hand to shush her.

"She left your grandmother a considerable sum. Your grandmother didn't want to touch it. She felt similar to you, Natalie." Victoria ventured a small smile. "But when she learnt she was sick and her health was only going to get worse, she reached out to me. She told me, when it was time, I was to tell you, make you listen and accept the help. It doesn't equate to forgiving the past. It was more important to her that you and Helena not struggle financially with caring for her. Maggie wanted the money to go towards putting her in a care facility. She wanted you two to live the life Billy couldn't"

"What? No!" Natalie stood up, outraged. This was ridiculous. They would find a way to keep Grams safe and living with them without the help of the O'Regans.

"I told you she wouldn't listen!" Helena stomped her foot.

Victoria narrowed her eyes at Helena like she was a naughty child.

"Well, she's *my* mother, the money should've come to me. I'd get Mum taken care of if you're going to continue being so selfish!" Helena turned on Natalie.

Natalie clenched her fists.

"Helena!" Grams had snapped back to attention, and everyone froze.

Natalie tried to calm the adrenalin and fury making her heart race.

"Sit down and hush," Grams said, in a tone leaving no room for argument. Natalie couldn't remember the last time she'd heard Grams raise her voice like that.

"Natalie, my moko, my love. This is what I want." Her voice came softer now.

"Grams! No. You belong here with us!"

"No. I don't. Vicky will help, won't you Vicky?"

Nodding, Victoria patted Grams's arm.

"I need to sleep," Grams said, snuggling down under the covers.

Natalie shared a look with Victoria.

"Okay, my friend. We'll sort it, don't you worry your head. We'll be in the other room if you need us," Victoria said before standing up. "Helena, Natalie." She gestured towards the door.

Natalie's natural instinct was to argue with her. How dare she tell her what to do? But Grams's eyelids were already closed, and she looked so peaceful. Natalie leaned in and kissed her forehead, then picked up the journals Victoria had given her.

Helena left the room first, and Victoria waited for Natalie to do the same before following suit.

Helena was furious. Her energy was spiking in such a way it reminded Natalie of a milder version of the shadow man when she'd first seen him. Once the door to Grams's bedroom was closed, she turned around to glare at both Natalie and Victoria.

"You were supposed to make her see sense!" she accused Victoria, arms waving in exasperation. "And you—" She turned to Natalie, letting out a half sob, and Natalie was shocked to see Helena's eyes were wet with tears. "You don't have to believe me, but I want Mum safe. And I want you to get a life! You're too young to be closing yourself off from the world like this. You might not think I care, but I do!" Helena's voice cracked; her chin angled at Natalie. "Whatever you decide doesn't just affect you, it affects all of us! And as Mum gave *you* power of attorney over her money" – Helena harrumphed – "try and make a decision based on more than some grudge against the O'Regans." She turned and stormed out the front door.

Natalie was shocked. Her mother's tantrums were commonplace, but this one had thrown her. Despite the sharpness of Helena's words, she had seen something else on her face. She was scared. In her own way, she was worried, not just about her mum but about Natalie too. She sounded like she genuinely cared.

The guilt of knowing that and being so dismissive of her mother's intentions weighed heavily on Natalie. When she took a step to follow Helena, to make some peace, Victoria grabbed her arm and stayed her.

"No!" Victoria said. "We need to talk."

Natalie looked back and forth between Victoria and the door her mother had just exited from, and with a sigh, her decision was made. She was angry. Angry at being ambushed. Angry at Victoria, forcing her way into their family business. Angry with herself. She wasn't making decisions based on what was best for everyone. She was making decisions based on pride.

Troy's words from the hospital came rushing back to her. He'd said the same thing. Their friendship was over because of her stubbornness. And as much as she liked to believe she had everything under control, that she could see them through this without putting Grams at risk, she couldn't. If she could, she would have already.

The memory of seeing her grandmother unmoving on the ground in the woods would haunt her forever. And hell, from the small paragraph she'd read in her grandmother's notebook, Natalie wasn't alone in having seen the shadow man. And if Grams had been tormented by him like Natalie had, then she had already failed in keeping her safe. How do you keep someone safe from a demon? A ghost? A malicious shadow who wanted to inflict harm?

The tears broke through her walls with a fury, swamping her, making her whole body shake, and all she could do was stand there facing the door, her grandmother's notebooks in her arms.

A deluge of grief, of hopelessness, regret, and guilt, threatened to drown her. And then beyond it all, she felt two thin warm arms, turn her around and pull her close.

"It's alright, Nat. We'll work it out. Everything's going to be okay," Victoria said.

And Natalie let Victoria lead her down the hall to the kitchen, her whole body dissolving with emotion. She couldn't imagine ever feeling okay again. How could she? Too many things were broken around her and within her. And so many people needed her right now and she didn't know how to help them.

CHAPTER 31

Natalie

It was late when Victoria finally went home.

After Natalie's break down, Victoria had sat her down in her grandmother's chair, taken the journals from Natalie's arms and placed a cup of hot tea in her hands instead. Natalie couldn't bring herself to speak. Once the tears stopped, she felt empty. Numb and empty, so Victoria filled the silence for the two of them.

She told Natalie about the fire. How impetuous she had been at nineteen. How Grams had tried to warn her about dating an older man. How she only went along on what Victoria had organised as a double date simply to look out for her best friend. How they had smoked, and drunk, and made out, except Grams hadn't really wanted to do any of it, so she went for a walk. And Arthur had been playing around with his lighter. Victoria had told him to stop. Something in his demeanour had chilled. Even JP had tried to warn him off as he started lighting and then stomping out the flames, until suddenly the flames caught. Really caught. Possibly it had found some of the spilled home-made liquor, but it just took off. Victoria had never seen anything like it. Everything was so dry, so she shouldn't have been surprised. It licked at their ankles as they scrambled to get out of its way, and it seemed to follow them as they ran further into the bush. And all the time Victoria had been screaming for Grams. JP too. But Arthur had only laughed. Even as they ran, he laughed. And despite the chaos, the fear, the adrenalin, Victoria remembered thinking how this wasn't Arthur. It couldn't be him. And then Arthur pulled her one way, towards the road, despite her protests, while JP took off deeper into the words, yelling and searching for Grams.

Arthur had dragged her onto the road and held her there, and they watched as the woods before them were engulfed in flames, the heat, even from the road, almost searing their skin. She had watched too, as the fire, possessed as it was, raged towards the school, and a sense of even deeper foreboding hit her. Like she had known something was terribly wrong, beyond the obvious, but was at odds to prevent it from happening. And then JP had dragged Grams out of the woods, and Victoria was overwhelmed with how scared she'd been. It had been an accident, she told Grams. And it had been, except there was still, hidden deep down, the fear that maybe it hadn't been.

Natalie listened, saying nothing, not knowing how to respond. As she gradually returned to her body, she sipped her tea.

Victoria told her how her and Grams had spent the night at the O'Regans and how they'd caught Arthur's mum, Peggy, pleading with her husband to make Arthur leave. She believed he had started the fire. That there was something wrong with him. Until she'd read Grams's journals, she'd completely forgotten Peggy making a comment about Arthur not being their son. And Grams and Victoria had argued. Grams had said there was a darkness around Arthur, but Victoria was in love. So what if he was a little rough around the edges? In her teenage mind, it just made him all the more attractive. Plus, she'd seen a side of him Grams hadn't. One of the few times he'd let his guard down was after smoking too much weed. He'd told her how scared he was that there was a darkness stalking him. It could change his mood in an instant. There were times he didn't feel himself, and he felt powerless to do differently. And his vulnerability in that moment made Victoria love him more.

Natalie listened. The words floated around her. She understood them but at the same time, they meant nothing. What did she care about Arthur O'Regan? She already knew how the story ended. Gavin Jenkins was found half incinerated, hiding beneath a badly burned classroom. No one had owned up to the fire. Gavin's family, his mother and his little sister, were bullied out of town by uneducated arseholes who believed the young boy's death was due to poor parenting on the mother's behalf, not negligence, vandalism and trespassing of four young adults.

Natalie already knew Grams had ended her friendship with Victoria. What else was there to know? It didn't help the fact that a boy was dead and now haunted a student of hers. A member of the O'Regan family went on to destroy Natalie's life by killing Anna and then got off with barely an investigation. Or that, right now, her grandmother needed fulltime care requiring money they just didn't have, unless they took money from the O'Regans. It was like signing a contract with the devil, despite the money being bequeathed to them.

"Peggy was a good person," Victoria said, bringing Natalie back to the conversation. "And she had a soft spot for your grandmother. I'd noticed it right off the bat, and I admit, I was a little jealous. It wasn't until earlier this year that I learnt the full story." She paused. Waiting to see that Natalie was still paying attention, she guessed.

"You don't like Riley much, do you?" Victoria said, shocking Natalie into almost dropping her mug.

"What's Riley got to do with anything?" Natalie asked, her voice raw.

"Riley's more like you than you realise, Nat. It's why I've wanted you to give her a chance."

Natalie highly doubted they had anything in common. How could they? She was dating the man who killed Anna.

"You might remember, she had a tough go of it at the beginning of the year. What you probably don't know is why."

Why would I care? Natalie thought, her snarkiness returning.

"Riley has a gift," Victoria went on. "She can also see people who have passed."

Natalie's eyes bugged, her jaw dropping. She'd suspected as much. But that also meant Victoria understood her secret now.

"Riley's seen Gavin?" Natalie asked, trying to keep her voice steady.

"No. I don't think so." Victoria pulled a chair out from the small dining table, placed it closer to Natalie and took a seat.

"Riley had some experiences with Gwen, the woman Peggy said Jake raped." Victoria winced as she said it.

Natalie's ears were pricked and listening now.

"She also said she'd seen your great uncle, Billy MacKenzie."

Natalie felt the floor drop out from under her. Newbie? Newbie had seen her uncle? It didn't make sense. Why Newbie? Why not Natalie? She was family, not Riley!

"A lot of things happened in the beginning of the school year, and I admit, I only learnt the full story much later, when Liam and Riley came to ask permission to put a plaque on the shed."

Of course. The plaque that she'd been standing near when the shadow man had appeared. The plaque Cole and Gavin played under because it was safe.

"I can't claim to see spirits," Victoria continued. "But I do believe there is more to this world than the things we see. And there have been times, I admit, where I think I've seen things at school, when no one's been around, albeit out of the corner of my eye. Your grandmother tried to tell me she had this gift. I didn't listen. I wouldn't listen. I refused to hear anything bad about Arthur, despite anything your grandmother said. Silly really, when you think about it, knowing now how things turned out."

Both Victoria and Arthur had married different people. Both ended up widowed. There was no happily ever after for either of them.

"What does this have to do with Peggy? What does this have to do with me?" Natalie asked, tiring of trying to make sense of everything.

"Thanks to Riley's efforts, I learnt more about Gwen, Billy's girl-friend at the time. About her being raped by Jake. That he got her pregnant. Gwen died not long after childbirth. It confirmed what Peggy had once alluded to and was unknown to anyone else at the time, including Arthur. Peggy and Hugh O'Regan claimed Gwen's child as their own."

Natalie inhaled sharply. "So, Arthur wasn't their son?"

Victoria shook her head. "No. He was Gwen and Jake's son. And because he was Gwen's, Peggy took him in, and Peggy and Hugh raised him as their own. The darkness that follows him, I can only guess, comes from his father. Not" – Victoria's tone grew stern – "that Arthur is *like* his father. He's not! He might be a grumpy old coot, but he's not a rapist or a murderer."

Something prickled in the back of Natalie's mind.

"So, it was Riley who worked all this out?" Natalie said, still somewhat disbelieving.

"And Liam." Victoria added. "And it's a good thing they did. Three restless spirits in a school are too many in my book. And now you've added Gavin to the list."

"Three?" Natalie repeated.

Victoria's eyes locked on Natalie's, and she nodded. "Gwen, your great uncle Billy, and ... Jake."

CHAPTER 32

Maggie

1964

It took a month before Maggie had the courage to return to the school. She had to. There was no real reasoning for it, just a need to see first-hand the damage they'd caused. To see the place where their fooling around had cost a young boy his life.

The classroom that had been destroyed in the fire was now just a bulldozed, scarred area of dirt, cordoned off by tall wire fences with a "Keep Out" sign. A couple of handpicked bouquets of flowers and a small teddy bear leant against the fence by one corner in memoriam.

The school was reopening in a week, extending the school holidays a little longer. From what Maggie had heard, the O'Regans had made a hefty donation to the school and been in talks with connections at the Department of Education to fast track a new classroom to be built on site in its place.

Surprisingly, the extent of the bush fire had been relatively contained. Almost like it had stalled its path of destruction on reaching the school. It had probably helped that the fire department had been so quick to respond, but despite knowing little about fires, Maggie couldn't understand how the fire hadn't taken out more of the acres and acres of wood and brush. But it hadn't.

Though Vicky had tried to reach out several times, Maggie couldn't bring herself to talk with her. Maggie knew what she had seen. There was some malevolent entity attached to Arthur. She still woke in the middle of the night, feeling his warm sour breath moistening her cheek, it chilled her blood just thinking about it. And she just couldn't reconcile the secrecy around their connection to the fire, particularly when a young child was dead. That was the worst of it for her. She'd heard the whispers, and the conversations even in the next town over, that Mrs Jenkins had been bullied out of town. What sort of mother let her mentally damaged child loose like that? It was her own fault he died, they said. Best for everyone. What sort of life could a child like that have anyway?

It made Maggie sick. How could people be so cruel? A mother had just lost a child. A little girl was going to grow up without her brother. She had only ever seen Gavin in passing. Sure, he was high spirited, but what nine-year-old boy wasn't? He was curious and happy and always laughing. So what if he couldn't always communicate clearly? Or that he didn't understand social norms like other children? No child, no mother, deserved to be treated and spoken of in such a harsh way.

The guilt Maggie carried for having not paid more attention that day, for having not followed his laughter or making some effort to take him back to his mother, ate at her. More and more, Maggie was sure, it had been Gavin she'd heard following them, laughing and running around in the bush. Had she gone to see ... maybe things would have been different.

And so she found herself at the school on a Saturday morning, staring at the spot where Gavin had lost his life.

She looked at the corner of the cordoned off area, where she imagined from reports that Gavin had been found. He had a habit of hiding when spooked. When he'd seen the fire, it was assumed he'd done just that. Climbed through the hatch leading under the classroom to get away, huddling in the corner. And even if he realised it wasn't safe, by then, it would have been too late. No other exit was available. Maggie could imagine the area filling with smoke, choking him. She remembered herself how the heat alone had been scorching; suffocating. And everything would have been dark.

Her bottom lip trembled, and she bit down on it to stay the wave of ever-present emotion. The tears escaped anyway. How she had any left to cry, she wasn't sure, but they slid down her face, and her body constricted against the sobs she held in by wrapping her arms around her body.

They had had no right being there. Hadn't going to the glade been Arthur's idea too? She couldn't remember. Yet who, at their age, went skulking around the woods to get wasted and make out? She felt another tremor of anger towards Vicky. And herself. How could she have been so stupid to go along with it? She should have just left Vicky to it.

Maggie wiped her face with the palm of her hand. Now what? She wasn't sure what she had been expecting being there. Some sort of closure maybe? Something to alleviate her guilt? There wasn't anything. Just a crippling hollow ache in her chest.

Maggie glanced around, suddenly self-conscious. What would someone think if they saw her there?

As expected, the school was empty, being a Saturday. Sometimes parents would bring their children, or children would find their own way there to play on the playground. Just like Mrs Jenkins had done on what would have started like any normal day, taking her kids for some fun on the playground equipment.

Without realising what she was doing, Maggie made her way towards the playground beside the main classroom block. She went and sat on one of the swings and moved backward and forward on the balls of her toes in a rocking motion.

There were a couple of wooden seesaws, a merry-go-round and, as a focal point, a large slide. A wooden tower allowed you to climb up and then you'd slide down to the thirty centimetre drop at the bottom. She remembered how hot the metal got in the summer sun.

Behind the playground was the forest, much of which for the first hundred metres or so, particularly behind where the destroyed classroom had been, was now blackened debris and ash. But beyond that, the wood continued all the way, Maggie knew, to her house. Podocarps and tree ferns, shrubs and vines. It didn't make much sense to her. With the speed the fire had taken, there should have been so much more damage.

For a moment, Maggie thought she saw someone hiding behind the chute of the slide. She put a hand up to shield her eyes from the sun's glare hitting its metal side. No one was there. The shadows were just shadows. She rocked a little more on her toes allowing the swing to move with her back and forth, back and forth. You could almost hear the laugh and chatter of children like white-noise or static, even when no one was there.

She pricked her ears. Yes. So quietly, almost indiscernible, it sounded like a child laughing. She stopped moving and listened. A bird maybe? Or someone walking down the road.

The laughter got slightly louder. A lilting chuckle. Almost warming, adding to the summer heat. It was a nice sound. Maggie closed her eyes for a moment, letting herself soak it in, and she felt a heaviness lift a little in her chest.

When she opened them again, she was surprised to see the sun had gone behind a cloud, and the day suddenly seemed a little darker, the colours a little more muted. A creaking sound drew her attention beside her. One of the swings, two swings down from her was swinging backwards and forwards, yet nothing else was moving. Not even a breeze tousled the leaves of the nearby gingko tree.

Crick. Creak.

The sound got louder as the swing gained momentum. And there it was again, a flicker of laughter almost out of earshot.

Maggie gripped the swing a little tighter. She was otherwise frozen, unsure whether to run or watch. It almost seemed safer to watch. If she kept her eye on the swing there would be no surprises, because more and more she was beginning to think someone was there, someone she couldn't see.

Finally, her voice cracking, she whispered one word, "Gavin?"

The swing stopped. Everything went deadly quiet as if the world were holding its breath. And then came the sound of feet running away from the swing, and a gentle chuckle hanging in its wake. And she was alone again.

Gavin was dead, she realised, her heart in her throat. But he wasn't gone.

CHAPTER 33

Natalie

Natalie woke with a start. It had been another fitful night's sleep. She'd spent hours skimming through Grams's notebooks, feeling a whole mixture of emotions she hadn't expected. Her grandmother had kept so much from her. She knew about Gavin's ghost and had blamed herself even though, to Natalie, that was ridiculous. How could she have expected herself to stop Arthur mucking around with his lighter if she wasn't even there? She was lucky to have gotten out alive. And she had experienced the same shadow man as Natalie had. The man she now knew for certain was Jake O'Regan. Grams had drawn her own conclusions that it was Jake, feeding off his O'Regan bloodline. It all made sense, particularly knowing Arthur was Jake's son, making Liam Jake's grandson. What wasn't clear was why Jake was still hanging around, inflicting pain on people. Why he had targeted Grams and then herself, so many years later? Grams had hypothesised it might be because he had recognised her bloodline to Billy, a man he had a complicated relationship with. And maybe Grams was right. In Te Tapu people often suffered at the hands of their bloodline, their reputations sullied by those family members who had walked before them.

Unless, of course, you were an O'Regan. Then only the good was remembered. Like Te Tapu's founding father, Ol' Man Tom. And Hugh and Peggy's contributions to almost every charity and community funding initiative known to man, if Grams's journal entries were anything to go by. She was now quite aware of just how much the family had buried.

What was more sickening to Natalie, was how so many people were willing to go along with it, even against their best judgement. Just like Grams had. The O'Regans were a wealthy family. They could make anything go away. Including murder. From reading Grams's journals, it seemed that even dead, the O'Regans were hell-bent on eliciting harm on those they didn't like.

Grams had never forgiven herself for the role she played in Gavin's death. And after feeling his presence that first time in the school playground, she made it her mission to keep going back to search for him. She hoped maybe she could find a way to help him to cross over, to find peace. But at every turn, she was met with Jake stopping her. She'd search the woods and instead find Jake, who, like a spider, would lull her to the centre of his web and play with her, mauling and threatening, scaring and scarring her. And he seemed to enjoy it too. Like he had with Natalie, taunting and touching with such misogynistic malevolent tendencies. She had no doubt he had raped Billy's lover, if not other women too. His wife for example. How had she survived?

Natalie's head ached. She rolled over towards her nightstand and grabbed the water bottle she'd put there a few days back. Lid unscrewed, she gulped it down until she had finished, and then felt the urgency to use the rest room. She stumbled out of bed, her eyes sore and swollen from all of the tears she'd cried. As she made her way down the hallway, a note on the sideboard caught her eye. It was from Helena. Natalie hadn't heard her come home, and yet the note proved she had. And then left again, by the looks of it. She was heading into Maramanui to run some errands and check some care facilities. She wasn't waiting for Natalie's approval, despite the money being entrusted to her. It was the most proactive she'd ever known her mother to be, and the uncharitable thought hit her: what was Helena planning to get out of all of this?

After cleaning up, Natalie checked in on her grandmother, knocking on the door first.

"Grams? Are you awake?"

There was a noise from inside the room, so Natalie opened the door and peered in.

"Hello, sweetheart. Did you sleep well?"

Her grandmother was sitting up in bed, a table tray with a plate with toast crusts and an almost empty glass of orange juice, lay on the bed beside her. Someone had pulled the curtains, and the sun was already streaming into the room. Most startling was that Grams looked as lively and lucid as ever. Natalie searched around the room for the time, before her eyes came to rest on the alarm clock on the bedside table. It was well past nine in the morning. Natalie had slept in a lot longer than she had expected.

"Hi, Grams. How are you feeling today?" Natalie answered, leaning over to give her a peck on the forehead.

"I'm a box of fluffy ducks," she said giving a wide smile. "Your mother was up early."

"So I see." Natalie scanned the room again.

"She's gone into town to do some errands for me."

Natalie narrowed her eyes.

"Oh, don't give me that look. It's time I went into a home. I'm fine with it. I truly am." She patted the edge of the bed for Natalie to take a seat.

"You remember us discussing it last night?" Natalie asked.

"Yes. The important stuff, I remember."

Natalie wasn't sure how she felt about that. "I read your journals. You could have told me all this years ago."

Grams's smile dropped. "I could have." She took Natalie's hand in her own. "But just like you've been trying to protect me by keeping me here, I've been trying to protect you by dealing with things on my own."

"Things? Like ... Jake?" Natalie whispered.

Grams's face got serious.

"Grams, I know you've been trying to help Gavin, but he's still there. At school. He's haunting one of the students in my class."

"He's a good boy," Grams protested. "I can't work out why he's still around."

"Maybe he just needs the truth to come out." Natalie let the statement hang there between them. She had no idea if that was what he needed. It was her best hope. Somewhere between reading the journals and her fitful sleep, the beginning of a plan had started to form. It was far-fetched. Absurd. But if something was somehow keeping both Gavin and Jake earthbound then she needed to try and do something to release them, send them on their way. Gavin needed to move on to another place, and that, Natalie was sure, would in turn help Cole move on and make friends. And Jake … she didn't care where he went but he needed to leave her family alone. And the only thing Natalie could think of that was holding these two spirits to the school, was the lies. O'Regan lies. Arthur's lack of accountability with starting the fire. The denial of Jake having murdered Grams's brother. Maybe "the truth will set you free" was more than a pithy idiom.

Grams's eyes were watery, and Natalie felt a stab of guilt that this was one of the few times Grams seemed completely coherent, and she was ruining it by bringing up the past.

"Grams. I have a plan. And I think I need you there."

Grams nodded.

"Like, really need you there," Natalie said. "I need you to stay with me, to not get lost inside … your mind," she finished.

Grams silently nodded again.

"Do you think you'll be up for a little bit of walking?" Natalie asked.

"It's my mind that's going, not my legs," she said with spark, and Natalie felt a weight lift.

She had no idea if what she was planning had any chance of working, or if at the end of the day it was going to make her look even crazier than she already had the budding reputation of being. But she had promised Riki she would try to help. And even if Grams and Helena got their way and Grams went into a home, she couldn't be sure she wouldn't go walking again or that Jake wouldn't terrorise her again.

Plus, Natalie had her own demons to exorcise, and that too, required the truth to be told.

CHAPTER 34

Natalie

It took most of the day to organise. Victoria was immediately on board and took over most of the phone calls for Natalie. There had been the risk that not everyone would be available, but now that Natalie had made the plan, and Grams was more coherent than not, she didn't want to allow any opportunity for things to change or for her to lose her nerve. It went against everything Natalie had fought so hard for: her independence. The truth was, she needed to cover all bases, which required a lot of people. People whom she'd have to let her guard down around. And what she was asking of them in turn was huge.

To get everyone there, different people needed to be told different things. Particularly Arthur. And although Natalie thought she could hear Victoria cringe on the other end of the phone when she said Arthur needed to be there, Victoria made it happen anyway. Not even Arthur O'Regan could say no to Victoria when she was in a certain mood. Liam would have to be there too. Natalie wasn't sure how much Victoria had told him. Despite Natalie's debate, Victoria had insisted that Riley be there. Natalie had called Riki and filled him in as much as she could over the phone. He had said he believed her that Cole was being haunted, and thankfully, that at least hadn't changed. Natalie wanted Cole to be there too. She was scared that without him, Gavin might not show. And if he didn't show, how would they be able to help him move on?

Helena had not been invited. Grams and Natalie agreed that she seemed unaffected by everything of that sort. Helena didn't seem to have inherited the ability to see the dead like Natalie and Grams had. And as she was out visiting retirement homes anyway, it was best to leave her out of it. And Natalie was relieved. Her mother could be like a bull in a china shop, and what they were planning to do was already likely to be emotionally charged.

Victoria, Liam and Riley were already there when Natalie pulled up to the school with Grams. They were standing by the caretaker's shed visible from the car park. Natalie felt her hackles go up. It didn't matter that she'd seen Liam a million times since Anna's death. A pool of hatred still stirred in her blood on seeing him. And Riley ... whatever spirits had haunted Te Tapu School had primarily kept to themselves until she arrived. Victoria had admitted Riley too could see the dead. If that were true, why was she so attached to Liam? Surely, she'd have seen Jake too? Granted, Natalie couldn't see him now, which was fine with her. Yet as often as she'd seen him hanging around Liam, the way Riley clung to his arm, she must have noticed Jake's attachment to him.

"This won't work if you're joining them with anger in your heart, sweetheart," Grams said, studying Natalie's face.

"He killed Anna," Natalie whispered, "and just like his father and his grandfather, he gets to go free."

"You don't know that, and right now you need to focus on the task at hand. We're here to help Gavin and his young living friend first. Then we'll deal with Jake ..."

Grams shivered involuntarily in saying his name, and Natalie couldn't blame her.

"... and we'll go from there. Jake feeds on anger though. He'll use it against you."

Natalie could believe it, but if there was a magical way to forgive the man who killed her soulmate, she didn't know it.

Concern clouded Gram's face.

They got out of the car, and although Grams was much sturdier on her legs than the day before, Natalie held her arm and walked with her. Riley sent a weak smile in Natalie's direction and involuntarily, Natalie scowled. She couldn't do this. Couldn't play all nicey-nice knowing her relationship with Liam.

"Natalie," Liam said by way of greeting, his face remaining stoic.

"Liam," she replied, fire leaping in her veins. Grams gave her arm a hard squeeze.

"Riley, Liam, this is Natalie's grandmother, Maggie," Victoria stepped in where Natalie couldn't. They all said their greetings, and Natalie wondered how much Victoria had shared with Liam and Riley. How was any of this going to play out? And how much more awkward was it going to be come Monday's staff meeting? There was also the distinct possibility that nothing would happen.

"Is Arthur coming?" Grams asked, and Natalie could feel her grandmother tense with the question. If Liam was Natalie's nemesis, it seemed Arthur was Grams's.

"He said he'll be here," Liam said.

"And you trust him?" Grams asked, making Natalie's jaw drop a little.

Liam shook his head, and Natalie's stomach dropped. Without him ... He was key.

Maybe catching the concern on Natalie's face, Victoria quickly responded. "I'll be driving down there and picking him up myself if I need to. He doesn't know what this is about; I thought it was best this way. But I threatened to make his life insufferable if he didn't get his butt down here."

The mood lightened somewhat. Victoria could be formidable when she wanted to be.

Next to arrive was Riki. He pulled up in his ute. For a moment Natalie couldn't see Cole, and she was suddenly scared it might all turn out to be a waste of time. But after a moment, the passenger side door opened, and a little figure dropped down onto the gravel road.

Riki caught her eye, and Natalie's cheeks flushed while her lips stretched into a smile. Her heart sped up a little in her chest. Yeesh. It was horribly disconcerting the effect he had on her. Yet at the same time, it was nice to take a breather from the tension and drama she wore the rest of the time.

"This is Riki and his son Cole, whom I've told you about," Victoria whispered to Liam and Riley.

Natalie couldn't bring herself to look at anyone else, her eyes were locked on Riki's. When she did glance down, she noticed Cole – now holding his dad's hand – kept his eyes on his feet as he walked. Natalie wondered what Riki had told him.

Riki introduced himself and Cole and went about shaking Grams, Riley and Liam's hands.

After the brief introductions, Victoria took charge, as she was apt to do. "Cole, maybe you could go play in the playground for a little bit while the adults have a bit of a chat."

Cole glanced up at his dad, eyes wide.

Riki gave him a smile and nod. "Off you go," he said. "I'll let you know when you're needed."

Cole ran off towards the closest swing, and Natalie was reminded of the entries in Grams's notebook, where she'd first met ghost-Gavin.

Victoria grabbed a fold-out chair she'd left leaning against the shed wall. After opening it, she gestured towards Grams, who gratefully accepted it. Something about Grams's eyes had Natalie worried. There was a transparency in them that she'd seen before when Grams's mind started to unravel.

An awkward silence fell over the group, and suddenly Natalie was overwhelmed with doubts. Could it really be so simple that the truth would fix everything? And if it didn't? She glanced over at Cole who was swinging back and forth, feet kicking into the air. Poor kid, she thought. He shouldn't be involved, and yet Natalie didn't know how else to get Gavin to appear. Cole was their best bet.

Riki was the first to speak. "I'm not altogether sure what we're supposed to do exactly?" He shuffled his feet, locking eyes with Natalie.

Natalie tried to find the words. All she had told him was she thought she might have a way of helping Cole by helping Gavin pass on. Now it all seemed ridiculous. How could a sharing of hearts help the dead? What had she been thinking?

A cloud drifted over the face of the sun, making the temperature dip slightly, and Natalie prepared herself. Everyone was on edge. She could feel it. When Grams rubbed her arms, Natalie moved behind her chair and rubbed them for her. "Are you okay?" she whispered.

"He's here," Grams whispered back.

The hairs on the back of Natalie's neck rose. Her eyes darted around the group and over to where Cole still swung back and forth, back and forth on the swing.

A dull thrum of a vehicle getting closer drew their attention to the car park, but the corner of the building and Riki's ute blocked their view. It didn't matter. Natalie knew who had pulled up, and judging by the tension in the air, so did the others.

"Right. Well, it sounds like Arthur's arrived," Victoria said. "I haven't told him any specifics. He doesn't know why he's here. Best you leave the talking to me." Victoria had donned her principal voice again.

Riley pulled closer to Liam, and Liam stood up a little bit straighter. It wasn't a secret that Liam and his father had a fraught relationship. Anna had told her the two fought a lot. Arthur had a nasty streak, and a big bone of contention was that Arthur wanted Liam to take over the family business, which Liam wanted nothing to do with.

Gossip had been rife through Te Tapu when Arthur had a stroke and Liam had returned to help him.

"Who's Arthur?" Riki asked. Natalie had done her best to give him the basics of what had happened, but even that had been a lot.

"My dad," Liam said.

"The man who started the fire that killed Gavin," Natalie said, earning a severe look from Victoria and a narrowing of eyes from Liam.

Well, that was what they were here for, wasn't it? The truth?

A slamming of a car door preceded the slow hobbling of an elderly man with a cane. Arthur rounded the building and on seeing them froze. His face drew into a scowl.

Victoria marched over to him, and from their animated faces Natalie saw words fly between them, too low to catch. Natalie stood up to her full height beside Grams, and Riki joined her side. Riley whispered something to Liam, but Liam stood stoic, staring in the direction of his father.

Whatever Victoria said must have won out, because Arthur continued his way towards their small group, with Victoria at his side.

Victoria made quick introductions for Natalie's and Riki's sake, and Arthur mumbled something in response, looking at neither of them. This wasn't her first-time meeting Arthur. He was now the king pin of Te Tapu, the oldest surviving O'Regan. She'd had a run-in with him at Anna's funeral. He'd refused her attendance. Had two goons in fact act as bouncers, not allowing her into the church. She'd yelled and screamed and made a hell of a racket. A rush of anger flared in her chest, and she did her best to push it down, for the moment at least, when Grams grabbed her arm.

Grams pulled herself to a standing position, and the temperature dropped another degree or two. A small breeze made the limbs of the feijoa tree overhanging the shed rustle against the corrugated iron roof.

"Arthur," Grams said, her voice stony.

Arthur glared at her. "What am I doing here?" he growled at Victoria.

"We're making amends," Victoria replied matter-of-factly. "There have been too many lies in this community for far too long, and they've hurt people. *Are* hurting people," she corrected herself.

"For fuck's sake ..." He pulled a pack of cigarettes from his front shirt pocket. Picking his walking stick up and tucking it under his arm he went about pulling out a smoke and a lighter he'd stashed in the box. He put the cigarette to his lips, shielded the end with one hand and flicked his lighter. A flame sprung to life and licked at the end of his cigarette. Natalie watched his every motion with increasing tension and anger. He put the lighter back in the packet and returned it to his shirt pocket.

A rhythmic creaking sound gradually drew their attention to the playground. Two swings, side by side, swung wildly back and forth, their occupants gone. The sun had well and truly disappeared. Concrete-coloured clouds crowded what had once been a perfect blue sky.

"Cole!" Riki said, panic flashing across his face.

"There's not enough of a breeze ..." Riley whispered half to herself.

No shit, Sherlock, Natalie thought. Victoria had filled her in on Riley's connection with Gwen. She'd started this whole thing, digging into the past. Before Riley, Natalie didn't remember there being any vengeful spirits causing havoc. The breeze hadn't set the second swing in motion. Gavin had shown up just as they'd hoped. Only now neither child was there.

Riki took off in a sprint across the field towards the playground.

"Stay here," Natalie said to Grams and took off after him. Footsteps followed close behind her, but she didn't bother looking. She knew who it was.

"Cole?!" Riki called out, on reaching the playground, his head whipping this way and that, searching for him.

"Cole?" Natalie added her voice to the mix, trying to keep the panic out of it.

Liam went around searching under the tower and climbing the ladder, knowing from his experience caretaking of all the places kids liked to hide.

This wasn't supposed to happen, Natalie thought. Gavin had said the caretaker's shed was where he felt safe, it was why they had congregated there. She'd thought that once they were all there, Cole could help encourage Gavin to show up, and maybe, somehow, Arthur, Vicky, even Grams, could apologise, do what they needed to help the little boy move on. She'd even tried to track down JP, but neither she nor Vicky had had any luck.

"Cole!" Riki's voice rang out against a breeze.

A stabbing of fear pricked in the pit of her stomach. If something happened to Cole ...

"Cole!" Natalie called out again. Where would he go? Where would Gavin take him?

The realisation hit her with a punch.

The rest of the group were making their way over to join them. Victoria led the group. Riley supported Grams with one arm looped around hers. A flash of anger rose up towards Riley, and Natalie had to remind herself Grams could be stubborn when she wanted to be.

And if Grams was right, anger was only going to make things worse. It explained the sudden worsening of weather.

To her surprise, Arthur wandered slowly behind.

"The woods," Natalie cried out to Riki. "Gavin likes to play in the woods."

Riki's face paled. The terror in his eyes made a lump form in her throat.

"No!" a voice called out from behind. Grams had broken away from Riley and was moving as fast as she could towards them.

"It's not safe," she said. "He'll be there!" Grams's eyes locked on to Natalie's, and she knew her grandmother wasn't talking about Gavin.

Riki didn't, and he took one look at the two of them, turned and ran towards the fence line separating the school boundary from the woods.

"This way," Liam yelled at him, redirecting him behind the pool. The make out spot Grams had described in her journals had fallen out of popularity recently, but when Natalie had been at school, it had still been used as a sort of hang out. Liam was headed towards that. In Grams's time, the pool hadn't been there. Had it been, the classroom might have survived. Gavin might have survived.

"Natalie!" Her grandmother was upon her, she gripped her forearm with such vice, Natalie let out a small squeal. "You can't go in there!" she said. "You have MacKenzie blood too. He'll find you."

Natalie shivered. He'd found her before. But Grams didn't know that. And maybe he would find her again, but Cole being here had been her idea.

Riki and Liam had already disappeared. She had to help.

"I'm sorry, Grams. Stay here with Riley." She gave Riley a look. Though they might not like each other, what other choice did she have? Riley gave her a small nod. Natalie dislodged her arm from her grandmother's grip.

Grams turned around, shooting daggers at Arthur with her eyes. "This is your fault!" she spat, and a gust of wind rose up shaking the gingko tree near them with a fury. Victoria stepped between Maggie and Arthur as Riley put an arm around Maggie's shoulders, trying to calm her. Natalie turned on her heel and followed where she knew the men had gone.

There wasn't much to differentiate between the school boundary and the wood. A rickety wire fence with wooden posts spanning the whole length of the school on that one side. She could hear Liam and Riki in the distance yelling Cole's name and thrashing through bush. The wind was getting stronger, and Natalie's hair whipped around her face. Brushing it from her eyes, she set about climbing the fence.

MacKenzie blood. If Jake was so intent on harming those with MacKenzie blood like Grams had alluded too, why was Gavin scared of him, the shadow man? Natalie followed the trampled path which she knew led to the grotto. She and her friends used to hang out there sometimes, before people considered her a freak.

It was getting harder and harder to hear Riki and Liam above the breeze. The long grass made way for the actual woods, and Natalie found it was difficult to follow where Liam and Riki had gone.

"Cole?" she called out, cupping her hands to her mouth. "Gavin?" She cringed even as she said his name. "Where the hell are you?" she muttered, gazing around. Behind her stood the school. If she walked far enough to her right, she'd end up at the road, to her left, the woods extended for miles, and not too far ahead was the glade.

A child's chuckle made Natalie spin around. She couldn't pinpoint where it had come from; it seemed to be moving all around her but nowhere at the same time.

"Cole? Gavin?" she tried again. The tall treetops swung as the wind gusted. A deep grumbling rumble made Natalie's heart jump into her throat. Thunder.

Oh shit! Don't let there be lightning!

Pinecones, needles, dried leaves and branches covered the ground. Lightning didn't often strike the woods, but all of Natalie's senses told her to forget whatever was the norm. As it was, she was trying to hunt down a ghost boy and his very real living friend, with a possible murderous dark entity out to hurt her and anyone related to her.

"Cole? Gavin?" she tried again. She couldn't hear Liam or Riki at all now. God, she hoped they'd stuck together. Riki was new to these parts, so getting lost was a very real possibility. A sudden realisation gut-punched her – how safe was Riki with Liam right now? Liam: Anna's murderer and Jake's grandson.

The thought propelled Natalie towards the glade with heightened urgency, calling the boys' names over and over as she did so. Nothing. Above her, the treetops whipped themselves into more of a frenzy.

The glade opened up before her. It hadn't changed much since she had last been there. Wooden stumps serving as stools were scattered around the place. The low table with rusted metal legs and a wooden top was still there along with some rubbish: a rotting comic book page by the looks of it, a chippy packet and a plastic drink bottle half buried by dirt and pine needles.

The boys weren't there. It was too much to hope for. Had they been there, Liam and Riki would have had them by now.

From the corner of her eye, she saw movement from behind a tree. "Hello?" she called out.

Laughter, more laughter. "Cole? Is that you?"

A crunching of leaves sent her wheeling to the other direction. Another flash of motion close by was followed by chuckling.

Natalie's heart raced. It wasn't Cole. This was Gavin. She knew it.

"Gavin?" she called out, trying to keep her voice steady. "Gavin, you need to help us find Cole." Natalie glanced around her, searching for any clue as to where either boy was. A deep rumbling from above drew her attention and then erupted into an earth-shaking boom, making her jump and close her eyes.

On opening them, she sucked in a breath.

He was here. Had he been alive, she could have touched him. The little boy stared at her. His brown hair hung across his forehead. One large brown eye peered at her. The other one was thankfully hidden by his hair. His face pulled into a lopsided smile. Gavin giggled, and Natalie's breath came in shallow pants. She tried to steady her heart, not wanting to startle him. Slowly, she crouched so she was more his height.

"Gavin?" she whispered softly

He giggled again.

"I need to find your friend Cole. Can you show me where he is?"

Gavin tilted his head to the side and studied her, and Natalie tried to stem the nausea creeping up her throat. No child deserved to die the way he had. His burns were still red and festering.

"Safe," he said. His mouth never moved; it was as if the word had simply implanted itself in her mind. "He's safe. No bad man." Gavin continued to stare at her.

"Where?" Natalie asked, willing him to tell her something specific. Once she knew Cole was really safe, then she'd find a way to help Gavin. He shouldn't be here.

"No bad man," he repeated. "No fire."

No fire? Natalie didn't understand. Was he thinking about how he died?

"There's no fire anymore. You're safe," she told him

"No!" he said, facing her straight on. "No, no, no! Bad man is here. Bad man is here!" His voice rose, growing all around her, and the tree-tops lashed at each other with even more ferocity as his voice rose to a scream. Natalie covered her ears with her hands; it was too much. She felt like her ear drums were going to rupture. Squeezing her eyes shut, she willed him to stop. Her head felt like it was about to split open, her own scream joining in, and another rumble of thunder rolled out across the skies. A flash of light painted the inside of her eyelids red, and she flung them open. Before her, little red embers drifted down from the sky. Her eyes followed where they'd come from. The top of one of the tall beech trees was glowing red. Lightning. Lightning must have struck; just has she had feared. The upmost branches of the trees were singed and smoking, sizzling as foliage and small branches drifted down to the forest floor, alight.

Oh shit! Oh shit!

Riki and Liam were God knew where in the wood, and Cole ... Cole must be back at school. It was the first thing she thought of when Gavin said Cole was safe and there wasn't any fire. Gavin thought he'd be safe under the classroom away from the fire. Is that where he'd hidden Cole?

She rifled in her back pocket for her phone. Her fingers shook as she searched her contacts for Riki's number. She had to warn him that the forest might be on fire. Would he believe her? Would he trust that Cole was back at school even though she had no proof?

Her hypothesising didn't matter. There was no reception. How was that even possible? She was barely a hundred metres from the school. The men on the other hand, she didn't know where they were. Please, God, let them be okay, she prayed. She might not like Liam. Hated him in fact. But there had already been too much death. What if he came back like his grandfather? She shook the thought from her mind. Unless he was somehow behind the change in weather, there hadn't been any sign of Jake.

Right now, she had to make a decision.

More embers floated down from the sky. One burnt a hole in her T-shirt, and she slapped at it with her hand. Others landed near her feet, and she stomped on them to put them out.

Who was in more danger right now? Cole? Or Riki and Liam? Her mind screamed at her to decide. Gavin had said Cole was safe. Could she trust him? He had thought he'd be safe hiding from the fire, and yet here he was. But Riki, she had no idea where Riki was. She cupped a hand to her mouth, summoning the loudest volume she could muster. "Riki!" she cried into the thick encircling of trees. "Liam!"

Another gust of wind sent the tree tops thrashing against each other, sparks now igniting from one treetop to the next.

Oh, God. She had to make a decision.

Before she could even move, a supernatural gust of air picked her up off her feet and threw her against the trunk of a rimu tree, sending a sharp pain through her shoulder and reverberating through her arm. Black dots danced before her eyes as her vision blurred. Her chest heaved for air, having been sucked right out of her lungs. What the fuck had happened?

Finally able to suck in a lungful of air, her vision cleared and her blood chilled. Less than two metres from where she landed at the foot of a tree stood the semblance of a man. At first, a dark cloud of swirling energy, a leering smile splitting his face, and red eyes that sucked the breath right out of her again. He took a step towards her, and Natalie shrank further against the tree. His image morphed, becoming more human like, until he looked as he may have when living. A tall, dark-haired man wearing pants and a dress shirt rolled at the arms. He might have even been considered handsome in his day but for his cold dark eyes locked on hers, and a sneer that contorted his face. His ugliness, she realised, was from within. He emanated it. Anger, and loathing, and ... evil. This, she realised, was Jake O'Regan.

CHAPTER 35

Maggie

Another deep rumble rolled overhead. Thunder. A storm was definitely on its way.

Maggie's anger had given her energy, and for a moment she felt like she was nineteen again, not sixty-nine. "This is your fault!" Her words were thorned, and Arthur stumbled under the weight of them.

"What the hell are you even talking about?" The corner of his mouth bent into a scowl.

"We're not doing this now," Vicky said, stepping in between them, hands up as if ready to hold them apart. "There'll be time enough to get everything out in the open once the boy's been found."

"Maggie, why don't we go sit down," a small voice said from behind her. Riley gently touched her arm. "I'm sure it won't take them long to find Cole, and then Natalie will be back ..."

"What's the big deal anyway," Arthur growled. "So the boy wandered off. It's what boys do." He took another puff of his smoke, exhaling a blue cloud that made Maggie cough involuntarily.

Vicky moved fully in front of Maggie then, back to her, using her body to get Arthur to move away. Anger burned in Maggie's chest, and she was ready to blow. She could feel it. And despite everything, she suspected her old friend did too.

"Come on, Arthur." Vicky gently tried to cajole him away.

A gust of wind took Maggie by surprise, and Riley grabbed her arm again to steady her.

"Please, Maggie. We can wait inside," she pleaded, her eyes were round. Frightened. She kept glancing around as if expecting someone else to join their group. Vicky had told her about some of Riley's experiences. She'd connected with Gwen, the woman who was in love with Maggie's late brother, Billy. If Vicky was to be believed, she'd even seen Billy a couple of times. Somehow, she'd reunited them in death. It had been enough to let both souls finally find their peace. But what did peace look like for Gavin? No one knew where his family had disappeared to. He was just a kid. Did he even know he was dead? And what about Jake? Jake who had tormented her from beyond the grave since the fire. Whom she suspected had been tormenting her granddaughter, Natalie as well. And this man, this man here, Jake's son ... he had lit the fire, set everything into motion.

The wind raged, making Riley cling to her to stop her from toppling. Maggie's hair whipped around her face, and through it she saw Vicky, her hands up against Arthur's chest seeking shelter.

Thunder rolled across the sky again, ending with what felt like a sonic boom. Maggie's heart leapt into her throat. Before Arthur had arrived, the sun had been out. It had been a warm, sunny day, but now, now a storm was brewing.

"Let's get inside," Riley called out, her voice fighting against the wind.

Maggie ignored her, and with all the volume she could muster she yelled at Arthur: "You started the fire! You killed the boy!"

Arthur pushed Vicky aside, and the wind backed off slightly, allowing them all to catch their breath.

"What the hell are you talking about? You're losing your mind, woman!"

Vicky stood up straighter, then, and Riley inhaled sharply beside Maggie.

"You listen here, Arthur O'Regan! You don't go talking to my friend like that. I told you it was time to make amends, and that starts with the *truth*! We did kill that boy. You lit the fire, and we covered it up!" Vicky shook, her finger jabbing Arthur in the chest. The wind died back down as if Vicky had sucker punched it.

"What boy?" Arthur shook his head vehemently; his forehead furrowed with confusion before realisation shifted his features. His face drained of colour, and he grasped his walking stick with two hands, trying to counteract the shaking that had overcome his legs.

"Inside!" Riley interrupted. "We need to get inside."

The sky suddenly lit up. A sheet of lightning haloed the dark clouds, which had closed in around them. The air was electric, menacing, unnatural. She could feel it. As Riley dragged her by the arm towards the nearest classroom, Maggie cocked her head, scouring the sky. A fork of lightning this time hit above the woods.

"It was an accident," Arthur mumbled. "It happened so long ago …"

Maggie couldn't look at him. Something wasn't right. A different sort of darkness was closing in now. And it wasn't with Arthur; it was out there in the woods. Riley was still tugging on her arm, and Maggie stumbled after her, yet her eyes were glued to the treeline where her granddaughter and the men had taken off to.

Distantly, she recognised Vicky was berating Arthur for playing with his lighter. They should have known better. Then they lied. They lied. They lied ....

Those words swirled in her mind. They had all lied. All of them. Maggie too. She'd covered up to protect her friend. They'd not been in the woods, she'd told the police and the fire service. They'd been at the school, yes. Just passing through on the way to the orchard. When they caught sight of the smoke, they'd made their way out to the road where Mr O'Regan found them. To Maggie's knowledge Mr O'Regan had corroborated their story even though he'd found them much further down the road than outside the school. But then, hadn't Mr O'Regan himself told them to say nothing, in front of the fire station?

And when they'd been interviewed, had they seen the boy, the little Jenkin's boy? They'd shaken their heads. All of them. They said no. Mrs Jenkins had heard them. Her hand clasped around the fist of her little girl, tears streaming down her face. Maggie didn't ever think she'd be able to forget the look of betrayal. They're lying, she screamed. They saw us walking through the school, towards the playground. It was too late. They'd said their story. *They* were at school, not Mrs Jenkin's and her kids. And there were four of them against one distraught woman and a toddler. Their story was believed because it had come from an O'Regan. Because Arthur had said so, and the O'Regans were always to be believed. Always.

They had lied.

Maggie stumbled as another bolt of lightning flared across the sky above the trees. This time, it hit. Sparks like fireworks lit the sky, and the tops of the tree spires glowed red.

Riley must have seen the same thing. For a split second, she let go of Maggie's arm, and that was all she needed. Suddenly Maggie was running. No longer an elderly woman, no longer a grandmother, but a girl of nineteen again, only this time she was running towards the forest, towards the fire, not away from it. This time, to save someone.

CHAPTER 36

Maggie

Though it was different than she remembered it, she knew where to go. Voices, distant echoes, resounded behind her, but she didn't turn back. This time would be different. This time she'd win.

The wind picked up her hair and tangled it. She climbed over the fence without a pause, limbs moving on adrenalin, living out her many dreams of being in a much younger body, only this time she wasn't being chased; she was the predator. The smoke made her nose and eyes itch. She couldn't tell if it was real smoke or the remnants of her nightmares wafting into her waking life.

She kept running, thrashing through the long grass and brush into the woods where branches and twigs lashed at her arms and legs and face. Still, she ran. Her lungs heaved with each breath, not used to such a workout. She was driven purely by the knowledge of two things: Jake was close, and Natalie needed her.

She heard a voice, a boy's voice, his words floating just out of reach: "Hurry. Bad man. Bad man. Hide. Hide."

She slowed a little. She could feel him. Jake. His energy stole the breath from her lungs more so than the run. He was close. There was crackling too. Crackling and popping and a choking ashy haziness coating the world.

Fire. The trees were on fire!

"Natalie?!" she tried yelling, her voice raspy, too quiet to be heard. "Natalie?" she tried again.

She rounded a tree into a clearing and saw them. Her granddaughter, balled up against a tree, one arm hanging lower than the other, her face so pale, so scared, and towering above her, the man who had tormented her in her dreams over and over again. Jake.

"Get away from her!" Maggie screamed.

"Run, Grams. Get out of here!" Natalie yelled, but Maggie ignored her.

Her focus was entirely on the monster slowly turning around to face her. He grinned, and Maggie stayed herself from shrinking backwards.

"Two," he drawled, taking a step towards her. "Seems fair. Two lives for one O'Regan."

"Go to hell!" Maggie retorted as more white ash and red embers floated down from the sky like swirling confetti. Maggie angled her face upwards; the branches above were on fire, and the wind served to fan the flames. Maggie coughed, her lungs sore from the run and the smoke.

"You know, you look a little like him. Older. Weaker ..." He drew his words out, almost slurred them, and took another step closer to Maggie.

Now what? Over his shoulder, Maggie could see Natalie trying to drag herself to a standing position. It wasn't just her shoulder injured. Her ankle appeared hurt too. Maggie needed to keep his attention on her, not her granddaughter. And think! Think Maggie, she prompted herself. The woods are on fire, and you need to get out of here.

"You killed, Billy, isn't that enough?" Maggie yelled at him.

Natalie picked up a broken branch and was using it to lean on.

"Wasn't that enough?" she repeated.

"I. Didn't. Kill. Billy!" he said, each word making the wind whip up into a stronger frenzy. The trees to her left were on fire now. The heat was sucking the remaining air from her lungs and searing her exposed skin.

"You did." Maggie's throat was raw, her voice croaking as she said the words. She coughed, her lungs wheezing and gasping for breath. "You killed him. You raped his girl. And you're jealous," she said between splutters. She didn't really know what she was saying; she just wanted to keep his focus, give Natalie a chance to escape and keep her own mind from wandering off.

"Jealous?" he said toying with the word. His palms closed into fists and then opened again.

Another boom of thunder made Maggie squeal. God, if it would just rain right now. At least get the fire under control. It was spreading. Before long, it would block their way back to the school.

"Because even dead, they're together again, and you have no one!" Maggie spat at him, taking another step back. Victoria had told her.

Riley had seen it. When she and Liam had hung the plaque on the caretaker's shed, she'd seen them. And they were at peace. Love prevailed.

At that moment, Natalie took hold of the branch in both hands, holding it like a bat. She swung it at Jake. It cut through the air, cut through Jake's midsection, and Natalie lost her balance and fell to the ground, crying out in pain.

Jake cackled, a deep, growling laugh, which combined again with the thunder overhead.

Around them, trees crackled and popped while the air fizzed, the heat getting stronger and stronger.

Jack ignored Natalie. "I. Didn't. Kill. Billy." He laughed again. Louder. The wind roared.

"Natalie!" a voice called out. Breaking through the woods behind Natalie two figures formed in the smoke. One coughing and wheezing. It was Riki, Natalie's friend. And a second later Maggie recognised Liam. No, no, no. It was too dangerous with him here! She wanted to yell at Liam to get away. None of them would survive if Jake got his hands on Liam. But she couldn't breathe, the smoke was suffocating her, and a pain in her chest was growing.

"What the fuck?!" Riki took in Jake's form. He could see him. God, that meant Jake was getting stronger.

Bent over coughing, Maggie tried to get his attention, waving her arms at him.

"Get Grams!" Natalie yelled at Riki. Maggie saw his eyes land on Natalie's form on the ground, then bounce to her, then Jake.

Liam came up behind them, his eyes also taking them all in.

"I didn't kill your brother," the monster spat at her, as another pain jolted her chest. "That whore of his killed him." He laughed again, and the sky flashed white as more lightning shot across the sky and the flames rose higher.

"He's right," Liam yelled over the din. "Gwen killed Billy. She killed your brother."

Another lie, Maggie thought. Another lie. Or else, why hadn't anyone told her? Her chest contracted again; her lungs refused to work. Natalie, she had to get to Natalie. But the darkness was too swift, too strong, it blacked out the flames, the fire, the noise. Everything.

CHAPTER 37

Natalie

"No!" Natalie screamed, trying desperately to scramble to her feet. The pain from her shoulder made her want to pass out, and the ache in her ankle did not prove much better. But Grams, she needed to get to Grams.

Strong arms grabbed her from behind and hauled her to her feet, and she coughed and gasped, retching as she fought for breath. The smoke filled her lungs and the heat from the flames scorched her throat.

"I've got you. We'll get you out of here."

It was Riki. He wrapped an arm around her waist and let her lean on him. She needed to get to Grams, who had collapsed, but he was taking her away from her.

"No," she cried. "We have to help her!"

"We will!" He nearly dragged her as she fought against him, and then she realised what was happening. Jake was focused on Liam. He'd grabbed his attention. Riki was trying to move her out of eyesight of Jake, making his way around the perimeter of the glade, staying far enough away that despite the searing heat, the flames at least wouldn't reach them.

Every step sent a jarring pain through her ankle and shoulder, and Natalie clenched her teeth against the rising nausea. They needed to get out of there. Needed to get Grams to safety, away from Jake.

Jake's back was towards them now. Another couple of metres and they'd be at Grams's side. Liam had been slowly moving, keeping Jake's eyes on him, away from her and Riki. She almost felt gratitude towards him. Anna had loved him, remember? The thought rose up. Yes, but then he'd killed her, she reminded her conscience, and she squealed as another jolt of pain coursed through her shoulder.

"Almost there," Riki said, his head close to hers.

"You know who I am?" Liam was asking Jake; his voice barely audible against the roar of the fire and wind.

"You're an O'Regan," Jake replied, a tinge of humour in his voice, and Natalie's blood chilled despite the suffocating heat.

"I'm your grandson!" Liam yelled back.

Natalie flinched. What was he doing? She'd seen Jake attach himself to Liam before. Why was he inviting that now?

They reached Grams's side, and Riki asked Natalie if she could stand on her own for a moment. Nodding, she extricated herself from his arms. Her ankle hurt like a mother, but she took her weight on her good foot to keep her balance as she cradled her busted arm.

Riki checked for vitals, called Maggie's name, felt for a pulse and leaned in close to feel for breathing.

Please, Grams, please be alive, Natalie pleaded with no one in particular. If there was a God, now would be a good time to show themself.

Riki scooped Grams up like cradling a baby. "She's breathing," he said turning away to cough. "But we need to get out of here."

Good plan, but Natalie wasn't sure how far she could get on her ankle.

She looked over her shoulder at Liam and Jake. Liam's hands were balled into fists, his shoulders tense. He was angry. Didn't he know anger would only fuel the monster? He was going to make things worse. And then what? She had to help him. The thought hit her with a gut-punch. She wasn't sure where it had come from, but with all certainty she knew.

Riki needed to get Grams out of there and find his son, and she ... she had to stay.

"Go!" Natalie turned back to Riki. "You need to leave. I'll follow behind. I'll be okay."

"No. Not going to happen," Riki yelled back. Sweat rolled down his face.

"I think I know where Cole is. He'll be hiding under my classroom. Or else by the caretaker's shed. Gavin said he's somewhere safe. Go!" she urged him on.

A million emotions whipped across Riki's face. His mouth moved as if to argue, and then looking down at the frail woman he held in his arms, then back up at Natalie and to Liam and Jake, he made his decision.

"You're going to follow, right?" He waited barely half a second. "Right?!"

She nodded. She would; she just had to do something first. Anna saw something good in Liam, enough to love him and worry about hurting him. Maybe Natalie had been wrong; maybe Anna's death really had been an accident. Maybe if she could believe that, she could forgive. And maybe that would kill the rift between the O'Regans and the Mackenzies.

"Liam," she yelled, pivoting to face him, putting as much weight on her back foot as she dared. Could she really with just a few words let go of a lifetime of hatred towards the O'Regans? No. Probably not. But maybe she could let go of a little.

Liam turned to face her. His jaw dropped. "Get out of here!" he yelled.

"You loved Anna!" Natalie yelled at him, choking on her name as she said it.

"What are you on about?"

Jake turned to her. His dark eyes locked on her face, confusion tattooing his brow. She could see the family resemblance. God, what was she doing?

If Riley had been telling the truth and somehow Billy and Gwen got to find their happily-ever-after after Gwen had killed him, then maybe there was a chance …

"You loved Anna!" she shouted. It wasn't a question. She just needed to hear him say it.

"Of course," he said, his face contorted with pain.

"Then I forgive you!" she yelled again; her voice hoarse from the smoke.

Jake cackled, his laugh reverberating all around them.

"I forgive you!" she yelled again. She wasn't sure what she expected to happen, but this wasn't it.

All the blood drained from Liam's face, and like lightning realisation hit.

"I didn't kill her!" he yelled back, his voice cracking, and this time Natalie was sure it was from emotion. "I didn't kill her," he repeated, and Jake roared with laughter.

A branch fell to the ground by the tree where Natalie had been flung by Jake. It smouldered and flamed. They needed to get out of there.

"*He* didn't kill her!" Jake said, his face contorted with amusement. "I killed her, with the help of my son!"

CHAPTER 38

Natalie

A loud crack preceded another flaming branch crashing to the ground. The smoke had become so thick not only was it becoming harder to breathe, it was becoming harder to see, and the flames had almost entirely engulfed the trees around them now.

Natalie's head spun. What had Jake meant? Arthur? Arthur had killed Anna? A new wave of grief and anger threatened, but there was just no time. Unless she planned on joining Anna in the afterlife right this second, they needed to leave. Liam seemed to have the same idea. He launched himself past Jake to where Natalie stood.

"Now! We need to leave now!" he said. "Can you walk?"

Natalie shook her head hopelessly, keeping one eye on Jake who seemed to be watching them, amused and yet doing nothing to stop them.

Liam bent down close to her. "Get on my back," he said.

It took her a moment to realise what he was asking. He was going to piggyback her out. Could she do it?

He barely waited for a reply. With one hand he hoisted her up. Another jolt shot through her shoulder making her stomach roll and fresh beads of sweat break out along her hairline, combining with those from the searing heat. She bit back against the pain and nausea. Her bad arm hung loosely at her side. This was not going to be good. He bounced her once to get a better grip around her legs, and she wrapped her good arm around his neck not too tightly as to allow him to breathe. Ignoring Jake completely, he took off, running for the one small gap where the fire hadn't spread. The path back to the school. Natalie desperately wanted to turn around to check on Jake. Why wasn't he following them? Why wasn't he trying to stop them?

Her plan hadn't worked. If Liam had been telling the truth and he hadn't killed Anna, then she couldn't be angry at him. If anything *he* should be angry with her. Anna cheated on him with her. Yet here he was trying to save her. And if Jake was telling the truth, Arthur was responsible for Anna's death ... and that ... did she have it in her to forgive Arthur? He was why they were here in the first place; to try and cross over the child he'd killed.

Liam raced through the woods. Branches whipped at her arms and legs, and she bent her head, feeling twigs like fingers clawing at her skull, but missing her eyes. Her arm hung loose slapping against them as they moved, every time making Natalie cry out in pain and fighting back the threat of unconsciousness. Not yet, she told herself. Not yet. She needed to make sure Grams was alright. And Cole.

The trees gave way to the grassland, and overhead thunder boomed again. But this time, the sky split open. A heavy downpour dropped on them, making Liam whoop.

Natalie's spirits lifted. Hope. There was hope. Rain ran into her eyes, soaked her clothes and cooled her skin, and despite the agony of her limbs, she smiled. Liam slowed a little as the ground became slippery. Again, Natalie wanted to look behind her. Was the rain putting out the fire? Would it wash away Jake too? Water was supposed to be purifying, wasn't it?

The fence to the school came into view, and near it stood a figure, waving and yelling. Sirens echoed in the background, dulled by the roar of the rain pelting the earth.

Liam slowed to a quick walk, his breath heavy and fast. Natalie shook her head, trying to dislodge the hair plastered to her face and hanging in her eyes. On reaching the fence, Liam let her down gently, her good foot first, and she clung to one of the fence batons for support. Her shoulder ached like nothing she had ever experienced before, but somehow the rain soothed it. And she realised she was sobbing. She wasn't sure if it was from relief or fear or pain or all of them, with each emotion intermingling in equal amounts.

"Help me get her over," Liam said to the figure on the other side of the fence.

"I don't know how much help I'll be," Vicky said, her thin arms reaching out towards Natalie anyway. Liam was still bent over, hands on thighs trying to catch his breath. With a shake, he stood up tall, and Natalie was aware of another figure running towards them from around the side of the building. She blinked, trying to see through her waterlogged vision.

Riki.

Her heart leapt on seeing him before a curtain of dread settled. Where was Grams? Was she okay? And Cole? Words were stolen from her by the roar of the rain and the sirens blaring in the background. Fire engine, police, ambulance? She wasn't sure.

Liam wasted no time in lifting her up in his arms. She screamed out, the pain taking her by surprise again, and then sobbed as she was handed over the fence into Riki's arms.

"Careful. I think she's dislocated her arm," Liam said.

Riki held her tightly, and she pressed her face into his chest for a moment, stifling her sobs and closing her eyes against the pain.

"Go!" Vicky ordered Riki, pointing towards the school. "I'll help Liam."

"Wait! Cole?" Natalie asked. "Did you find him? And how is Gram's?"

Riki scooped her up, her head resting against him. He cleared his throat. "Yeah. Cole's unharmed. He's with the others."

She couldn't hold back her cry of relief. And yet ... "And Grams?"

A pause. "The ambulance is here. They'll do everything they can," he rumbled against her temple.

Her heart lodged somewhere outside of her ribs as he carried her around the side of the building.

A police car was parked on the courts, lights flashing, but she couldn't see anyone. A fire engine sped past the school. Easier access to the fire from the road. God, she hoped the rain had stopped the worst of it.

More sirens. Different ones this time. An ambulance came into view. It pulled up the school drive. A figure ran out of Natalie's class just as Riki stepped up onto the deck. He ran out to the court and waved his arms, trying to get the ambulance driver's attention. Troy? Was that Troy? Riki hesitated, Natalie guessed, weighing up his options. Classroom or ambulance.

"Classroom," she said. She needed to see Grams. Natalie's injuries at least weren't life threatening.

Riki looked at her, and she saw the questioning in his eyes, but he did what she asked. The room was dark. Power out, Natalie guessed. Luckily, it was still light enough to see by.

It was eerily quiet. She scanned the room. Arthur sat in her chair in one corner. His head resting in his hands; Cole sat at his feet playing with some of the wooden blocks. She felt a surge of relief. Cole really was okay. Gavin, she noted, was nowhere to be seen. Riley was kneeling on the floor beside a figure positioned in the recovery position. Grams. Her Grams.

Natalie struggled in Riki's arms, but he held her tight. Riley, face drawn, held one of Grams's hands between hers, and she looked up at Natalie, her eyes wet with tears, her bottom lip trembling.

No. She needed to get to Grams; she struggled against Riki's grasp.

Riki held her tighter. "It's okay," he whispered.

Voices carried from outside, almost yelling. And Riki stepped aside with Natalie in tow as more people rushed into the room. Three paramedics with a stretcher and Troy. He glanced at her, and his face broke before he quickly turned away, moving with the paramedics. Two went to Maggie, one stayed behind, blocking Natalie's view. The paramedic was talking to her, but she couldn't hear anything. There was so much noise. So much going on. So many thoughts thrashing around her head.

Riki set her down gently on the edge of a desk, back towards Maggie, while the paramedic went about assessing her, asking her questions, poking, prodding. Natalie fought, calling out for her grandmother.

Liam and Victoria were there too, side by side, and Liam had his arm around her. They had Maggie on the stretcher. Natalie couldn't see her face, just her form, and they were heading out the door. Riki held her the best he could without touching her arm, but she struggled and wriggled, and tried to get up.

"I'm going to give her something for the pain and to calm her down," the woman in front of her said.

There was so much yelling. Who was yelling? Make them stop! She glanced around. Arthur hadn't moved, his face hidden. Riley had her back towards them, her arms around Cole, guiding him towards the door that fed through to Brittany's room.

Natalie squealed as something pricked her arm.

"It's going to make her quite sleepy, but it'll help us get her to the hospital," the woman was saying.

There was another face. A face right in front of her. Troy. Troy was there bending down to her height. Had he been crying? She couldn't tell, everything was so blurry, colours were muted. She was so confused. Where was Grams? Grams should be here?

"I'm so sorry, Nat." Troy was talking, but she didn't understand. Why was he sorry?

He wiped his eyes with his palm. He *was* crying. This wasn't making sense.

"Should I get the stretcher?" a women's voice said.

There were voices, but they were too far away to hear, and somehow
everything was disappearing, shrinking away into nothingness.

CHAPTER 39

Natalie

"You know I'm still going to visit, don't you?"

Anna picked a daisy from amongst the grass, brought it to her nose, and sniffed. She tucked it behind her ear, and Natalie found herself wondering how it was she'd gotten so lucky.

They were picnicking again in their spot. And they'd chosen the perfect day for it, with clear views of Te Tapu in every direction. Nary a cloud in the sky, and just enough of a gentle breeze to keep the sun from heating their skin. The tendrils of the willow above them swayed in a gentle lullabiac motion.

"You're not going to visit me," Natalie said, shaking her head. What a stupid thing to say. "We'll kick out Helena, and you and I – and Grams of course – will live happily-ever-after." Natalie smiled. She was teasing of course. Helena could have the house. They'd get their own. Make their own memories. Create their own home. With Grams, unless Grams had other plans.

Anna watched her for a moment, a smile playing on her lips, then she turned away to pluck another daisy from the grass beside the picnic blanket. She leant forward and placed it behind Natalie's ear. Her fingers lingered for a second on the side of Natalie's cheek, and Natalie closed her eyes and nestled into it. This was paradise, Natalie thought, a warmth bubbling up inside her.

"I love you so much," Anna whispered, and Natalie opened her eyes. Anna pulled her hand back, a hint of sadness tainting her smile.

"And that's why we're doing this. Why you're getting the divorce," Natalie said, her eyes automatically dragging to Anna's ring finger. It wasn't there. She must have removed it.

"I want you to forgive," she said, her head tilted.

"Forgive?" Natalie was confused. Who did she need to forgive?

"None of this was Liam's fault. He didn't ask for any of this. In fact, he saved you," she said. And Natalie found herself chuckling. What was she talking about? Liam hadn't saved her from anything.

"And you're going to forgive Arthur too."

Arthur? A small seed of panic began to grow inside her. Natalie wracked her brain. Why did she have to forgive Arthur? What had he done? It was there but she couldn't quite hold onto the memory.

"Jake was always stronger than him. Sowing seeds in his mind about how he had to protect the O'Regan name, but a name doesn't need to be protected. He just didn't understand that," Anna said, sadness pulling at her voice. "It took him a long time to piece together who I was, but by then Liam and I were already married."

"I'm not understanding ..." Natalie said, the feeling of dread was growing, and yet the sun was still shining, the sky was still blue, and a bird was flitting around and chirping in the branches above them. Natalie glanced up, trying to find it. A pīwakawaka. It saw her watching and flitted to a closer branch, where it cocked its head to inspect her.

"Remember how I told you how my family had once lived in Te Tapu, many, many years ago? My mother was just a little girl at the time. Her brother had died in a fire at the school ..."

"You never told me that," Natalie said. Somewhere in the back of her brain alarm bells went off. What wasn't she remembering?

"You're right. I never told you about the fire or the death of my uncle. My family never spoke about it. It was only recently that I learnt all the details. How my mother and grandmother were run out of Te Tapu. Funny, how Arthur knew more about my family than I did. I think he was scared, always scared someone would work it out one day."

Strange random images flashed in Natalie's mind. A car upside down in a ditch, sirens and lights, and a little boy with half his face half melted away ...

"When he found out I'd applied for a divorce—"

A scene of her and Anna flashed in Natalie's mind. They were sitting inside her car outside Ol' Tom's Garage. She felt so warm. So happy. Giddy with excitement that they were about to start their lives together ... only ... something had happened.

"Do you remember yet?" Anna asked shuffling a little closer.

Natalie bit her lip. Her memories were so disjointed. They weren't making sense.

"He'll be punished, Natalie. You don't need to worry about that. Arthur will spend the rest of his life behind bars, and there won't be anyone left to cover it up. There'll be no more lies. But, if you can forgive him, Nat, you'll free yourself. Not all O'Regans are horrible."

She chuckled and slid her hand over top of Natalie's. Then, turning it over, she pressed Natalie's hand to her lips to kiss.

"I want you to live a long and happy life, Nat. And fall in love again." The corners of Anna's mouth pulled upwards, and she kissed her hand again. "He's cute," she said. "I approve." And she winked.

The pīwakawaka chirped and flitted above them. And suddenly everything came flooding back. Natalie felt a ball of emotion well up inside her.

"I'm not leaving you," Anna said pulling Natalie closer until she could wrap her arms around her. "I'll always be here, watching over you, but you won't see me. You don't need to. I'm at peace. I was loved by you. What more could a girl want?" she teased, nuzzling into Natalie's neck.

"And Grams?" Natalie asked her voice shaking, fresh tears rolling down her cheeks. "Will I see Grams again?"

"Maybe," she said. "I don't know. Maggie has things to do. It was her choice though. She wants you to remember that. She's going to keep Jake in line. It's easier to do from this side. He doesn't scare her anymore. Her brother's here too. He's going to help. Bad people only have the power we give them. She wanted me to tell you that you can help by forgiving and opening your heart again. You are worth loving, Nat. Maggie knows it, and I know it, and if you open your eyes, you'll see other people know it too." She fell silent for a moment, letting her words soak in.

Natalie sobbed full-body sobs and pulled Anna's arms around her tighter.

When her crying had ebbed, Anna spoke again. "Oh, and Maggie wants you to be nicer to Helena." She chuckled, and Natalie couldn't help but fight off a smile.

"But I'll miss you both," Natalie's words broke through her grief.

"I know, my love. I know."

The pīwakawaka circled around their heads again, this time dropping one of its tail feathers. It lazily floated toward them, rocking gently back and forth on the breeze, until Natalie was able to reach out and grab it.

Anna pulled Natalie around to face her and brushed her lips with her own.

CHAPTER 40

Natalie

Those first few weeks after the incident were harrowing. So much had changed in the shortest of time. Natalie woke in the hospital. Helena was slumped forward in a chair, her head resting on folded arms on the hospital bed. That in itself told Natalie things would never be the same; Helena was here by her bedside.

When Helena woke, her eyes were swollen and red. She'd been the one to break it to her. Grams had passed. A heart attack. And for a moment, Natalie had wanted to blame herself. Grams had taken on Jake to protect her. But then she remembered what Anna had told her in her dream, if it had been a dream, and she found a way to grieve fully without blame.

Natalie only had to stay in one night and was released the next day. Helena had been there, on time too, to pick her up. Natalie's arm was in a sling. Liam had been right; it was a dislocated shoulder. And thankfully Natalie's ankle was just a bad sprain. She was given crutches and told to stay off it as much as possible for the next week or so.

Those first few days were a blur. Their house became a train station of people coming and going, of flower deliveries and food drop offs. Of tears and hugs and kind words. So many times, Natalie wanted to rage and howl and shut herself in her room and avoid everyone ... but she didn't. Grams had wanted her to live. And sometimes living meant hurting and not shutting herself off from the world, so she swallowed her pride, and she did just that.

Grams had been explicit about not wanting a funeral. She was to be cremated and then what happened to her ashes could be decided by Helena and Natalie at a later date. For the moment they kept them in an urn, high up on a shelf where Poe wouldn't be likely to knock them over. Just having her ashes close by made Natalie feel better, like her grandmother was somehow still around.

Helena and Natalie leaned on each other, maybe more than they ever had. There was a lot to attend to. Paperwork. Money. Being the shoulder for others to cry on. And sometimes, being the shoulder for each other to cry on. Helena took time off from the tavern and swapped some of her night shifts for day shifts, and it surprised Natalie when a month had passed, and she realised Helena was going out less and less. She wasn't coming home drunk any more either. Things *were* changing.

Victoria was at the house a lot, fussing around, cooking and tidying. She was hurting, Natalie knew. Maggie had been her best friend for so many years, and even after their falling out, Victoria had never stopped caring for her. The double whammy had been when Arthur was arrested. Natalie had shared with her what Anna had said in her dream, and to Natalie's surprise, Victoria believed her. She had broken down in tears, but once her tears were spent, she had marched around to the O'Regans and had it out with Arthur. Victoria told her later that Liam had walked in during their argument. And to everyone's surprise, Arthur had fessed up. He had one of his mechanics mess with Anna's brakes, changed the paperwork, and started the rumours about a drunk driver. He told them everything. Even that he had tried to stop Liam from marrying Anna once he learnt she was related to Gavin Jenkins. It was to protect the family from scandal, he'd cried.

But scandal was unavoidable.

Arthur was put on home detention, complete with an ankle bracelet while he awaited his trial. Natalie had heard rumours that he had hopes his lawyer would put forth an insanity plea. He was suddenly very vocal about a dark entity placing thoughts into his mind, making him do stuff he didn't want to do. Natalie knew the jurors wouldn't buy it. Anna had said as much. Arthur would live out the rest of his days in jail, and Natalie believed her.

She wasn't at the stage of forgiving him. Not yet, anyway. However, she could admit she did pity the man. Jake was a formidable foe. Not only did Arthur carry his genes but also some of his personality. It had likely drawn them together and made it easier for Jake to get inside his head.

That might also be why he wasn't able to manipulate Liam in the same way.

Liam, Natalie was coming to realise, wasn't the bad guy she'd thought him to be. He'd literally carried her through flames away from his demented, dead grandfather. He'd risked his own life for a MacKenzie. And, he told her when it was just the two of them left alone, that he'd known about Natalie's affair with Anna. He'd known for a long time. He suspected most people had. He'd seen the way they looked at each other, and the way Anna spoke about Natalie. To him, it was obvious what they had was more than friendship. It had broken his heart, and he'd been angry at them both. But in the end, he had accepted it. He'd been ready to bring up the idea of divorce himself. It wasn't until a few weeks after the funeral, the divorce papers Anna had gone to collect arrived in the mailbox. A new intern had sent them, not knowing the circumstances at the time. It opened a new wound. She'd beat him to it. So he'd held his grief close to his chest and he'd left. Disappeared. Until Arthur took a turn, sending him right back here to where it all started: Te Tapu.

Natalie had even found a way to make amends with Riley and Troy too. In both instances it had been super awkward.

Riley had offered her condolences, and Natalie had thanked her for being there with her grandmother at the end. For being there for her great-uncle too. Overtime, Riley filled her in on everything that had happened at the beginning of the year, when Gwen had started haunting her. Riley had thought she had somehow been protecting Gwen by not telling anyone but Liam that it had been Gwen who had inadvertently killed Billy. It still seemed to Natalie, that if it hadn't been for Jake, Gwen would have never picked up the axe.

Unlike Natalie, Riley's move to Te Tapu was her first induction to the spirit world. It hadn't been a pleasant one either. But she'd made it through. She'd really thought once Gwen and Billy had been united it would all be over. The plaque had seemed a good idea at the time. She wasn't to know it would stir up Jake's animosity even more. They'd discussed removing it, with Victoria and Liam, and Riki in the room.

They'd tried bringing Helena into the fold, but she wanted nothing to do with it. Life was for the living, she said. Talking about the dead just creeped her out.

In the end, they decided on keeping the plaque and maybe adding two more. One in memoriam of Maggie. The other, for Gavin.

Troy visited her in the hospital. He brought her flowers and placed them on the stand beside her bed, standing there saying nothing until Natalie could muster the composure to say thank you without completely dissolving into tears.

While she couldn't say much, her thank you was heavy with gratitude. He'd been there even at the end, even when he said he wouldn't. Without him, saying goodbye to Grams might have come so much sooner. She gestured him closer and pulled him to her with her good arm, and as he bent down, she kissed him gently on the head.

"I'm really sorry," he said, pulling away. His eyes bloodshot and glassy.

Natalie shook her head. There was nothing for him to be sorry about. She had been in the wrong. He'd only been trying to help, and the way she had led him on ...

She didn't have the words. Not right now. But she'd find a way over the next few weeks to tell him how she really felt, and just how grateful she truly was.

And then there was Riki.

Victoria had given him Natalie's address, and he arrived that evening after she'd gotten out of hospital. People had already been coming and going and Natalie was exhausted, so another knock at the door meant nothing to her. Until she saw him, standing in the doorway to the living room. He carried a bouquet of flowers – pinks and reds and yellows. His face was drawn, and he shuffled awkwardly on his feet. And Natalie found herself aching for him as much as she ached for herself. Helena got up from the chair opposite Natalie and made an excuse to help Victoria in the kitchen, leaving just the two of them alone.

"How's your arm feeling?" he asked.

"Not too bad. They've given me some pretty potent painkillers."

Smiling weakly, he gestured with the flowers and glanced around. Natalie directed him to the coffee table. Already the room was heady with condolence bouquets. Vicky, she knew, would find a vase for them later.

He took the chair Helena had been sitting in.

"I'm so very sorry for your loss," he said, his eyes downcast.

Did he blame himself, she wondered? They'd been there to help Gavin and Cole, but Grams's death hadn't been caused by either. A jolt of anger grew as Jake crept back into her mind, and she pushed it away.

"How is Cole?" Natalie asked.

Riki lifted his eyes, holding her gaze for a moment, and Natalie could almost hear Anna's words again: "He's cute. I approve." A warmth overtook the anger she had felt.

"He's remarkably okay," he said, a lightness returning briefly to his face. "I have no idea what happened out in the woods after I left. I still don't understand what it was I saw." He cracked his knuckles, and Natalie could see the cogs of his brain turning over.

"But I want to tell you some of what I experienced," he said. "I can't make sense of it all ... But maybe now's not the right time?"

"I want to know," Natalie said, and she chewed on her lip, scared of what he was going to say.

"Your grandmother was still breathing," he said. "I ran as fast as I could. I was really so torn; I didn't know if Cole was back at the school or lost in the woods. My brain was scrambled. When I got to the school, Victoria and Riley saw me and helped me. We got Maggie as comfortable as we could in your classroom, and Victoria called 111. I wanted to stay to make sure Maggie was okay, but I needed to find Cole." His words flew out and his face looked pained again.

"It's okay," Natalie said. "Cole's your son, and there was nothing else you could do for Grams." Her voice cracked. Knowing it was true didn't dull the pain. Had she not had an arm in a sling and a leg propped up on a footstool, she would have moved closer to comfort him.

"The first place I checked was under the classroom like you said. I was yelling for him, but he couldn't have heard. Between the thunder and the wind ..." He massaged his brow with his hand. "I was in such a panic. In the distance, the treetops were glowing red. All I could think was what if it happened again? Another child killed in a school fire."

Natalie swallowed hard. It must have been horrible for him.

"I kept looking for a way under the building, and I couldn't find anything. Had I been thinking straight, I would've asked Riley or Victoria, but I ... And then something ... something happened ..."

He started playing with his knuckles again and colour flushed his cheeks.

"The whole time, I'd been praying, right? Asking for his mum, or God, or any bloody thing to help me, and I was getting more and more frustrated. So I ... I asked Gavin."

Gavin.

"Did you see him?" Natalie whispered. She could only imagine how confronting seeing Gavin might have been right then, particularly when you're trying to save your son from the same fate.

"No. Not exactly. But I called out his name. I told him I needed his help. That Cole was in danger. I needed him to show me where Cole was. And then I heard him. Giggles. Laughter, like a child. I know it sounds crazy."

Natalie shook her head; with everything they experienced that day, it was the least of all the crazy.

"It was like Gavin had heard me, wanted to help me. Except he was leading me away from the classroom. At first, I didn't want to go. The fire was heading towards the school. If Cole was under the building and I couldn't get to him in time ..." His voice broke, and Natalie's eyes welled up again.

"But something ... like invisible hands pushing me ... I don't know. But I followed him to the shed."

Natalie's heart thundered in her chest. She knew the outcome. Knew Cole had been found safe and sound huddled under the plaque, but she hadn't known the terror and pain Riki had endured during his search for him.

He shifted in his seat, scrubbing his palm over his face before continuing. "The thing is ... Cole wasn't alone when I got there."

So he did see Gavin, Natalie thought.

"Maggie was there."

"What?" It took her a moment. Warmth flooded Natalie's body, like a comforting hug. Of course Grams would have found a way to be with him. Of course she would. Tears slipped down her cheeks.

"It didn't make any sense to me at first, as I'd left her back in the classroom, but my boy was safe." He swiped his eyes and sniffed. "I'm sorry," he said. "I just ..." He wiped his face again. "Maggie ... she looked good. Healthy even. I still don't understand it. Yet there she was, one hand on Cole's shoulder, and another little boy was with her, half hiding behind her. She had an arm around him too. And then I knew ... but I didn't really until we got back to the classroom after. So Cole, he came running towards me, talking non-stop. He said this was where the bad man couldn't get them. And Maggie, she was just smiling."

Tears streamed down Natalie's cheeks, and she wanted to say so much, but she listened on.

"I went to ask her how she'd found them. How she'd recovered so quickly. But she put a finger to her mouth to shush me and said she was taking Gavin home. He had family waiting for him."

He broke down, and Natalie ached to throw her arms around him. Instead, she wiped at her own face.

When he'd regained his composure again, he continued. "She said Arthur needed to admit his wrongs. Jake thrived on all the lies, and then she told me ... to look after you."

Tears flowed unchecked down Natalie's face. "Did you see her leave?" she asked.

He shook his head. "It suddenly started pouring, and Cole was tugging on my arm. We ran back towards the classroom, and I saw movement out by the fence line, so I sent Cole to join them inside, and I made a beeline for what I hoped was you returning. Victoria was already there. And I saw you and ..."

He couldn't finish, and Natalie didn't need him too.

He'd seen Grams. She'd been there with Cole. Taking care of him and Gavin. Natalie wondered if the family she was taking Gavin to included Anna. Her heart both warmed and broke at the thought.

They'd done it. Grams had done it. Gavin had moved on, Cole was safe, the truth, it was out there – set free from all the lies, and Jake …

She shivered. It was too easy to still see him glowering. Laughing. Enjoying their pain. But somehow Liam had escaped him. Maybe it was simply that he was a better person than his father, than his grandfather. Maybe Anna was looking out for him. Arthur would, if Anna was right, live out his days in prison. If Jake visited him there, so be it. He couldn't torment Grams anymore, Natalie knew that, and she'd do her darned best to stop him tormenting her.

Despite the heaviness of grief, despite everything in fact, there was a seed of lightness growing inside her. Everything had come full circle. It was time for her to let go of some of the darkness too.

Natalie looked across at Riki.

"Thank you," she said, warmth growing stronger in her chest. He'd given her more than he could know.

A fluttering noise at the window behind her made her turn the best she could in her chair.

"It's a fantail," Riki said. "A pīwakawaka."

It flitted back and forth like she'd remembered one doing so, so many years ago when she was just a child and she'd been baking with Grams.

"It's okay," she said, remembering the words her Grams had told her all those years ago. "It's just a spirit come visiting."

Free Ebook!

Thanks for reading *Broken Lies*.

I hope you enjoyed it!

If you would like to stay updated about future books, be sure to visit my website and join my newsletter at https://jobuer.com.

By joining my newsletter you'll be the first to learn of new releases and special offers, and you'll get a behind-the-scenes glimpse of my life as an author. I'll also send you a free copy of my gothic short story collection, *Between the Shadows*!

And if you enjoyed this book, please be sure to leave a review. This helps put my books in front of new readers, and in turn, allows me to write more.

Thanks again for your support!

Jo xx

Author's Note

Unspoken Truths, the precursor to *Broken Lies*, was a true passion project, a book of my heart. When the first idea for *Unspoken Truths* came to me, I had just started a career as a teacher at a small country school. Due to the nature of the job, there were times I was onsite alone after dark, and, like Natalie and Maggie mention in *Broken Lies*, schools can be eerie places when devoid of children.

On a number of occasions at this school, I experienced things I couldn't explain – footsteps following me on the deck when no one was there, a voice in my ear as I locked up one evening, and hearing a woman singing that neither my colleague nor I could explain. And trust me, we tried to find a rational explanation for our ghostly singer. We spent a decent amount of time scouring the school, hypothesising one rational idea after another, before my colleague's nerves got the better of her, and she bolted for her car, leaving me alone, giggling at her reaction. Suffice to say, things that go bump in the night don't scare me as much as they do the people around me.

One day, walking along the deck to my classroom, a clear image came to mind of a young woman, obviously distressed, holding an axe. Where the image came from, I have no idea, but I never forgot it, and many years later, that image, and those experiences, sowed the seeds for *Unspoken Truths*, a book that insisted I go to the darkest parts of me to dredge up the experiences of the two main characters, Riley and Gwen.

Writing *Unspoken Truths* took a toll on me. Emotionally, it stripped me bare. To recover, I tried my hand at something lighter, not so serious, not so dark, and hence I wrote *Hades's Haunt*, my first fun paranormal cozy. But the thing was, *Unspoken Truths*, its characters and the little village of Te Tapu, still haunted me. When my editor mentioned she wanted to learn more about Natalie and Victoria, I knew there was more story to tell.

From the beginning, I had felt an affinity towards Natalie. I knew her bitchiness towards Riley had a bigger story behind it. "Hurt people, hurt people", as the saying goes. I just didn't know what her story was. Natalie also reminded me of myself. After a time of feeling like life's punching bag, feeling "different" and misunderstood, I knew how easy it was to act out – to punch back in ugly ways – as a form of protection and self-preservation.

The only other clue I had as to where *Broken Lies* might take me, was my conviction that I'd once been told that a classroom I'd worked in had been built on the spot where a previous classroom had burnt down. No lives lost, fortunately. I was so sure someone had told me about this fire, only I couldn't for the life of me remember who. Annoyingly, when I asked around, seeking confirmation, everyone looked at me weirdly, like I'd made the whole thing up. Which, in retrospect, maybe I had. Maybe I had imagined being told there had been a fire. Regardless, it was the inspiration I needed to start writing.

Broken Lies has been a beast of a book to write … and rewrite, and rewrite again. I am not a "Plotter" but what I call a "Discovery Writer", which means my notes on *Unspoken Truths* were a total mess of random thoughts as the story only unfolded as I wrote it. I had no series bible to refer to for characters' eye colours or other descriptive nuances. Sure, I had the actual book, but checking for consistency between the two books was time-consuming work.

Broken Lies was also stalled by a year of insanity in my personal life, the drama of which kept me zapped of energy and away from the page. And as any author knows, the longer we're away from the page, the harsher imposter syndrome can hit when we get back to writing. On top of this, *Broken Lies* had, just like its precursor, turned into a book of my heart. I cannot tell you how many times the story within these pages, these characters, made me cry. I often forgot I authored their stories, as they seemed so much bigger, more real than what I could create from imagination alone. But also, Te Tapu and its residents, are such a part of me, it's honestly hard to let them go.

But here they are.

Although *Broken Lies* is considerably different in form from *Unspoken Truths*, I hope you enjoy it just as much. Part of me hopes you cry just as much as I do, reading their stories, forgetting, as I do, that they are characters of imagination only. There is no greater gift as an author, to evoke emotion in my readers through story. And if this story moves you, please consider leaving a review, so it can reach other readers in need of a good emotional undoing too.

On a final note:

This book exists in large part because my editor wanted to hear Victoria and Natalie's stories. If there were to be a third book (just hypothesising), I would love to hear your thoughts on whose story you would like to read next. Is it that of our sweet friend-zoned copper, Troy? Or Arthur's villain origin story? He can't be all bad, surely? Or would you like to travel back in time to Ol' Man Tom – the founder of Te Tapu and the O'Regan who started it all? The thing is, I know firsthand that once you visit Te Tapu, it's hard to leave. So if you'd like to see a third book in the series, you can send me your thoughts to jo@jobuer.com. Who knows what secrets and lies Te Tapu still has to share.

Jo xx

Also by Jo Buer

Gothic Suspense

Unspoken Truths (The Prequel to *Broken Lies*)

Rest Easy Resort

Between (A Gothic Novella)

Voices (A Collection of Short Stories)

Between the Shadows (A Collection of Short Stories)

Paranormal Cozy Mystery

Hades's Haunt (A Widdershins Magical Mystery Book 1)

About the Author

Jo Buer is a Kiwi-Canadian gothic suspense and paranormal mystery author. She writes stories with gothic heart and ghostly mystery, with a dash of romance ... and maybe a cat or two.

Jo is also the host of Alchemy for Authors - a podcast on manifestation and mindset for authors.

Jo lives in Aotearoa New Zealand with her wonderful husband and four free-spirited felines.

Connect with Jo at www.jobuer.com and join her newsletter for book updates and exclusive content.

Find all of Jo's books on her website, at https://books2read.com/jobuer or request from your local library.